the last christian on earth

OS GUINNESS

Bestselling Author of *The Call, Dining with the Devil* and *Unspeakable*

the last

christian

on earth

Uncover the Enemy's Plot to Undermine the Church

Regal

From Gospel Light
Ventura, California, U.S.A.

Published by Regal
From Gospel Light
Ventura, California, U.S.A.
www.regalbooks.com
Printed in the U.S.A.

Formerly published as *The Gravedigger File: Papers on the Subversion of the Modern Church*
(InterVarsity Press, 1983).

Library of Congress Cataloging-in-Publication Data
Guinness, Os.
The last Christian on earth : uncover the enemy's plot to
undermine the church / Os Guinness. — [New ed.].
p. cm.
Rev. ed. of: The gravedigger file. 21983.
Includes bibliographical references and index.
ISBN 978-0-8307-5125-9 (trade paper : alk. paper)
1. Christianity—20th century. 2. Christianity—21st century.
3. Secularization (Theology) I. Guinness, Os. Gravedigger file. II. Title.
BR481.G84 2010
270.8'3—dc22
2009034665

1 2 3 4 5 6 7 8 9 10 11 12 13 14 15 / 15 14 13 12 11 10 09

Rights for publishing this book outside the U.S.A. or in non-English languages are administered
by Gospel Light Worldwide, an international not-for-profit ministry. For additional information,
please visit www.glww.org, email info@glww.org, or write to Gospel Light Worldwide,
1957 Eastman Avenue, Ventura, CA 93003, U.S.A.

DOM

and to CJ and his generation,
who are the ones to make the critical
difference on these issues

Contents

Author's Introduction to the New Edition

Some years ago, I had the privilege of addressing a forum of Chinese CEOs in the business school of one of China's leading universities. As we were walking back to the conference after a magnificent dinner, the dean asked me the most searching question of the day.

"What am I missing?" he said. "We in China are fascinated by the Christian roots of the Western past, in order to see what we can learn for China's future. But you in the West are cutting yourself off from your roots. What am I missing?"

The dean's question highlights one of the most urgent questions facing Western Christians in the advanced modern global era. *We are living in the global era. The global era is a product of the West, just as the West is largely a product of the Christian faith. And the Christian faith is the world's first truly global faith. But what is wrong with the Church in the West if the Church is exploding in the global South and around the world but is increasingly faithless and failing in the West?*

I was born in China, and the area where I grew up has witnessed the most explosive growth of the Christian Church in 2,000 years. I am an Anglican Evangelical, and a member of a church that is decadent or withering in many parts of the West but exploding in Africa and Asia. And not only that, but the courageous and faithful sisters and brothers in Africa and Asia who were led to faith by missionaries from the West are in their turn riding to the rescue of the Western Church that has fallen captive to the most heretical and apostate forms of faith in 2,000 years of Christian history.

The Episcopal Church in the U.S. is an extreme case, but what has gone wrong elsewhere in the West? How are we to make sense of the spiritually barren situation in Western Europe, Canada, Australia and

New Zealand? Or of the fact that in the United States, where Evangelicals, the people of the good news, are still strong numerically, they have become one of the shallowest, noisiest and most corrupt parts of the Christian Church, bringing down an unprecedented avalanche of disdain on their heads—almost none of which has anything to do with Jesus?

For five decades now I have been a follower of Jesus and an Evangelical, one who has always sought to define myself, my faith and my life according to the good news Jesus announced and demonstrated. Not once has God ever let me down, and the central and overwhelming response of my life is joy, gratitude and trust for the greatness and goodness of God. But, a constant lesser theme on my journey has been sorrow over the weakness and follies of the Church in the West, both in Europe, where I have spent many years, and in America, where I live now.

The core challenge to the Western Church can be expressed in three words: "integrity," "credibility" and "civility," though the greatest of these is integrity. In relation to Jesus Christ our Lord, we must regain the integrity of our faith; in relation to educated outsiders, we must regain the credibility of our faith; and in relation to people of other faiths, we must regain the civility of our faith. This is the sum of our challenge to be utterly faithful to our Lord while at the same time utterly and properly engaged in life in this astonishing modern world.

The Search for the Deepest Answer

There are Christian books by the hundreds that tell us we have problems in the Church and that appeal to the disillusioned and stir the angry. But there are few that say why. What has caused the problems, or what Martin Luther would have called the new "Babylonian captivity," of the Western Church? There are many answers to this question and many of them are obviously inadequate or wrong. We simply cannot trace all of the problems back to theological liberalism or secular humanism or godless education or sexual permissiveness or coarse television or corrupt politicians or outmoded pastors, or whoever and whatever is purported to be the villain of the day. There has to be a deeper, more comprehensive and more damaging reason than any of these answers.

I believe there is such an answer. What Luther called "Babylonian Captivity" is a falling for the spirit, style and system of the age, which is also a worldliness and an unfaithfulness that both saps the strength of the Church and brings it under the judgment of God. How have we done that? Ironically, we in the Western Christian Church have been undermined by the very modern world that the Christian faith was so instrumental in helping to create.

This notion has mostly been studied in the social sciences, which is why Evangelicals have mostly missed it until recently. The notion might be called the "gravedigger thesis," and it can be put simply: *The Christian faith contributed decisively to the rise of the modern world, but it has been undermined decisively by the modern world it helped to create. The Christian faith has become its own gravedigger.*

When I began to understand the significance of this analysis many decades ago, it threw such light on the weaknesses and follies of the Church today that I wanted to share it with fellow Christians. But much of the analysis was buried in academic books and papers that were impenetrable to ordinary readers. Hence *The Gravedigger File,* the first edition of this book that I wrote in 1983. It was a grand summary and simplification of much that has been written in the social sciences on the state of modern religion, but with a crucial difference: I translated it all into a form that looks at the issues from the perspective of faith and discipleship, rather than sociology.

I am not a subscriber to apocalyptic alarmism or to conspiracy theories. On the contrary, I adhere strongly to the most repeated assertion of the entire Bible: "Have faith in God. Have no fear." But I used the literary device of writing memoranda from one spy to another spy on how to undermine the Church for a simple reason. I did so deliberately, in order to challenge us as Christians to wrench ourselves out of our shortsightedness, so that we can see things from an outside point of view. Worldliness is always a spiritual myopia. It falls for the spirit and system of the age and fails to correct itself through the correcting lenses of the perspective of the global (the Church in other continents), the historical (the Church in other centuries), and above all, the eternal (the Word of God across all places and times).

Over the years, many readers have asked whether my model was C.S. Lewis's *The Screwtape Letters,* and wondered who is "the old Fool" mentioned in the story. I owe a great deal to the famous Oxford don, including his decisive nudge toward my coming to faith in the first place. But my inspiration here was not Lewis but John le Carré and his brilliant depictions of the grey world of intelligence. As for the "old Fool," he is Malcolm Muggeridge, who was alive and well when I first wrote the book, and a dear friend. His utterly hilarious, but deadly serious, brand of fool making has long been an inspiration to my lifelong passion for Christian persuasion. He is now in heaven, but he read the book when it first came out and his kind commendation has always meant the world to me.

Timelier than Ever

Twenty-five years later, some may like to evoke associations with other and newer types of secret agents, but they are always only devices. The central challenge, however, remains. Since *The Gravedigger File* was first published in 1983, the world has changed considerably—including such dramatic events as the fall of the Soviet Union, the rise of the computer age, the re-emergence of China and India, the rise of Islamic terrorism, and the worldwide revitalization and politicization of religion. But the central point of the gravedigger thesis remains the same and it raises an inescapable question for followers of Jesus in the Western world today: *Can we regain the full integrity of faith in Christ while fully and properly engaged in the advanced modern world?*

This new and re-titled edition should be read with that question in mind from the start. Sadly, the central argument is not only unchanged but more urgent than ever, which underscores the challenge. Only a few more recent illustrations have been added to underscore what has happened since the book first came out and where we are today. To be sure, many Christians are now more aware of the contributions of the social sciences than when I first wrote, though this has its snags too.

First, much of the new awareness stops at an obsession with statistics, which itself is often a form of reductionism and even of worldliness. It misses the deeper understanding that comes only from wise theory and deeper analysis.

Second, too much of the awareness is uncritical, so that Evangelicals have swung from an earlier ignorance of the social sciences to an acceptance that is sometimes equally uncritical. I have heard sermons in American churches with more taken from pollsters than from the Bible. The old three-step Christian approach of "discern, assess, and engage" is still the better way.

And third, many have become so adept in using the important tools of the social sciences that they never go back to seeing things from a biblical point of view. This point is true too of many of the academic disciplines, so that the laudable increase in distinguished Christian scholarship is offset by the decrease in faithful Christian thinking.

The title of this new edition of the book, *The Last Christian on Earth*, plays off the gravedigger thesis as well as the words of our Lord in the Gospel of Luke: "When the Son of Man comes, will he find faith on the earth?"[1] Growing up in China, where I was witness to the beginnings of the terrible persecution that Mao Tse-Tung unleashed against the Church, I once thought Jesus was referring to the results of a time of dreadful persecution. I now think it is more likely that Jesus was warning of a time when there could be millions of people who ostensibly name his name but are unrecognizable as the followers he called to follow his way. Parts of the Western Church are already in that condition now.

For American Evangelicals, the new edition is particularly timely because of watershed changes in Evangelicalism after the Republican debacle in the 2008 election and the role of the Christian right in its defeat. For many decades in the twentieth century, the Evangelical faith in America was deeply *privatized*—"privately engaging but publicly irrelevant," as one critic put it. Then, after the wake-up year of 1973

(Watergate, Roe v. Wade and the OPEC crisis), the pendulum swung strongly to the other side.

Since then, the Evangelical faith has been deeply *politicized* through its identification with the religious right. Both extremes have been unfaithful to God as well as a failure in practice. The second era is now coming to an end, and the question is: which stance should Evangelicals take in public life now? It would be as bad to be politicized from the left as from the right, but which is the better way? That is a burning question, and it is raised here along with many other vital issues.

Memorandum 4 speaks directly to these issues, just as it did when *The Gravedigger File* first came out. Perhaps the needed current debate will be wiser and more biblical than the heedless mid-seventies rush to political engagement at any cost. But the issues are set out here for thoughtful believers to engage.

Unquestionably, this issue and many of the issues raised in this book are controversial, and the times we live in make them urgent. But the book is back to speak for itself. As Jesus said so many times, "Whoever has ears to hear, let him hear."

There are many Christians so caught up in the way things have always been or so caught up in the excitement of their new "rush to relevance" that they have no time to stop and think. But for those who sorrow over the state of the Western Church, this book is a passionate and open plea for reformation and revival. It is written and now re-issued to help with the wrestling with the world, which is the preparation for the fervent prayer, which is the prelude to the costly discipleship, which will be the springboard for a faithful and effective prevailing over the greatest challenge the Church of Christ has ever faced: modernity. May it be so—and may it be soon.

Os Guinness
Washington, DC
January 2009

How These Papers Came Into My Hands

My wife and I have known the source of these papers for five or six years, first in the setting of his graduate philosophy seminars, then in the wider context of university life and, more recently, as an occasional dinner guest in our own home. To all appearances, he was a typical university don, genial, witty and (when occasion served) penetrating in his insights and criticism. Not once in all these years has he ever given us a clue that this was a mask for an altogether different self.

We had sometimes talked quite deeply, though always agreeing to differ over the question of our respective convictions. Trained, as I realize now, to withstand forms of interrogation somewhat stronger than philosophy seminars, he must have listened to us and nonchalantly parried the questions we raised like an adult playing chess with children.

The break came when we were dining together at his college, after an invitation that was uncharacteristically late and insistent. I noticed that he seemed distracted, almost agitated. He chose to sit at the end of the table, well out of the central conversation. Once the main course had been served and the conversation level was rising around the dining hall, he dropped his voice, a sudden edge entering it.

"Look," he said, "I need your help. Listen to me carefully, but show no sign of any special attention. It's possible that I'm being watched. I suggested meeting here in public because it was less conspicuous than coming to your home."

"I believe I can trust you," he continued. "I've come to see where your North Star lies. And there's one other person I know I can trust . . . Old Fool indeed!"

The last three words were said more to himself than to me. They trailed off into the unlit world of his own thoughts. In response to my questioning look, he spoke the name of a distinguished writer whom he knew I had recently interviewed.

"I will soon need to get something to him urgently, without fail. I gather you've met him. Are you willing to do it?" If so, he continued, he would contact me again in the course of the next week. He was waiting for the arrival of news that would allow him to act.

His call to my cell phone came earlier than I expected. At home the next evening, he phoned me as I let myself in. He wanted me to meet him that night. "Radcliffe Square. Catte Street entrance, 11:00 P.M.," he said, and rang off without further explanation.

The deep bell of the University Church was tolling over the almost deserted square as he loomed out of the misty November night under the winter-flowering cherry tree. He shook hands with me strongly, and as he did so he pressed something small and metallic into my palm. Then, seizing my arm, he piloted me brusquely across the square and on toward Broad Street.

We walked together for less than 15 minutes before he slipped into the darkness as silently as he had arrived. What he had given me was a memory stick, and in it a series of top-secret memos directed to him, which he instructed me to take the next morning to the writer he had mentioned. Together we should review them and get them published without delay. He was emphatic about the urgency. He would be missed as soon as he failed to turn up for a flight at Heathrow, so 12 hours were all that were left him. The writer would not be expecting the memos, but would know what to do. He had been a journalist in his time, and had also worked in intelligence, so he would appreciate immediately what he was dealing with.

"With the proviso that you add an afterword of your own," he said, "you must publish the memos just as they stand. For several years now you've been arguing the case for the Christian faith and saying there was another side to the Church; that my facts weren't all the facts. Now you must write about it to put these papers in perspective. But the papers must be published at once. It's urgent that Christians should realize what's happening." And then he added cryptically, "We'll see whether the Director is right or whether the Church can wake in time."

He told me many things besides this, things which have weighed on my mind ever since, some of which I will discuss in the afterword. Finally, he said he would be leaving Oxford that night to go into hiding on the Continent. From there he would contact me after the public response to the papers was clear. He would be very interested to see the official response, but that was not his ultimate concern. It was the popular response that would prove decisive.

Also on the memory stick were some cartoons that were his own doodled commentary on the papers. The best one has been published too, for in a sense the seeds of his defection were nurtured by the comic perspective that lay behind them. There were no footnotes in the original papers. I have traced the references wherever possible and added them to the text for those wishing to delve more deeply into the thinking behind the papers.

I have followed the instructions given me to the letter, and with the cooperation of the writer am now presenting these papers to a wider audience so that, just as our source urgently requested, the papers can speak for themselves.

The last thing he said to me was this: "Maybe even the Doomsday clock has more time than the Western Church." I think not, but we shall see.

Os Guinness
Oxford

Operation Gravedigger

FROM: Deputy Director, Central Security Council
TO: Director Designate, Los Angeles Bureau
CLASSIFICATION: *ULTRA SECRET*

Warmest congratulations, both on your appointment as head of the Los Angeles Bureau and on your election to the Central Security Council. I have followed your steady rise in the service for some time. I have also consistently argued that Los Angeles deserves permanent representation on the Council. As you are well aware, not everyone takes this position. But we are confident that you will soon convince those who have reservations about you personally as well as those who fail to see the strategic importance of upgrading the L.A. Bureau. I say *we* advisedly. With the Director favoring it, your election was a formality and went through on the nod.

Naturally, it will be a wrench for you to leave Oxford. You may not miss the mist and rain, but what other place rivals its intellectual sophistication, its urbanity and wit, all wreathed in the smoke of endless pipes and washed down with sherry and port? Los Angeles has its own compensations, but my excitement for you goes beyond a question of place. Moving from Oxford to L.A. is more than a change of cities. It will mean a switch in strategies that you will find engrossing.

You are taking over in Los Angeles just when it is becoming crucial to our plans. Many people think only of the film industry and consider

Hollywood's greatest days to be over. They miss the point. Our sights are on the wider influence of what has been called the "Sillywood Revolution"—the combined power of Hollywood and Silicon Valley that is shaping the global infotainment of the future and creating the totally mediated world of "real virtuality." L.A. has long been the entertainment (and porn) capital of the world. Soon it will be one of the most vital nodes in the world's media networks and a bellwether city of the wired world of tomorrow. The old talk of the "Los Angelization" of the world was a little far-fetched, but the California connection will undoubtedly become one of our hottest centers of activity.

The Director himself has asked me to brief you on our top priority operation. You have three more months in England before you take up your new post. This will allow you to give the Operation your undivided attention, as well as to fit in some advance trips to L.A. It will take some work catching up on the background, which I will be sending you. Master the details, but don't lose sight of the forest for the trees. The big picture is what counts.

Operation Gravedigger

We are poised on the brink of a staggering victory, one of our most glittering prizes in history. Reports from all fronts of the modernized sector of the world indicate that, after 250 years of painstaking planning and successful execution, the payoff is very close. Operation Gravedigger is moving smoothly and inexorably toward its climax. Its goal—the complete neutralization of the advanced modern Western Church by subversion from within—is in sight and almost in our grasp.

I will be sending you memos from week to week to brief you on the Operation and the part your Bureau is to play. In this first memo, I will define the Operation, its objectives and assumptions.

I will also outline aspects of the Operation that will be examined more fully in subsequent memoranda.

The underlying strategy of Operation Gravedigger is as stark in its simplicity as it is devastating in its results. It may be stated like this: *The*

Christian faith contributed to the rise of the modern world, but the Christian faith has been undermined by the modern world it helped to create. The Christian faith thus becomes its own gravedigger.[1]

The strategy turns on this monumental irony, and the victory we are so close to realizing depends on two elementary insights. First, the Christian faith is now captive to the very modern world it helped to create. Second, our interests are best served, not by working *against* the Church, but by working *with* it. The more the Church becomes one with the modern world, the more it becomes compromised, and the deeper the grave it digs for itself.

Having joined the Operation when it was well underway, my own contribution has all been in the execution, not in the planning. So my use of the word *we* in these memos is in the broad organizational sense. But as you will come to recognize, the very relentlessness of the way the strategy is being carried out betrays its mastermind. Only one mind is capable of such audacity of vision and sheer force of will. "The devil is in the details," people say casually. If only they knew.

A Fall Beyond Belief

Now that the final phase of the Operation is beginning, a wider distribution of information is natural, and the Operation will soon be downgraded from "ultra secret" to "top secret." This is not to be taken as a sign of relaxing urgency. The art of "controlled leaks" has become a finely tuned instrument of state policy, but incidents such as the disclosure of the Pentagon Papers show how leak-prone classified information still is. Governments have long lamented that the ship of state is the only vessel that leaks from the top and not the bottom. Now, with the invention of emails and photocopying, the vessel is holed irreparably.

Our own record over security leaks is unrivaled and will remain so. But there are several on the Council who query whether the enemy still has the capacity to profit from any disclosure of the Operation. Most Christians are simply too lethargic to care. There is no question of our

risking the strategy by putting this belief to the test, but at the same time the reasons for such a belief are compelling.

For one thing, there is a psychological reason. Even if the details of the Operation were leaked at this stage, the Christians' most likely reaction would be disbelief. I will explain later why we are able to count on such a response, but it allows us to press forward, rather as Hitler was able to discount possible Allied reaction to news about Auschwitz and the Final Solution: "But they will never believe it." You can take this complacency (or its opposite extreme, the credulity that believes in any and every conspiracy) as a measure of our success so far.

In any case, most Christians would never take the trouble to make sense of these papers. "Christians," as that crusty old philosopher Bertrand Russell used to quip, "would sooner die than think—in fact they do." That is all too true. If sections of their handbook, such as the letter to the Romans, had been addressed to an American Church, they would be rejected as "far too complicated and intellectual." Everything in America has to be said in one-page summaries or in camera-ready form for PowerPoint presentations. Longer than that, and they are lost—and we are safe.

The Director was the first to maintain that even if this material were leaked, it would not cause a stir. I have learned to bow to his judgment. With sales up and serious thought down, and with marketing triumphing over mission, Christian publishing and reading are approaching the point where inspiring reflection and reformation will be beyond the Bible itself. The conspiracy-prone fringe and the complacent majority are as bad as each other. The former cannot see clearly because they only see red; the latter do not read seriously, so they cannot see at all.

There is also a strategic reason for our confidence. The Operation is moving into a phase that is almost irreversible. History tends to mock the finality of judgments such as "irresistible" and "irreversible," yet such claims are not far off. Your role in Operation Gravedigger is not to be a theoretician, let alone historian, so I will spare you a lengthy historical overview. However, to give yourself some simple historical back-bearings, it is useful to chart the development of the Operation against the course of the first and second phases of modernization.

The Darkest Hour Just Before Dawn

I call the Industrial Revolution, "Modernization, Phase One," and the Information Revolution, "Modernization, Phase Two." Obviously, the former was centered on production and was symbolized by the factory, whereas the latter is centered on communication and is symbolized by the computer. What matters for us is that when the Industrial Revolution took off in England in the mid-eighteenth century, we were caught unawares, and for a time the situation threatened to get out of control.

The reason was that the technological advances accompanied a massive spiritual awakening that swept Britain and the American colonies under the leadership of John Wesley, George Whitefield and Jonathan Edwards (the first two, incidentally, were both Oxford men—a lamentable stain on the record of your former Bureau).

This period of spiritual awakening coincided with rapid economic, social and technological progress, as well as a new burst of European influence around the world. And not long after, it was followed by one of the greatest periods of reform in human history—even temporarily reversing the age-old human habit of slavery (though, thankfully, we are now back to the norm and there are more slaves today than when the abolitionists started). In other words, the "power of the Spirit" and the "power of steam" combined to form a devastating partnership. They created the danger that the newly energized Christian faith would be welcomed as the leading contributor to what the rest of the world would see as one of the greatest advances in human history. That we could not afford.

The threat that we faced was partly fulfilled in early nineteenth-century England and America. The Evangelical faith of the heirs of Wesley and Whitefield grew so strong (especially as inspired by the example of William Wilberforce) that it was actually described as "the single, most widespread influence in Victorian England"[2] and "the rock on which the character of the nineteenth century English was founded."[3] At the same time, the first half of the nineteenth century in the U.S. has been called the "Evangelical Century" because of the striking Evangelical contributions to education, philanthropy and reform.

That dark hour in the mid-eighteenth century was our Dunkirk, and it forced the Council into the radical rethinking from which Operation Gravedigger was launched. We could not forestall such a momentous convergence of spiritual revival and social revolution—at least not in the English-speaking world. But if our counter-offensive succeeded, we could channel that power so that it would eventually become self-subverting—and on a scale never seen in history so far.

Now, more than two centuries later, we are well into the Information Revolution. The development of computers and the Internet has shifted the emphasis from production to communication—from a technology of muscle to one of mind—and the lead society today is no longer Britain but the United States.

We are at the decisive stage in the course of Operation Gravedigger. Curiously, ever since the mid-1970s, American Evangelicals have attempted to come to center stage in the U.S. just as they did in England 150 years ago, but the difference is comically plain. They are not Wilberforces but Don Quixotes tilting at windmills—and angry Quixotes at that. Not only have they failed abjectly to do what they set out to achieve, but they have also brought down around their heads the greatest anti-Christian hostility in American history, which will soon marginalize them for good.

In other words, we are almost home. The combined effect of all the forces of modernization unleashed over the past 250 years, and the Church's succumbing to it, is about to ensure the success of Operation Gravedigger.

This prediction may strike you as sweeping and overconfident. But once I have outlined the entire operation, you will appreciate the powerful evidence on which it rests. You may still be doubtful that so complete a collapse can be achieved in so short a time. This reaction comes from a weakness in the "intellectualist" tradition in which you have been trained. I will pick that up later.

For the moment, simply savor the breathtaking prospect of the Church in checkmate. Our ancient knights and rooks are pressing deep into the defense that surrounds the Christian king. The Director has withdrawn into himself with a concentration and a stillness that can be felt. The present stage of the Operation is charged with high-voltage tension like the moment between lightning and thunder.

The Way of the Fox, Not the Lion

Although Operation Gravedigger is essentially simple and its impact obvious, its underlying assumptions are quite subtle. In planning the Operation, we found two principles especially important. The first was "the way of the fox."

When Louis XIV went out to battle, he inscribed on his cannons, *"ultima ratio regum"* ("the final argument of kings"). There, in a nutshell, is the philosophy of realpolitik: the big stick and the big battalions—a style of thinking that lives on to this day in brash slogans such as "shock and awe" and "mission accomplished." Unfortunately for the Sun King, the Duke of Marlborough carried an even bigger stick and commanded even stronger battalions.

It is not in our nature to make mistakes like that. We knew that open warfare against the Church could not succeed. It depends on the basic maxim, "If you don't win, you lose," and the late-eighteenth-century alliance of Spirit and steam had left us horribly outnumbered and outgunned in the English-speaking world. The situation was different in France, of course—thanks to our skeptical friends such as Voltaire and to the oppressive corruptions of the Roman Catholic Church. But our first concern was Protestant England and its colonies, represented by its newly revived Evangelical wing. We could rely on some heavy artillery in the English-speaking world (such as the skepticism of David Hume from north of the border), but taking everything into account, an all-out attack was not an attractive proposition. There was never any suggestion of open persecution, let alone a massacre on the order of the St. Bartholomew's Day slaughter of the Huguenots in France.

The secret of clandestine warfare, by contrast, lies in the maxim, "If you don't lose, you win." Ever since Machiavelli, Western statesmen and politicians have been fascinated with the idea of combining the wiles of the fox with the strength of the lion. We have always used both to effect, but this time we knew victory lay in the way of the fox. If war (in Clausewitz's dictum) is the extension of politics by other means, clandestine war is the extension of conventional war by other means.

As you will see when you read through these emails, neither persecution nor discrimination is an essential part of our strategy. They are too crass. There is a time for bringing out a Nero, a Diocletian or Mao Tse-Tung, but not today. They are too crude, and their hostility too obvious. In mid-twentieth century China, where modernity was hardly advanced, there were no televisions, let alone cell phones and an Internet, to broadcast what Mao was doing in the Cultural Revolution. But even so, his heavy-handed persecution was horribly counterproductive. "The blood of the martyrs," as Christians defiantly insist, "was once again the seed of the Church."

The brilliance of seduction through modernization is that it succeeds when modernity is at its best, not its worst. The insights and technologies of modernity are devastating because they are so powerful, so positive and so beneficial. After all, who can argue against his own tools after they have brought such convenience and success?

We never use modern insights and technologies to deny or defy the Adversary openly. That would be blatant—we simply replace him. These insights and technologies of modernity work so well that Christians who rely on them have "no need of God." As we shall see, they can run their lives, repair their relationships, grow their churches and reach their dreams without any practical need for the Adversary at all. We have come as close as we ever have to creating a world in which humans can truly live contentedly "by bread alone."

Stages in Subversion

This strategy of subversion through worldliness has followed certain overlapping stages, some of which we are completing only in the present generation.

The first stage is *penetration* (or "worming in"). This is the stage through which our agents infiltrate Christian groups and organizations with a view to influencing and manipulating them over the long haul.

The second stage is *demoralization* (or "softening up"). This is the stage at which we work to ruin the fabric of the Church's spiritual and social life through such things as deviant teaching and public scandals. As this happens, Christian morale sags and Christians slowly become incapable of simple, instinctive resistance. For example, it was recently said of the Christian right in America that "its leaders are too often found with their foot in their mouth and their pants down." Every such scandal is hypocrisy exposed and, better still, it is discouragement deepened. "The thing now"—as Marx described his rather crude version of the tactic—"is to instill poison wherever possible."[4]

The third stage is *subversion* (or "winning over"). This is the stage through which we work to win the hearts and minds of key leaders of the Church and, through their "radical" or "daring" (read "revisionist" and "unfaithful") new ideas, to rattle and unnerve the faithful who are committed to the old ways of seeing and doing things. Behind this move is the recognition that the Church's morale and will to resist depend on its loyalty to the Adversary and to certain of his symbols, such as his Word or his sacraments. These are the flag and emblems of the Christian nation, and it is loyalty to these that we have to undermine.

We will never subvert all Christians, of course, but we do not need to do so. All we need is a *passive acceptance* of the corruption by the general body of Christians on the one hand and a *positive allegiance* to it from a carefully cultivated counter-elite on the other. Without such a counter-elite, we could never hope to win, let alone establish, our own rule. More on that later, but as you see when you cross the Atlantic, such Christian leaders as the current Presiding Bishop of the Episcopal Church in America are a dream for us.

The fourth stage is *defection* (or "bringing over" individual Christians). This is the stage through which we keep up sustained propaganda efforts that have been specifically designed to make the most of notorious defections from the Christian side (counter-conversions, if you like). The high tide for this sort of brain drain in Europe was during late-nineteenth century (it has been one of the factors in the current shortage of serious Evangelical thinking ever since). But we are working on a new wave of defections in America today, when headlines such as "Thousands of atheist de-baptisms" and "Former Fundamentalist Denies the Authenticity of the Bible" are making a splash again.

Do not overrate such defections, however. Like that of defectors and émigrés in the recent Cold War, the value of counter-conversions and anti-testimonies rapidly diminishes with time. Today the shock headline; tomorrow the old bore and the chronic refugee. It is the enduring lies of the Enemy that we are battling.

The final stage, which still lies ahead, is *liberation* (or the "taking over" of the whole Church). This is the stage at which the degree of our influence will become absolute and the secret operation will become public—through *coup d'état*. The Church, in short, will become completely unfaithful to the Adversary while still pretending to be in his camp. That, obviously, is our supreme objective and the one we are actually approaching in this momentous generation.

Subvert Strength Rather than Attack Weakness

The second principle behind Operation Gravedigger takes the first principle even further, and it has proved to be most effective. The Church's most crucial weakness is found at the point of her most conspicuous strength.

The tactic is as old as time: A person or a group's strong point often becomes an unguarded point. This, as any English schoolboy knows, is amply illustrated in military disasters from the fall of Croesus's "impregnable" Sardis in 549 B.C. to the fall of Singapore in 1942. (The British Empire's mightiest naval base fell ignominiously to "little men on bicycles" who easily stormed the notorious 15-inch guns that were facing the wrong way.[5]) Each was unguarded at its strongest point. But there is something less obvious and more important to us: A person's true strengths are not only likely to be left exposed; they can easily be turned inside out and made into real weaknesses.

Inversion, or turning things inside out and upside-down, is, of course, the heart of the revolution we are out to promote. The relative is made to bear the weight of the absolute, and finite people and things are given the place of the infinite (the "creature rather than the Creator," as their handbook puts it).[6]

What happens when one strand of reality is singled out and stretched too far is hardly surprising. Wider reality springs back and has the last laugh. Pressed too far, for example, reason becomes rationalism and rebounds into mysticism; or freedom becomes anarchy and rebounds into authoritarianism. We thus become masters of irony and connoisseurs of the art of the side effect, the unintended consequence and the unknown aftermath. Reality rebounds, and things turn out the opposite of what they seem and what people expect. Strength becomes weakness; love becomes pornography; pleasure becomes boredom; and so on.

We have had classic successes with this tactic in the lives of individuals. You might call it the "Samson Syndrome," because you see the cycle so clearly in the namesake. Trace the line from Samson's early promise, to his extraordinary exploits, to his careless delinquency and ultimate downfall. Samson could become prodigal only because his strength was prodigious. When his gifts became his master, they were the key to his undoing. *Et voilà*, strength turned to weakness. "All men that are ruined," said Edmund Burke, "are ruined on the side of their natural propensities."[7]

We have sometimes pulled this off with whole nations, but it usually takes longer, and in the mid-eighteenth century time was what we lacked. What if, through an authentic revival, the Christian faith were to gain a decisive influence in Britain, America and the English-speaking world at the very time when those places (through modernization) were gaining a decisive influence in the world? In one leap, the Adversary would have been around the world with a new freedom and power, and centuries of work would have been undone. There was no time to lose. We had to put out the fire of Western revival where it started, before its sparks could be carried to some dry corner of the world less easily dealt with.

Our long-term objective was clear: to work out the best way to turn the Church's strengths into weaknesses and turn their sudden advantage into a disadvantage. Once we found this, we could parody their own approach ("perverting" rather than "perfecting" their strength in weakness) and use it to plan our boldest operation.

This is how the Council's thinking developed. To begin, the researchers and archivists were set to work on a full-scale re-examination and analysis of Christian beliefs and behavioral requirements. Despite the accepted wisdom that the ideal attack-point was faith, we insisted on starting from scratch and hunting for any new lines of inquiry that might have provided us with background on the problem at hand. Might there be some key flaw or potential stress-point we had overlooked in earlier studies?

The "burrowers" were magnificent. No lines of inquiry were overlooked. Personal files, subject files, method files, background files. They rechecked every last one. Never have they worked over anything with such thoroughness, but their findings were always the same. The crucial point of strain for Christians is ultimately their faith.

The job then was to crack the secret of the workings of faith. Or, as it is put in the trade, to analyze their handwriting—trade jargon for their habits and patterns of behavior. As you know, the philosophical strength of the Christian faith lies in *its claim to truth,* whereas the social strength of the Christian faith lies in *its challenge to tension.* It was at this second point that the break came. Let me explain.

Part of the root meaning of the word "faith" is "tension" or "tautness." There, in two words, is an accurate picture of the faith required of

Christians. And there, too, is the rub. Loyalty to the Adversary in a world liberated by us makes their lives a kind of "double wrestling."[8] Faithfulness to him has to mean foreignness in the world. As they were taught by him, they are to live in a way that is clearly distinct in terms of space ("in" the world but not "of it") and in terms of time ("no longer" what they were, "not yet" what they will be). Their unenviable role, as one of them has put it, is to be *against the world for the world.*"[9] Let them try telling that to their next-door neighbors.

Such a high-wire balancing act would be precarious at best, even if the poise it involves were all that is required of them. But that is not the case, and here a further element is introduced. The Adversary has actually *commanded* them to be identified with the world. From his perspective, there are still a great number of positive reasons for their being in the world, the most basic of which is to seek to reclaim it for him.

Here is where we saw their ancient Achilles' heel at its most exposed. If any of these "positive" purposes of cultural involvement could be overdeveloped, they would serve to obscure the growing negative side effects. For instance, if their *desire to witness* leads to cultural engagement, that engagement could lead in turn to the *danger of worldliness.* The price of contact would be contamination.

This cultural contamination could happen in any culture. How much easier, though, would it be to achieve in a culture that Christians regard as good because they themselves had contributed to its creation?

What the Council envisaged has worked out exactly. From the initial research to the present moment, no operation has ever gone better, and Operation Gravedigger is sure to become a classic in subversion through culture. The textbook procedure has been followed with such ease that you, with your philosophical training as a counter-apologist, would find it absurd. The Church contributed to the creation of the modern world. Soon she was committed to that world without reservation. Before long she was hopelessly contaminated— in the world and up to her neck.

We have moved easily through the standard levels of subversion, each level leaving the Church deeper in cultural captivity. First, we encouraged the complete identification of the Church with culture so that she could not see where one ended and the other began. This is the *culture-blind* level, the level at which we have neutralized her integrity.

Second, we developed this identification of Church and culture to the point where she had no strength to act independently. This is the *culture-bound* level, the level at which we have neutralized her effectiveness either to do anything distinctively different from the culture or to be seen as different by others.

Now we are approaching the *culture-burnt* level. This is the level at which it becomes apparent (too late) that, through her uncritical identification with culture, the Church has been badly burned and must live with the consequences. Our supreme prize at this level is the complete devastation of the Church by getting the Adversary to judge her himself.

Here you see the devilry of the Council's design. To this point the focus has been on the Church's being subverted as her cultural strengths are turned into weaknesses. But now, enter the Adversary. When we manage to see that his gifts, such as the fruits of culture, are subtly changed and become revered in his place—which he then calls "idols"—he changes too: from giver to judge. In fact, some of his most severe judgments in history have been against *his own gifts and works once he sees they have been "idolized."*

The clearest precedents for this are found in their own records. It is most revealing to follow them through. Who killed a man for daring to touch the ark of his covenant, but carelessly let it fall into enemy hands when it was treated as a talisman? Who was most against the first Temple in Jerusalem (which he himself designed) once it was abused? Who attacked the rules surrounding the Sabbath that he himself had ordained? Or the Law that he himself had laid down? Who keeps reiterating the theme of destroying what he himself has built and uprooting what he has planted? When his own gifts and works are misused, no one is more against them than the Adversary.[10]

There lay the guarantee of our success. Under certain circumstances, the Adversary could be counted on to act as a sort of "agent extraordinaire" and do our work for us. All that remained was to find the most suitable gifts against which he would be forced to move once they were perverted. *His own transcendence would then become subversive. There is nothing, short of himself, which he might not have to judge and destroy.*

Here, in a stroke, is the beauty of subversion through worldliness and its infinite superiority to persecution. Persecution is the world's drastic action to deal with the foreign body in its midst; judgment is the Adversary's drastic action to deal with the foreignness in the midst of his body. But if the Adversary is to judge his own people, who are we to complain?

Echoes of an Earlier Glory

For anyone with a feel for history, Operation Gravedigger duplicates the dynamics of our monumental victory over the Church in its early days. I am sure that it will also prove to be as decisive. As you know, the fledgling Church grew at an alarming rate once it came free from the constrictions of its Jewish parentage—a bad example, I admit, of over-playing our hand with excessive persecution. After three centuries, the Church was actually bidding to become the powerful force in the Roman Empire, and thus automatically a powerful force for the whole world. We were naturally concerned—until we saw that one of the Church's main strengths, its unique new stance toward culture, was also its Achilles' heel—if it could be relaxed. The cultural challenge of the feisty early Christians would then slump into an amiable cultural compliance.

That is how we achieved our magnificent victory in A.D. 312 when Constantine won the battle of Milvian Bridge and went on to declare the Roman Empire "Christian." It opened the door to one of the greatest subversions of all time. *The Christianization of Rome led to the Romanization of the Christian faith and away from the way of Jesus.* That was a fateful detour, and we exploited it with great relish right down to the eighteenth century, when the massive Enlightenment reactions to established churches made it a tricky card to play. Operation Gravedigger is a similar subversion through cultural captivity on a monumental scale today: *The Christianization of the modern world is leading to the modernization of the Christian faith and away from the way of Jesus. Similarly, as we shall see, the Christianization of America has led to the Americanization of the Christian faith and away from the way of Jesus.*

Operation Outline

I can only outline the Operation here, but I will take up the details in later memoranda. Your overall briefing will be divided into three main parts.

Part one covers the *conception of the project.* I have just dealt with this briefly here, but I will elaborate in a second memo.

Part two analyzes the rise of the modern world and the overwhelming pressures it brings to bear on the Christian faith. The three key pressures to be discussed are *secularization,* or the Cheshire-cat factor; *privatization,* or the private-zoo factor; and *pluralization,* or the smorgasbord factor. This second section will deal with *concentrating pressures* on the Church.

Part three will analyze what contamination by culture has meant for Christian institutions, Christian ideas and Christian involvement in the world. This section will deal with *creating problems* for the Church.

The stage we have reached is critical. New environments have challenged the Christian faith before, but it has never faced as massive a threat as it faces from modernization now. No age, no culture, no civilization has ever represented such immeasurable and unmanageable realities or carried such an unparalleled capacity to shape the lives of its members. In the spirit of modernity, the spirit of faith does not know what it is up against. Down the centuries the Church has been the most influential culture-shaping force in all history, but it has finally met its match.

The modern world has risen up through and reached beyond the Christian faith, and now it is essentially no longer Christian. Our progress will never be reversed. Their earlier authority can never be recalled. The father has produced a son; and now the son has come of age and will soon knock the father off his throne.

With the dawn of the computer revolution, the countdown of Operation Gravedigger has begun. You could hardly have been more fortunate in the timing of your promotion. Again, my congratulations. The prospect of working with you gives me great pleasure.

The Sandman Effect

FROM: Deputy Director, Central Security Council
TO: Director Designate, Los Angeles Bureau
CLASSIFICATION: *ULTRA SECRET*

Your response to my memo was exactly what I had hoped. I anticipated the intense interest with which you responded to Operation Gravedigger, as well as your questions. Not for nothing does your dossier include the comment: "Loves philosophic jousting." I also wanted to see how you would take my needling over your intellectualism.

Some agents never succeed in adapting from counter-apologetics to cultural subversion, and a major reason is their snobbery. Once trained in the sophisticated methods of intellectual subversion, they consider other approaches beneath them and miss the chance to use simpler but equally effective strategies. European skepticism has proved to be a deadly weapon, but its use is extremely limited. Being groomed for the highest posts, as you are, you would do well to add to it a complete mastery of the approach I am outlining.

A Surprising Discovery

Let me pick up the story again and elaborate on a key contribution to our success so far—the Church's extraordinary vulnerability to our approach. This is also the best reply to the questions you raised about the strategy. Your point is well taken that irony is not the exclusive property of either side, and that Philistines throwing parties should beware of Samsons who lean on pillars. Who had the last laugh in that case is therefore a moot point, and one that is not at stake here. As you will see, our Samson is asleep. Due to what we call the Sandman Effect, Operation Gravedigger proceeds *while Christians sleep.*

In the beginning of the project, when the Council had agreed on the main objectives and strategy of the Operation, they sent an outline of the plans to various central departments for preliminary testing and development. The Department of Intelligence and the Department of Propaganda and Disinformation were the top priority, since their respective roles in the Operation were recognized as primary.

The response was remarkable. The traditional independence, if not rivalry, of these two departments is well known and has long provided us at the CSC with an extra source of criticism for all our planning. But in this case their reports revealed an unusual, early degree of consensus.

Each had arrived independently at the same conclusion. The plan to subvert the Church by infiltrating it through culture was not only a *striking strategic opportunity* as we had expected; it also exposed the surprising *defensive vulnerability* of the Church. All our data and experience since then have confirmed the accuracy of those early reports. In our subversion through culture, we had stumbled on a front where the Church was habitually asleep and nearly defenseless. Hence "the sandman effect"; the way in which contemporary Christians have a habit of falling asleep, even in the face of extreme danger.

Doubtless you have read regular intelligence reports on the derelict state of the Christian mind. In the early days the Council had checked similar reports to see whether the Church was likely to respond critically and coherently if our proposed approach through culture were to be discovered. (Of course, your former Bureau has played a magnificent part in creating the disarray that has existed since the Enlightenment. I need not remind you of that.) It was then that we found what no one had anticipated. The Church's defensive vulnerability in the area of culture was so complete that Christians were never likely even to detect our operation, let alone to respond. That is still the case.

In the end, what finally convinced several of the Council to proceed with Operation Gravedigger was the unusually low budget submitted by Propaganda and Disinformation. For once they had proposed no grandiose schemes and no padded expense accounts. Their plans were built on the recognition that, once the process of cultural subversion had gained momentum, little extra effort would be required. Ninety percent of the resources needed to dig the Church's grave would be its own.

Their original assessment of the Church's vulnerability to cultural subversion was based on two crucial factors. Taken together, these factors produce the curious sandman effect. Instead of the Church becoming more alert as cultural danger approaches, she falls into a deeper and deeper sleep. This makes it almost impossible for her to detect any subversion along cultural lines. I want to lay these factors out for you here, partly to demonstrate how the Operation has proceeded and partly to show you what this switch in strategies will mean for you personally. Remarkably enough, the two factors are as relevant today as they were at the genesis of the Operation 250 years ago.

Forgotten Dimensions of Believing

Not surprisingly, Christians see themselves as "believers," and for most of them that is about all that matters. They may be vague about what they believe, and vaguer still about why they believe, but they believe, and that is all they worry about. Fortunately for us, very few of them bother to look into the deeper dimensions of believing. After all, how can they be expected to understand the subtleties of belief in a world in which believing itself is hard enough? Down the centuries a dedicated minority always explored the intellectual dimensions of belief, and this has been dangerous to us at times. But even they mostly tended to overlook the social dimensions. This oversight was our opportunity.

Let me tell you a little of my own experience to make clear what I mean by this first factor. It will also show that I appreciate how demanding the switch in strategies will be for you. You may know that before being appointed to the CSC, I had worked for more than 20 years on the Left Bank in Paris. What you would not guess is that it was there, in that high-octane cerebral atmosphere, that I learned to go beyond subversion by purely intellectual means.

You can imagine my pleasure when, straight out of training, I was assigned not only to France but also to Paris, and that tiny strip of Paris from which has flowed so much of its brilliance, creativity and skepticism. At first, the assignment was all I had expected and more. The Bureau chief was a protégé of the Director. It was the early 1930s, and a dazzling array of "committed intellectuals" was assembling—Gide, Picasso, Malraux, Buñuel, Sartre, de Beauvoir, and a score of lesser lights.

The combination of illustrious minds, formidable gifts, passionate debate and international influence was intoxicating. Every gesture and word from the Rive Gauche seemed to secure an immediate worldwide audience. I thought that there in that scintillating "republic of professors" was the potential for a worldwide movement of militant skepticism in the best tradition of earlier Left Bank heroes such as Voltaire.

I could not have been more naive. The Left Bank was to be a crucial influence, all right—for two-and-a-half fascinating decades—but not at all in the way I had expected. In spite of all the reputations and the promise, no great work of art was produced by those committed intellectuals during those years. Only loners, such as Camus, were exceptions. (The London equivalent of this—"Soho-itis"—was the contagious disease of talking books and art but never getting any work done.[1]) More extraordinarily still, our Bureau chief hardly bothered to encourage any major arguments against faith. He was after a different end.

The longer I served in Paris the more I understood and respected his strategy. In the first place, he was always as much interested in intellectual style as in the substance of intellectual debate. Long after the details of arguments were forgotten, he said, their aftertaste would linger, affecting the memory far more than the details ever had.

Think of the reputation of the Left Bank in the 1930s and 1940s. Yes, there was brilliance, but its darker side was the empty rhetoric, the hypocritical poses, the shabby compromises, the betrayal of friends and causes, with some people fellow-traveling with the Communists, and others more or less sleeping with fascism.

As the chief anticipated, the legacy of this kind of general mood became a more effective inoculation against faith than a hundred Voltairean arguments. The desire for truth itself went out of fashion and the way was paved for the postmodern movement, which itself is more a mood than a clear philosophy.

Also, and here again I came to see the influence of the Director, the chief was always more concerned with creating a whole world of skepticism than with merely producing a handful of skeptical individuals one by one. This was the finesse of his strategy on the Left Bank. He knew that seen one way, the Left Bank was just a narrow strip of old houses and even older streets along the Seine where writers and artists lived and worked. But seen another way, it was a world of shared schools, such as the Sorbonne and the École Normale Supérieure, shared literary salons, shared bookshops and publishing houses, and shared cafes, such as the Deux Magots, the Flore and Brasserie Lipp.

What was the effect? The Left Bank was not so much an address as an ambiance and an attitude of mind, not so much a place as a philosophy of life. "Revolution," as Clara Malraux observed, "is seeing each other a lot."[2]

Plausibility, Not Just Credibility

Do you see how all this applies to you? Los Angeles (or London or Shanghai or Dubai, for that matter) is important to us, not so much as a location as a mentality, a way of life, a world of its own. Yet that is exactly what Christians overlook, because they have no feel for the social dimension of believing. Let me explain.

In a world unaffected by either our infiltration or our propaganda, the credibility of any belief would be determined simply by whether it were true or false. It would be believed if, and only if, it were objectively true; and if it were false, it would be quite literally incredible. I don't need to belabor the point. If something were true, it would be true even if nobody believed it. If it were false, it would be false even if everyone believed it.

Needless to say, such a state of affairs would eventually place us in rather an awkward light. But an excellent consequence of an earlier operation, which Christians aptly call "the Fall," has been that this handicap has been lifted. It does not take a cynic to see that, since the truth requirement has been lifted, a climate has been created in which flagrant nonsense or complete error can be believed, and incontrovertible truth, in turn, can be disbelieved—*without the question of their being objectively true or false being raised at all.* In short, we have created a climate in which a thing's *seeming* to be true is often mistaken for its *being* true.

How have we done this? By stressing and distorting non-rational dimensions of believing. The best-known cases of this are from the field of psychology. It's common knowledge now that people have non-rational, psychological grounds for believing and disbelieving things. A person may be an atheist, for example, without ever looking into the truth or falsity of faith, but simply because his or her father was a religious hypocrite who alienated the family from God as much as from himself. Such psychological factors lie behind the ostensible reasons they give for believing a particular thing and have nothing whatever to do with the beliefs being objectively true or false. A particular belief merely seems true or seems false because of a psychological state of mind that wishes or fears it to be so.

Freud called attention to this as "rationalizing," and his well-known exposé of the technique threatened to uncover our work. What has saved us is that the category of rationalization has been applied so selectively, partly because of Freud's own bias. When believers wanted or needed their faith to be true, skeptics derided it as "rationalizing." But when unbelievers wanted or needed faith to be untrue, the same skeptics, abandoning their skepticism, described it as tough-minded and applauded.

In the shuffle, of course, we have conveniently obscured the fact that the Christian faith actually claims to *be* true.

Fortunately, Christians are almost completely unaware of sociological examples of the same thing. Again it was touch and go as to whether our cover might be blown; and, curiously, the person who has best uncovered the importance of the social dimension of believing is one of their own intelligence experts—Peter Berger, of Boston University.[3] As he has seen correctly, the degree to which a belief (or disbelief) seems convincing is directly related to its "plausibility structure"—that is, the group or community that provides the social and psychological support for the belief. If the support structure is strong, it is easy to believe; if the support structure is weak, it is difficult to believe. The question of whether the group's belief is actually true or not may never become an issue.

You see, then, how our Parisian skepticism was more likely to *seem* true on the Left Bank than on the Right. On the Left Bank it was a whole, shared, inevitable-seeming world, not just an intellectual idea that you could choose to believe or not believe. In the same way, Roman Catholicism is more likely to *seem* true in the Vatican than in Las Vegas, just as Mormonism is in Salt Lake City than in Singapore, and Marxism in North Korea than in North Dakota. In each case, plausibility comes from a world of shared support. Coach it with care, and plausibility will upstage credibility. It then becomes for the belief not just a cradle but also a crutch without which the believer would be stranded.

This is why the Left Bank philosophy could never cross the Seine, but reigned supreme on its own bank. And this is the real reason why the "new atheists," such as Richard Dawkins and Sam Harris, have been so troubling to Christians. The danger does not lie in their arguments. As we all know, their arguments alone are often as weak as they are strident and intolerant. The danger lies in the ambiance in which they speak. In circles sick to the teeth of fundamentalists and fanatics—"faith-heads," as Dawkins calls them—any glass raised to the demise of faith is guaranteed an approving toast, just as any witty rant is accorded an instant "Hear, hear!" just as if it were a verified truth.

If this social dimension was vital in an intellectual milieu like the Left Bank (it is also true in Oxford, if you think about it), how much more will it be true in an area like Los Angeles, which puts such a premium on things with no substance—image, gossip and celebrities ("well known for being well known" and all that).

Fortunately too, although the clearest analysis of plausibility is by an enemy expert, his own side will be the last to see it. Even that diehard band of Christians still concerned to defend the faith intellectually are almost totally preoccupied with the credibility of the faith (an intellectual problem) and have little concern for the Church's plausibility (a problem with social dimensions as well). To be sure, there is some slight new interest in "cultural apologetics," but we are working to block its growth.

There is a double irony in this preoccupation with the intellectual: first, that Christians, who are generally so resistant to thinking, have developed an intellectualist bias of any kind; and second, that they have gone overboard by being too theoretical, even though the Adversary's warnings against this are so clear. He himself is no stranger to the idea of "fleshing out" theory. His directive was always that faith be truth that is practiced (giving it the necessary social dimension) and not merely professed, propounded, proclaimed (or some other purely theoretical response). It was once hard work to break the hold of this idea in the Church.

Even their arch theoretician, that bombastic little Jew from Tarsus, saw this point clearly. He knew it was the Church itself, not theory, which was "the pillar and bulwark of the truth."[4] Of course he did not mean that the Christian faith was true because the Church was strong. He was not stupid, only stubborn. He would have believed his faith was objectively true if he had been the last one left convinced of it. But just as the Party is the plausibility structure for Marxism, and the Senior Common Room (or "faculty lounge" as you will have to call it now) can be the same for secular humanism, the Church is the plausibility structure for the Christian faith.

That wretch Paul realized this. The Church is the Christian faith's working model; its pilot plant; its future in embryo; its colonial outpost. So, if we can work on the Church as a social body until it is weak, shallow, distorted, hypocritical, or whatever, then it's all up with the truth of the faith. Christian apologists can muster all the best arguments in the world, but they will not seem true. More accurately, they may be credible intellectually. But they won't be plausible, and credibility without plausibility is tinny and unconvincing.

You can understand, then, our need to undermine the Christian faith through the Church, not so much at the level of truth as at the level of plausibility. Uproot Christians physically from a well-functioning community or alienate them inwardly from a poorly functioning one, and the rest of our job will take care of itself. There is a French saying that the Breton peasant checks his faith at the left-luggage office in the Gare Montparnasse on arriving in Paris.[5] But the same is true of the student from a Christian home checking his faith at his first university seminar, or of anyone changing worlds. On entering the new world, the old becomes implausible, and soon its faith becomes incredible too.

Irony apart, the Church's preoccupation with credibility and neglect of plausibility is typical of her cultural weakness. Without a feel for the social dimension of believing, the Church is like a person paralyzed from the neck down—quite insensible to the further damage being inflicted on her.

Wrong Tool for the Job

"If you want to know what water is, why is a fish the last one to ask?" The old Chinese riddle captures an essential difficulty that Christians have in becoming aware of their cultural context—they know it so well that they do not know it. Put differently, they have no counter-environment to give them a perspective on their environment. But I might add another old saying: "To the man with a hammer, everything is a nail." If Christians have a tool that works, they tend to use it and use it and use it, including in situations where it does not do the job.

These two simple points are an excellent introduction to the second reason we can subvert the Church while Christians sleep: They are not using the right tool.

It is relatively easy to understand an exotic culture—in other words, the culture of another people, especially when it is sufficiently distant or different. In that sense, culture, if understood as primitive African masks or the sexual habits of South Sea Islanders, would be easy for Christians to grasp. It is conveniently distant in time and space. But understanding their own culture is quite different. It is the water in which they swim and the mold by which they are shaped, so it is not easy for them even to see it. Culture is therefore a ridiculously easy way to influence Christians without their realizing it.

In theory, that should not be so. Culture-blindness should be less of a problem for Christians than for other faiths. You would expect them to deduce from their own notion of "worldliness" that they do not live in a vacuum, that their cultural context is never neutral, and that the worst dangers are often the least obvious. But then, of course, today's sophisticated Christians have consigned "the world," along with "the flesh and the devil," to the doctrinal attic to collect dust. So they are not on the lookout.

Reducing worldliness from a serious to a trivial category was a subtle but easy step that we completed in the 1960s. Slowly, Christians liberated from the old legalisms began to talk disdainfully of worldliness as something they were freed from. It was always a matter of "those old no-nos": "Don't drink. Don't dance. Don't smoke. Don't play cards." After that, it was simple to dismiss the notion of worldliness as one of the despised legalisms of the "bad old days" before Christian freedom dawned. From our viewpoint, that was a simple but devastating shift.

An understanding of their cultural context should be a basic stock in trade for Christians. Such an awareness would affect not only their notion of worldliness and witnessing but also their discipleship, theological self-understanding, missionary outreach and ethical decision-making. Occasional stirrings toward cultural analysis do occur from time to time, and in fact, such a stirring is happening in mission circles today. This might pose a serious threat to us, were it not for two things.

In the first place, the new Christian interest in cultural analysis is almost completely restricted to intellectuals. Under the pressure of the so-called knowledge industry, there has been such a drive toward specialization that their own analyses are becoming more rarefied and less intelligible to ordinary people. Congresses, consultations, reports and papers are proliferating, and an impressive new jargon is emerging. Sophisticated talk of "evangelologists" and "missiological hermeneutics" is replacing tactless, old-fashioned phrases like "passion for the lost." But their mission is no more effective.

This flurry of cultural analysis will not cause us problems. We should even work *with* this trend, so that Christian evangelism suffers the same fate as apologetics and becomes an almost purely theoretical exercise— well staffed and monitored by a growing band of scholars, experts and consultants who know everything there is to know about evangelism, but never do it.

Dirty Word, Essential Tool

More importantly, Christians are using tools of analysis that do not have a chance of detecting where our most damaging work is being done. As you know, in intellectual circles today there are three main approaches to analyzing culture: the history of ideas, which traces the family tree and intellectual pedigree of thought; cultural anthropology, which interprets thought in the setting of human cultures and customs; and the sociology of knowledge, which interprets the impact of everyday experience on all that passes for knowledge. Fortunately, they have almost completely overlooked the last, which would lead them straight to the heart of our Operation.

Anyone who stopped to think would see that all three approaches are necessary. They do not compete; they complement each other. But if one should be overlooked, far better for us it be the third. It is the least used, but it would be the most useful for the Church at the present moment.

If we can keep Christians working away like beavers on the other two approaches, they will not notice the limitations. Cultural anthropology may be helpful in describing the less-developed world (or the "mission field" as they used to describe it), but is difficult to transfer to the modern world. Similarly, analyzing the history of ideas has its own shortcomings and it has practical difficulties. It is hard enough to do and harder still to make useful sense of to the average person. (After all, how do Kant, Hegel and Kierkegaard *really* influence the nine-to-five world of the exuberant Pentecostal in Buenos Aires or the staid Baptist in Birmingham, Alabama?)

It would be tricky for us, however, if they ever cotton onto the sociology of knowledge.[6] It would present them with no such drawbacks. It deals with the modern world and insists on seeing it from the perspective of ordinary experience. Fortunately, the very name "sociology of knowledge" is off-putting enough to sound like a dirty word. And although the core idea is simple and practical, it can easily be surrounded with enough jargon to make it unintelligible. Keeping a smoke screen around the sociology of knowledge is crucial. Once Christians see it as a simple tool and begin to use it, our position is at risk.

Forgive me if I insult you by belaboring the difference between the history of ideas and the sociology of knowledge, but many philosophers have never bothered to grasp it. They only use the former. *The history of ideas* traces the genealogy or family ancestry of an idea. It follows the line from a "thinker" to his or her "thoughts" to their impact on "the world"—how ideas "wash down in the rain," as it is put. *The sociology of knowledge* does the opposite. It traces the line back from people's "social setting" to their "thoughts," and shows how the former shape the latter.

As I said, the two approaches are complimentary, not contradictory. Both are needed and both are useful. But when only one is used, large parts of life are not understood properly, which is precisely our secret advantage with Operation Gravedigger. We can subvert the Church through culture because Christians do not use the tool that best analyzes culture at an ordinary level.

There is a delicious irony here. Christians are weak precisely where they should be strong. Because if they were to think about it, they would see that the best proponents of the sociology of knowledge have been Christians—Blaise Pascal and Peter Berger supremely—and that the tool is only an elaboration on what the clearest Christian thinkers have seen all along: that truth seemingly "changes color as it changes climate," as Pascal put it.[7] That said, this is the sort of analysis we dare not let them regain.

There are obviously some areas in which the history of ideas is the very tool they need, so Christians can scrape by without using the sociology of knowledge at all. For example, if they stick to discussing worldviews as ideas only—secularism, humanism, communism, and so on—then the history of ideas approach goes a long way. But many worldviews are comprised of far more than philosophical ideas, and the extent to which social contexts play a part would surprise them.

The Answer Is on Your Wrist

In many areas of the modern world, the history of ideas comes up badly short. For example, try asking an average Christian which thinkers have shaped their modern view of time in the crazy, pressured, 24/7 "fast-life" of the advanced modern world in which they find themselves.

"Aha!" they would rush to reply, furiously wracking their brains to recall the details of the latest brilliant Christian worldview seminar that has recently been the rage in Evangelical circles. "The modern view of time is linear and progressive, and is a result of the biblical view of time as it has been interpreted by Augustine and reinterpreted by contemporary thinkers such as Einstein—and then secularized, of course, through scientific time-and-motion, efficiency experts such as Frederick Taylor."

Such an answer would be right, of course, but only up to a very limited point. What the earnest believer would miss would be a far more obvious shaper of modern time right under his nose—or more accurately, on his wrist: watches and clocks, and such children of the clock as schedules, timetables, diaries, calendars, business plans, efficiency, measurable outcomes, and the like.

Probably our earnest Christian would overlook these things because they are not part of "worldview thinking" and they are so obvious that they are hardly worth attention. But there he would be wrong. The clock has been described as the most important invention in the West, and a central secret of the power of the West. Reinforced and accelerated today by the computer and by nanotechnology, today's fast-life includes turbo-capitalism, business at the speed of light and war at warp speed. Accelerated time is one of the primary shapers of our modern world, and far more influential than any individual modern thinker. Today's Westerners are the first generation to organize life at a speed far beyond human comprehension.

Much closer to the mark in understanding the modern view of time would be the Filipino description of Westerners as "people with gods on their wrists." One quick look, and they're off. Or the Kenyan saying—"All Westerners have watches. Africans have time."

Do you know Jean-François Millet's painting *The Angelus*?[8] As the sun sets and the Angelus rings out, two peasants stop and bow reverently amidst their work in the fields. You could not have a greater contrast than with modern fast-life. Earlier, "sacred time" could even break into the world of work. Today, the secular time of accelerated fast-life routinely breaks into every area of life, including worship and Sunday.

In other areas, the history of ideas has little or nothing to say, so many Christians are hopelessly at sea. Take certain mundane but hardly inconsequential areas which we have monitored over the years, such as the craze for the drive-in church in the 1960s ("Come as you are—in the family car"). It would be futile to try to analyze such four-wheel fellowship solely from the history of ideas.

Some nimble interpreters might claim to "discover" that all along the Adversary's handbook should have read, "Praise God in the chariot!" But they would miss the obvious point: a culture of mobility plus convenience—Los Angeles par excellence—leads quite naturally not only to drive-in theaters and banks but also to drive-in churches. Driving-in is as natural as breathing to your future fellow citizens on the west coast. Many of the L.A. churches are really commuter fellowships. Walking to church only means walking from the parking lot.

These may be trivial examples, and the drive-in church, unlike the impact of fast-life, did not last long. But they all illustrate the same point. Overlay upon overlay, the effect in molding lives through culture looks trivial but is radical. The slow, subtle but all-powerful shaping of culture has all the advantages of a complete philosophical revolution with none of the disadvantages of intellectual sweat.

That suits us down to the ground. Without a proper grasp of the sociology of knowledge, it is highly unlikely that Christians will detect our work before it is too late. Some enemy analysts have recently succeeded in drumming into their people's minds, "As a man thinks, so he is." That in itself will not disturb the Operation. But it is absolutely essential that the true relationship of thought and culture as a two-way conversation remains well obscured.

Not Only in California

"While Christians sleep." Count on the Sandman effect. Together, the two factors I have outlined make the Western Church almost totally defenseless and vulnerable to our subversion. The Church is in a coma.

I must return to your original point, however, and end with a note of caution. We would be piling irony upon irony if our strategy, which is built on subverting strength, were itself subverted at its strongest point. Subversion works best when the process is slow and subtle. It must never be recognizable until it is irreversible. This means that all sectors of the modern Church are to be subverted at once, although obviously in different ways and at somewhat different speeds. The situation must never arise in which the dire subversion of one sector becomes so exaggerated that it is obvious and acts as an alarm to rouse the rest of the Church.

You must take special note of this. The danger of exaggeration is particularly strong in cities such as Los Angeles or Las Vegas, where the local culture is so powerful and distinctive. It is all too easy to produce the bizarre. Your temptation will be to confuse *extreme* with *effective,* and so to overplay your hand and give the game away. Strictly between us, this was precisely the mistake made by your predecessor, and the reason why he was "promoted" to another region. Had it not been for the prompt intervention of the Disinformation Department, our whole Operation might have been in jeopardy. As parts of the Church began to stir at the extraordinary things they saw in L.A., Disinformation covered his excesses by soothingly repeating, "Only in California. It could only happen in California . . ."

The fact is that we are making the Church captive not only in California but also all around America and all around the modern world. For lasting results, remember finesse. Subtle compromise is always better than sudden captivity. See that their dreams are undisturbed.

The Cheshire-Cat Factor

FROM: DEPUTY DIRECTOR, CENTRAL SECURITY COUNCIL
TO: DIRECTOR DESIGNATE, LOS ANGELES BUREAU
CLASSIFICATION: *ULTRA SECRET*

Have you acquired a taste for Lewis Carroll while you have been in Oxford? He could not be more different from the French writers I was working with, but I quite enjoy him for light reading. At any rate, you will remember his celebrated Cheshire cat and the giddying effect it had on Alice. Slowly, beginning with the end of its tail, the cat began to vanish until there was nothing left except the grin, which remained some time after the rest of it had gone.

"Well," thought Alice in surprise, "I've often seen a cat without a grin, but a grin without a cat! It's the most curious thing I ever saw in my life!"

That is an excellent picture of our success in subverting the modern Church. Unlike the Cheshire cat, however, the Church is not vanishing of its own accord and cannot reappear at will. Think of it. Less than three centuries since our Operation began, and we have drained the reality out of the Western Church. Where it has not vanished entirely—in fact even where it appears to be flourishing numerically—what is left is little more than an empty, lingering grin—empty, certainly, by contrast with what it once was and it was supposed to be.

Our greatest triumph is in what has long been the Church's heart-land—"Christian Europe." For the last six centuries the history of the world was virtually European history, and whoever rules the world of to-morrow will rule a world pried loose from its own traditional past by European ideas, European tools and European precedents. Yet as André Malraux said in the last century, "The death of Europe is the central fact of our time."[1] Do you think it is only a coincidence that the death of Europe followed so closely upon the stilling of the faith that was its heart beat, and that we now have "Christian America" close to a similar tipping point?

"Eurosecularity" is now a settled condition, even a cliché. From Scandinavia to the Mediterranean and from the Atlantic to the Urals, the dawning of the modern world has reduced the Church in Europe to a condition that, measured by its former standards, is one of virtual collapse. Even in countries like England, shaped unmistakably by centuries of reformation and renewal, less than one adult in ten attends church each week.[2]

But how about the Church in the United States, that super-Europe or Europe-across-the-water? At first glance, the picture of Christian faith and practice looks better there. More than eighty five percent of Americans still identify themselves as Christians, and in areas like the upper Midwest, roughly three-quarters of the population are church members.[3] But a closer look shows that the boom is curiously limited. The burgeoning movements are in the suburbs and among the middle class, but they are conspicuously absent from the key leadership institutions of the world's lead society. Where, for instance, are Christians in the universities, the press and media, and the professional associations?

Even where the Church appears to be doing well, the Operation is actually succeeding. The coming of the modern world has led to vital changes within the Christian faith in America *even where it is booming*, such as the megachurches, so that numerical strength masks spiritual weakness. The same historic Christian words are said and sung in church, but what is shown in Christian lives tells a different story. The indicators of faith are still up (buoyant numbers, increased giving, high spiritual interest and so on). But contrary to the popular impression, the impact of faith on moral, social and political life is declining. One out of every three Americans now claims to have been "born again," yet that now means everything and nothing and American life goes on much as before.

We are at the point where there may actually be more Christians in America than ever before, with more money at their disposal, more powerful technologies to use, more positions of national influence to fill, and a greater global opportunity with which to respond. But with the corruptions from within, the opportunities will be squandered. With many Christians little or no different from their "pagan neighbors," much of American Christendom is more modern and more American than it is any longer decisively Christian.

Take an example that I have dined on for a while. There have never been more Evangelicals in any recent presidential administration than under George W. Bush. The President himself, the Secretary of State, two Attorney Generals, the Speaker of the House, the Whip, the Senate Majority leader, and so on—all were Evangelicals, and all in their turn were pronounced inept. So many, so high, and all to such little effect. It would be tempting to stop and gloat, but that is a tiny triumph in the overall picture.

Imagine showing the Church of today to the Christian of yesterday, to that old renegade Paul of Tarsus, for example, or those hyperventilating intellectuals, Augustine, Calvin or Pascal. Misguided as they might have been, they would rub their eyes in disbelief. Compared with the solid body of the Christian thing they knew, what's left of the Church, as one of her present agents laments, is little more than a "disembodied wraith."[4] If the Adversary were to return to the earth, as he threatened, would he recognize as his followers those who claim his name?

I will explain as we go on how we have pulled off this historic success, and how we can now exploit it to the full. But bear in mind that the Cheshire-cat factor is only the first of three pressures which we have brought to bear on the Church. You will appreciate the full extent of the damage only when you can stand back and survey the impact of all three pressures together.

This first pressure happens to be the most important, since it is the earliest and most basic. But it is also the trickiest to grasp, and even the confusion works to our advantage. It may not be quick to reveal its secrets, but master it because it is breathtaking when you understand it.

Chaos and Confusion

The technical term for the Cheshire-cat factor is "secularization." But I have to say at once that this idea has been surrounded with such confusion that many people have given up on the notion completely and now assert that there is no such thing. As you can imagine, this delightful chaos serves us superbly, and it can be traced back to the superb work of the Department of Disinformation.

The idea of secularization has been around for more than two centuries. Put simply, it is the claim that the more modern the world becomes, the less religious it will be. According to this view, Europe is the pacesetter and the future of the world, whereas America is the exception. For its own reasons, the U.S. was said to be out of line. Somehow it was both the most modern country in the world and the most religious of modern countries.

As was bound to show through eventually, this statement of secularization was both exaggerated and biased—not surprisingly, because it was put out by agents on our side as part of an overall Enlightenment assault on religion. As the world modernized, they said, religion was declining and disappearing. Secularization was all about the decline and disappearance of religion.

The advocates of this view were on our side, but they were headstrong and not inclined to listen, and for a while no one looked too closely at their claims. Eventually, one of the Enemy analysts did, and the overstatement was exposed for what it was. It was both biased, with its secularist assumptions showing through, and it was also comically

incorrect in terms of the facts. Beginning with the eruption of fundamentalism in the Iranian revolution in 1979, it became apparent beyond dispute that religion is very much alive and well in the modern
world—simultaneously revitalized and re-politicized. The early secularization theorists were well intentioned, but they had an agenda, they
had got it badly wrong, and the theory itself came under scrutiny.

At that point, we moved in quickly and sowed confusion. Some
thinkers—mostly secularists themselves—doggedly held to the original
idea, twisting and turning to re-shape it to match every objection raised.
Other thinkers, however, at once swung to the opposite extreme, pronounced the world incurably religious, and renounced the idea of secularization altogether. All this chaos worked for us magnificently.
Needless to say, the goal of secularization in our strategy was never the
disappearance of religion but its decisive *distortion,* and that is beyond
contradiction.

A Process, Not a Philosophy

We must never succumb to our own propaganda, so it is important to
keep the proper definition clearly in mind. *By "secularization" I mean the
process through which, starting from the center and moving outward, successive
sectors of society and culture have been freed from the decisive influence of religious ideas and institutions.*[5] In other words, secularization is the process
by which we have neutralized the social and cultural significance of religion in the central areas of modern society, such as the worlds of science, economics, technology, bureaucracy, and so on, *making religious
ideas less meaningful and religious institutions more marginal.* Our goals in this
are simple but far-reaching: to negate the centrality of faith in life and to
neutralize the Adversary's rule.

Defined this way, secularization is deadly to the Church because a
central requirement of the Adversary's rule is integration: the integration of faith and the whole of life, a requirement Christians share with
the other members of the Abrahamic family of faiths. Jews are required
to integrate their faith under the Torah and Muslims under the Qu'ran.

Similarly, Christians are required to integrate their faith and the whole of their lives under the rule of the Adversary. This they can no longer do.

This definition of secularization begs a number of questions, but let me leave them on one side for the moment and turn to a remarkable fact. Since 1900, the percentage of the world's atheistic and nonreligious peoples (agnostics, materialists, Communists and so on) has grown from less than one percent to more than twenty percent; in fact, from a mere one-fifth of one percent to over one-fifth of the world's population.[6] Entire countries such as the Czech Republic now have a huge majority of secularists.

This explosion of secularists is the most dramatic change on the religious map of the twentieth century. Even Christian findings affirm this now, although the gloomiest of Christian prophets did not foresee such a possibility in 1900. Atheistic and nonreligious peoples now form the third largest bloc in the world, behind only Christians and Muslims, and catching up with them fast. (Eight and a half million "converts" each year to be precise.)

But what does this fact mean? "Come now," you are probably saying. "You can't take credit for that. That success is due to the improved performance of the Counter-Apologetics Division. All you are describing is the dramatic rise in secular alternatives to religious belief."

Of course, of course. Your old department deserves some credit, but that obscures the real reason this has happened. As I have defined it, secularization is not the same thing as secularism, so it cannot be measured by a Dow Jones index of rising or falling atheism.

Secularism is a *philosophy* and has all the strengths and weaknesses of any 'ism or philosophy, not least that it demands some effort of mind or will. Secularization, by contrast, is not a philosophy; it is a *process*. More important still, its roots are not in an intellectual concept but in institutional change. It is a process that has actually taken place in the structures of society. Secularization has its subjective and its intellectual side—a very important part that might be called modern consciousness or the modern mentality—but this is the result and not the root of the process.

Unlike a secularist philosophy, such as atheism or naturalism, this secularized mentality is not something people think about or choose. Rather, it rubs off on them. It comes as part and parcel of objective, institutional changes that have actually occurred through modernization and cannot be avoided or simply wished away. Secularization is therefore contagious in a way that secularism never is. Wherever modernization goes, some degree of infection is inevitable.

The fact is, secularization promotes and improves on the old weapon of secularism in two important ways: it goes deeper and reaches further. Secularization (the process) goes deeper in that it provides the perfect setting for secularism (the philosophy).

Imagine a sports shop in a ski resort that wants to improve its sale of ski wear. What would help it most would be to have not only attractive designs but also good snow conditions. Even the best designs would sell poorly in the Sahara. Similarly, secularization provides the perfect conditions for secularism. It is the new context that enhances the old concept, making secularism seem natural, even necessary.

Therefore, with due respect, your counter-apologists cannot take full credit for the recent surge of secularism. We have had secularism around for millennia, but it has never before caught on like this, because it lacked the ideal conditions. Look at nineteenth-century skepticism, either in England or on the Continent. When it stuck to largely intellectual arguments, as the noisy secularist societies did and the New Atheists still do, it appealed only to a tiny minority. But when it caught the imagination of the masses through other means, people were converted without any serious argument or extensive reading. The soil was well prepared. As one enemy historian notes, secularism and secularization are not the same problem. "Enlightenment was of the few. Secularization is of the many."[7]

Up to the nineteenth century, discussion of religion had been continued in roughly the same context for thousands of years. An intelligent Roman would have been as much at home discussing the Christian faith with Pascal or Voltaire as with his contemporaries. But today's conditions would amaze them all. The truth is that a whole gamut of things has gone into the breeding of all these recent agnostics and materialists, including in the Soviet era some old-fashioned persuasion, KGB-style. But in all of it, argument has played the lesser role and atmosphere the greater. The contribution of secularization has been decisive.

Importantly too, secularization reaches further than secularism in that *it affects and influences religious people too.* Secularization is a silent process that simply happens, rather than a philosophy that can be chosen or rejected. So, it subtly shapes even those people (Christians included) who would never knowingly subscribe to such a philosophy and turns them into subconscious secularists. Marx's sidekick Engels noted wryly how English religion and respectability were infected by nineteenth-century skepticism: "The introduction of salad oil has been accompanied by a fateful spread of Continental skepticism in matters religious."[8] But secularization today has come under a more sophisticated cover and is far more devastating.

Thus, secularization works for us because of a double thrust: it *compounds secularism,* thereby increasing its power, but it also *constricts religion,* thereby decreasing the power of religion. Both secularization and secularism serve the same objective in our strategies, but secularization is the stronger, surer, subtler means of reaching our goal.

Bad Religion, No Religion

So far I have said more about what secularization is not than about what it is. But one further point before we explore the latter. Our use of secularization as a weapon marks a key departure from our usual tactics against the Enemy. For the first time in history, we are attacking not only the Christian faith but also all religion in the modern world. For secularization affects all religions.

Some of the old guard on the Council saw this as unnecessarily risky. After all, it has been a standard operating principle from the beginning that *bad religion is more damaging to true faith than no religion.* Generally speaking, this still holds true. But bear in mind certain things about Operation Gravedigger. In the first place, it is more than just another operation. If it succeeds, the Western Church will be in our pocket, and it will be the curtain raiser to the final thrust for victory over the Church worldwide.

The fact is that the present moment of maximum secularization is only an interim period between the passing of the Christian age and the rise of a new religious era. Trendy theologians may play up a "religionless future" and talk of secularization as the "exorcism" of everything in the tradition they do not like, but only because of the secularization of their own theology. No one will be more dismayed by the number of new gods and old ghosts that crowd in as squatters in the conveniently emptied house.

Also, remember that we are promoting secularization not to remove the Christian faith altogether, but to reduce its influence in areas essential to its integrity and effectiveness. By putting an end to Christian influence in the central sectors of modern society, we level a body blow to the Adversary's authority. He no longer rules over the whole of his followers' lives. Once that happens, whatever faith is left is limited and inconsequential, and lacks the mental and moral muscle to resist us. In fact, once domesticated, such faith will be a useful workhorse for the society we have in mind. The "pit pony" of tomorrow's world, as the Director likes to say.

Rebellion by Any Other Name

Field agents who have never served anywhere but on the modern front do not appreciate the magnitude of what we have accomplished. We have pulled off something in the last three centuries that is little short of revolutionary, but latecomers take it as routine. What we have achieved is both a revolution in human affairs and a revolution against the Adversary's rule. Scholars use fancy words such as "differentiation" and "fragmentation" to describe the new situation, the way in which traditional religion has lost its authority in more and more spheres of life. Let them each choose their own terms. Let them measure secularization in a thousand different ways, and debate the fine distinctions. All that matters to us is the outcome. Rebellion against the Adversary by any other name is just as sweet.

Our progress becomes apparent if you compare the situation we have engineered with what was typical in the past. For example, compare the state of the Christian faith in twentieth-century Europe or America with that in the nineteenth, eighteenth, seventeenth or sixteenth centuries. The numbers of Christians in these earlier times might have varied, spiritual vitality might have ebbed or flowed, and compromise and hypocrisy might at times have been more evident than fidelity. But where there was faith, however small numerically, it had a characteristic social and cultural influence because it mulishly insisted on applying the Adversary's rule to all of life. The benighted faithful uttered such slogans to themselves as, "If Jesus Christ is not lord of all, he is not lord at all."

That, as they say, was then. Modern faith, however large it is in numbers (as in America), almost never has this integrated view. Call the result *differentiation*, or simply call it fragmentation. But it is secularization that has made the difference. More and more spheres of life have been liberated from the Adversary's interfering rule. Now, those Christians who try to reverse the fragmentation are met with outraged cries that are music to our ears. What right do Christians have to "impose" their views on others? What used to be integration is now "imposition." Worse still for them, they are told they are "coercing" others who do not share their values.

A World Without Windows

What I have described so far is the objective and institutional side of secularization. Let me pick up the equally important subjective impact. Humans have always been open to a world beyond the world of the natural, the visible and the tangible.[9] In other words, they always believed there was a world beyond the world of the five senses, and what they could see, touch, taste, smell, measure and calculate.

Certainly, most people spent most of their lives in the "seven-to-eleven waking world" of mundane, everyday concerns and interests. Certainly, there were varying degrees of openness to anything beyond, with most people fitting comfortably between the extremes of skeptic and mystic. Certainly, many of the experiences that went beyond ordinary reality (for example dreams) were not necessarily considered to be religious.

But in the traditional world there was always a world that was *beyond*. Indeed, experiences that were held to be "religious," "sacred," "other" or "transcendent" were held to be the deepest human experiences of all. Such experiences called ordinary life into question and cast a religious frame of meaning around the everyday world. Pursuits as down-to-earth as business deals, making love, farming and politics were all seen in the light of the world beyond. Human worlds enjoyed the shelter under the shade of divine truth, however that was understood.

Secularization has changed all that. Today, for some people all of the time, and for most people some of the time, *secularization ensures that ordinary reality is not just the official reality but also the only reality*. Beyond what modern people can see, touch, taste and smell—in other words, the world brought to us by science and the five senses—is quite simply *nothing that matters*.

One of the Enemy analysts puts the point with graphic simplicity. Human life has traditionally been lived in a house with windows to other worlds. These windows may have sometimes become dirty, broken or boarded up, but they were always there. Only in the modern world do humans live in what he calls "a world without windows."[10] Shut off from transcendence, modern people are shut up to triviality.

Once you see this, you get a very different perspective on all the exaggerated talk of Christian energy in America or the new religious consciousness in the West. The energy is there, of course, but it is harmless because it is faith in a shrunken form, faith shorn of the genuinely supernatural. More and more of modern American faith is "under the sun," as old King Solomon used to say. The worship, the preaching, the publishing and the conferences are all about realities that are *this side of the ceiling*. The ceiling is rarely punctured.

Put the impact of the subjective and the objective together, and the result is devastating for the Church. In some parts of the world the Christian faith has become contentious and controversial, so radioactive that Christians are quite unable to go about their work and simply be. But in more and more of the world, the Christian faith has become irrelevant to a degree that is unique in human history, an achievement we owe mainly to secularization.

The Blowout and the Fallout

I would be intrigued to know what you had already glimpsed of the Cheshire-cat factor, though I suspect that as a veteran counter-apologist, you credited the wrong source. Some agents kick themselves when it is first explained. The thing had been going on right before their eyes, but they had been trying to interpret it in overly intellectual frameworks that ignore cultural infiltration and concentrate on concepts rather than context.

You may not have made that mistake. But a precise mind like yours will want to get down to more than a general definition of secularization, and look more closely at its character, causes and long-term results. You will also need to examine the overall process of modernization that has carried this secularizing effect.

Keep in the back of your mind that secularization is not produced by any one cause. This is the secret of its elusiveness and power. The fact that it cannot be traced to any single cause works to our advantage in various ways. Enemy analysts sometimes hunt for a clear explanation that can be verified with scientific precision. Failing to find it, they pronounce the search impossible or the danger a hoax. We are eternally indebted to them for diverting people's attention from the problem.

Other intelligence experts, determined to be less simplistic, seek to account for the secularizing effect with a complex chain of causes and subtle reasoning. Obviously we have to keep track of their work much more closely; there is always a slight chance they could break through to a correct understanding. But the reality is terribly slippery. Often, as a result, their complications thicken, their subtleties grow more and more refined, the number of their variable factors slowly mounts, while the explanation grows more elusive still. In the end, the search becomes a goal in itself. The fox escapes, but the excitement of the chase is strong, and the hunt goes on and on.

The top field agents who will return to the Summer Training Seminars this year will have a course on the full complexity of the dynamics of secularization. But here I want simply to draw your attention to the two most important trends behind it. These are only two of many trends that could be cited, and secularization cannot be traced back to either of them in a single straight line. Yet these trends are fundamental, and their contribution to secularization is like the combined effect of a volcanic explosion and the fallout of acid rain.

1. The Displacement of Religion

Have you ever seen a silhouette of the London skyline in the eighteenth century? Compare it with the same skyline today. The contrast in Paris is equally striking. What is dramatic about the earlier skylines is the dominance of Church architecture. Abbeys and cathedrals tower above the other buildings, representing the social power of the Church, while spires and steeples, symbolizing the human spirit, thrust upward to a world beyond.

Today, by contrast, the churches are dwarfed by skyscraping office blocks and crouch down somewhere between the banks and insurance buildings, cramped and overshadowed by a host of competing institutions.

Here is a vivid picture of the effect of the first trend: the movement in modernization toward *explosive diversification*. As modernization gathers speed and the rate of change quickens, the scale and complexity of institutions and ideas continue to mount. The result is a volcanic explosion of diversification. Specialized, separate areas are thrown up, each with its own premises, its own priorities and procedures—in a word, its own autonomy.

You can see this process most clearly on a physical level. Between 1861 and 1905, for example, the number of Christian parishes in Paris grew by a phenomenal 33 percent, and the number of priests by a respectable 30 percent. The trouble for Christians was that the population of Paris grew by nearly 100 percent, so the Church was always left behind.[11] Statistics for London show a similar picture. The Church was neither ready nor able to cope with the explosion, so it lagged further and further behind and became yesterday's institution.

I was reminded of this almost daily living in France. There is no more striking sight in the environs of Paris and other cities than the little church, intended for a village but now feebly trying to serve a sprawling urban area. Inadequate in itself, it is marooned from the main currents of modern life and left to its own irrelevance.

I am not suggesting that secularization was a result of the collapse of the parish system. But the failure of the old parishes to deal with the new population was a symptom of the Church's failure to keep up with the explosive diversification on all fronts. Whole sectors of activity (such as the place of work) and whole segments of the population (such as the poor and the working class) were wrenched out of the control and concern of the Church. The coziness of the traditional world, with its geographical concentration, social integration and conservative thought, was gone for good. The slums of the new cities were a symbol of Christian failure on a physical level. But a score of other equally uncared-for areas of thought and life were a sign that most Christians had been swept away by the explosion of modernity and had given up the unequal struggle to keep abreast.

Thus, modern work and the modern working class were both born in a century when the traditional Christian Church was largely absent from the center of the stage.[12] Other ideologies were not so reticent, but despite the social and theoretical reverberations from this failure, the Church has not pulled itself together to regain the ground.

This process of explosive diversification has a secularizing effect on religion, which is felt as *displacement*. Once the lava settled, society's structural shape had changed beyond recognition. Religion no longer presides over much of society as it did in the past nor participates in all of life as the Christian faith is required to do. As a result, Christian institutions and ideas are displaced from the center of modern society and relegated to the margins. At one stroke, discipleship, in the sense of the Adversary's claim to rule over the whole spectrum of life, has been effectively neutralized.

2. The Disenchantment of Religion

As a useful introduction to this second trend, consider the growing alarm about acid rain. Borne on the shifting winds of expanding industrialization, acid rain is becoming a problem of planetary dimensions. A leisurely but lethal atmospheric plague, it brings silent devastation not only to lakes, forests and wildlife but also to the world's great buildings and statues.

Secularization is the acid rain of the spirit, the atmospheric cancer of the mind and the imagination. Vented into the air not only by industrial chimneys but also by computer terminals, marketing techniques and management insights, it is washed down shower by shower, the deadliest destroyer of religious life the world has ever seen.

Consider for a moment what was involved in the Apollo moon landing in 1969. No operation could be more characteristically modern, yet it was really no different in principle from designing a car or marketing a perfume. Strip away the awesomeness of the vision and the pride of achievement and what remains? A vast assembly of plans and procedures, all carefully calculated and minutely controlled, in which *nothing is left to chance.* By the same token, *nothing is left to human spontaneity or divine intervention.*

This is typical of the acid rain effect of the second trend: the modern movement toward *extensive rationalization.* Far from being an incidental consequence of modernization, this is one of its essential characteristics.

As modernization drives forward, more and more of what was formerly left to God or human initiative or the processes of nature is classified, calculated and controlled by the use of reason. This is not a matter of philosophical rationalism but of functional rationality. In other words, reason used for practical rather than theoretical ends;

reason as the servant of technology and development rather than of theology and philosophy.

Notice once again that as modernization expands, so also does that portion of life that is covered and controlled by the systematic application of reason and technique. "Simply figure it out," says the engineer. "Anything can be made." "Simply figure it out," says the salesman. "Anything can be marketed." In other words, the systematic application of reason is seen as the best tool for mastering reality, and this movement of extensive rationalization is at the heart of the imperialistic spread of science and technology.

Check for yourself. You can now find how-to manuals not only for running factories and repairing cars but also for making love, converting souls, restyling your personality and growing a megachurch—all in five easy lessons. The evangelistic training manual and the church growth pastors conference may seem poles away from the Industrial Revolution, but the former is only the latter writ small. Look closely at its style and its assumptions. Under the regimental control of reason and technique, wisdom has been reduced to know-how, fruitfulness to skill and measurable outcomes, and an arduous apprenticeship under a master to a breezy weekend seminar from an expert.

The overall result? If the impact of the *exploding diversification* is felt as *displacement*, with Christian institutions forced to become more marginal in modern society, then the impact of the *extending rationalization* is felt as *disenchantment*, and Christian ideas are forced to become less meaningful in modern society.

By disenchantment I mean simply that, as the controlling hand of practical reason stretches further and further, all the "magic and mystery" of life are reduced and removed. When reason has harnessed all the facts, figures and forces, divine intervention is as unwelcome as accident, divine law as antiquated as the divine right of kings. Human spontaneity becomes "the human factor," the weak link in the chain of procedures. Wonder, along with humility and notions about the sanctity of things, is totally out of place. Problem solving, twentieth and twenty-first century style, is a matter of working a Rubik's Cube rather than unlocking the riddle of the universe.

Do you see how this has a secularizing effect? Medieval Christians could use the maxim, "I dress their wounds, but God heals them." But how many modern Christians doing agricultural service in Africa would think of saying, "I irrigated the desert, but God made it grow"? *The problem for the Christian in the modern world is not that practical reason is irreligious, but that in more and more areas of life religion is practically irrelevant.* Total indifference to religion is characteristic of the central and expanding areas of modern life. The deadly rain has fallen and all the spiritual life it falls on is dead, stunted or deformed.

I said earlier that our goals were to neutralize discipleship and negate worship. The first is easy. Not all Christians enter the central areas of modern society, but all who do are constricted by secularization, even if unawares. Secularization, therefore, affects far more than the overt secularist. It touches the most spiritual people too.

Today, only the very conscientious and young hothead still attempts to carry faith out into the secular world. Most believers are as used to being frisked by secular society's reality guards as they are to being checked for weapons before boarding an airplane, so the chances of Christians taking over any modern society are accordingly reduced to zero.

Some Christians half realize that this has happened, but they do not fully appreciate what it means. Other Christians are themselves the best testimonies to our success. The founder of McDonald's hamburgers, for example, was recently quoted as saying, "I speak of faith in McDonald's as if it were a religion. I believe in God, family and McDonald's—*and in the office that order is reversed.*"[13] Our own Propaganda Department could not have put it better.

Our second goal, negating worship, is more difficult to achieve. This is partly because the setting of worship lies outside the central and more secularized areas of society, and partly because some people seek compensation in worship for secularization in work. They hunger for an overwhelming sense of transcendence in worship to make up for a distinctly underwhelming sense of triviality in work.

In an increasing number of cases, however, secularization from the central areas has spilled over even into worship. Take the conservative preoccupation with church growth, or the liberal rage for cultural relevance (read Saturday's newspaper and you have Sunday's liturgy). Or go to your local congregations with their Blackberry busyness and distractions. With pressures and priorities like theirs, the last thing they can afford is to be "lost in wonder, love, and praise." Their minds as well as their watches are synchronized with the "real world" and in "real time." Securely earthed in day-to-day life, not for a moment are they in danger of being "heavened." Talk about "a world without windows." All this sort of worship is "under the sun." We are not in danger from a worship that never "punctures the ceiling."

In sum, it is sometimes said that the religious difference between Europe and America is like the contrast between the Arctic and the tropics. We have certainly already cooled the spiritual temperature in Europe to an Arctic level where only the hardiest of believers can survive, and then only by huddling together in their spiritual igloos. ("Always winter, never Christmas," as one of their agents laments.) But, as you will soon discover, the steamy, equatorial spiritual heat of the United States has its advantages—not least in allowing us to cultivate exotic, poisonous hybrids that would thrive in no other climate. In fact, secularization is behind both outcomes, though we are using it in different ways.

This first main pressure, secularization, or the Cheshire-cat factor, is by far the most difficult to understand. But, as you can see, it is also the most basic and devastating. Once its work has been done, the way is open for the other two pressures to operate. Where secularization has occurred, we gain far more than a beachhead on the fringes of the modern world. We are able to neutralize the Adversary's power at its very command center.

The Private-Zoo Factor

FROM: Deputy Director, Central Security Council
TO: Director Designate, Los Angeles Bureau
CLASSIFICATION: *ULTRA SECRET*

"I believe in the discipline of silence," said George Bernard Shaw about the original Quaker style of worship, "and could talk about it for hours." Shaw's wit fastens here on the sort of contradictions that are basic to human nature. Have you noticed, though, how the number of such human contradictions is increasing dramatically in the modern world?

You can see this supremely in what might be called "sunset values." These are values that modern people prize highly and hold passionately, but which really gain their intensity from the fact that they are about to disappear or be changed forever. Like the setting sun, such values make a flamboyant show at the end.

Take, for instance, the contradiction in the mounting concern for wildlife and the wilderness. As humans destroy more and more species, and modern world encroaches on more and more of the natural world, they are getting to the point where the only wildlife left will be in zoos. Conservation will then justify captivity. What an irony. How else, it will be argued, can wild creatures be preserved from the advancing jaws of development?

But the question is: What will "preserved" mean then? How wild is a Bengal tiger in a wildlife park? Or the lone seal bulleting around its circular pond? Or the elephant on its ritual route behind the moat? How wild is wildlife in captivity?

I will leave you to ponder the ironies, a major preoccupation of yours, it seems. What I am getting at is that wild animals, once savage and dangerous to human beings, have become little more than pets. But what has happened to wildlife is nothing compared with the taming of religion.

Look at it from the point of view of religious believers. Religion was once life's central mystery, its worship life's most awesome experience, its beliefs life's broadest canopy of meaning as well as its deepest guarantee of belonging. Yet today, where religion still survives in the modern world, no matter how passionate or committed the believer, it amounts to little more than a private preference, a spare-time hobby, and a leisure pursuit.

The Cheshire-cat factor has paved the way, but the damage is mainly the work of the second great pressure that modernization has brought to bear on religion. This, which in many ways is the reverse side of the Cheshire-cat factor, is the private-zoo factor, so called because it domesticates the hitherto untamable world of the spirit and fences in the once unbounded provinces of the Adversary. Religious variety, color and life still remain. But here, too, the price of conservation is captivity.

Incidentally, I could sense in your response to the last memo your evident distaste for the notion of new gods and old ghosts "squatting" in the post-Christian house. That is your support for a fastidious secularism coming through. Do not forget that from the slave-based Athens of Pericles to the leisured, aristocratic world of the Enlightenment *philosophes,* pure secularist philosophies have always been a minority interest. I agree with you that the "exorcism" of the Christian house may introduce some post-Christian squatters of a rather unsavory sort. But be assured: Such scruffy spirituality will also be in strict captivity. And the Director has plans for it too.

The private-zoo factor is a tricky one to work with and requires a rare blend of cool thinking and deft handling. To be candid (and I will be, since these emails are for your eyes only), this is one area where I sometimes feel less than sanguine. Not that I think we have miscalculated. But

I do suspect that several on the Council and many of the Bureau directors underestimate the risks and the skill required to use this pressure to our advantage.

Can you imagine a hunter relaxing when he has cornered his tiger? He might be seconds away from capturing a prize quarry, but those seconds are the most dangerous of all. We face a similar risk at this stage of the Operation. The risk is that in cornering faith and driving it toward captivity, we may accidentally arouse its ancient energy and vision. Then, in an instinctive last stand, it could elude our capture and break loose again and dart in some new direction.

Make no mistake. Faith is never more dangerous than when it senses danger. In fighting for life, the conscience, the will, the mind and the emotions of an individual can be fanned into a blaze of pent-up conviction. The Christian faith grew strong this way in the first place, and periods of revival have always had this same personal element at their heart. So for religion to be personal is for religion to be powerful—but if, and only if it does not stop there.

That is our cue. If we can ensure that faith is *personal but no more,* then we can quietly coax it into a corner from which it will never emerge. On the whole, we are managing to do this, and so far the private-zoo factor is working well for us. And as I shall describe in a minute, if faith should burst out of captivity, we quickly have to coax that escape into becoming an extreme reaction that is as bad, if not worse.

What I am saying is that, unlike the Cheshire-cat factor, this second pressure is not automatic; and, unlike the smorgasbord factor, it is not easy. I would therefore advise you to keep a constant watch on your agents in this Operation. Mistakes are likely to be costly, and they are not likely to be forgiven. Success has a hundred fathers; defeat is an orphan, as the Director allows no one to forget.

The Heart of the Matter

The technical term for the private-zoo factor is *privatization.* By privatization, I mean the process by which modernization produces a cleavage between the public and the private spheres of life and focuses the private sphere as the special arena for the expansion of individual freedom and fulfillment—forcing religion to become a matter of purely private concern.[1]

Naturally, there has always been a distinction between the more personal and the more public areas of life, but until recently the relationship between them was marked by a continuum rather than a cleavage. Today it might as well be the Grand Canyon.

On one side of the cleavage is the public sphere.[2] This is the macro-world outside the home, comprised of giant institutions (government departments such as the Treasury, large corporations such as Sony, General Motors, and Microsoft, and military complexes such as the Pentagon). To many people, this public world is large and impersonal, anonymous in its character and incomprehensible in its inner workings.

That is not to say that people are necessarily lost or alienated in such a world. Modern corporations have become adept at making work more "fun and fulfilling." People do their jobs and earn their incomes there. But by no stretch of the imagination do most people see their work as the place where they find their identity and exercise their freedom.

On the other side of the cleavage is the private sphere. This is the micro-world of the family and private associations, the world of personal tastes, sports, hobbies and other leisure pursuits. Significantly, it is on this side of the divide that the Church has made her home.

Two developments have contributed to the special emphasis on the family in this private sphere. First, there has been a crucial *shrinkage* of the family's place in the wider world. Fragmented in terms of what it means (the extended family giving way to the nuclear family, and the traditional family to a myriad of alternative families), it has also been reduced to its smallest size ever and relieved of many of its former roles (such as its part in education and economic production—the "cottage industry").

Second, there has been an equally crucial *shift* to a new role for the family. The private sphere, in general, and the family, in particular, now have one overriding concern: to serve the personal needs, expectations and fulfillment of individuals. At the same time, the private sphere has become the sphere of spending rather than earning, consumption rather than production. This fateful convergence creates the possibility of "conspicuous consumption"[3]—spending that is not a matter of need but an expression of identity, a material consumption that is the badge of status and success.

All this means that modern people experience the private sphere as an island where the "real self" lives. To be sure, the computer revolution is now blurring this effect. Emails and text messages, for example, have obscured the hard and fast distinction between work and family, and private and public. The good news, as they say, is that you can work anywhere. The bad news is that you can work anywhere. Some corporations have expressed a concern that private matters will eat into the world of work, as friends email friends from work. But for most people, the effect is the opposite—the world of work never stops, either in the evening or during the weekend. The ability to work anywhere means that work can be with us everywhere. Needless to say, this is no problem to the Operation. Blackberrys may cover more and more of life and the world, so long as the Bible never does.

Negative Side Effects

None of the three main pressures of modernization originated with us, though they work decisively in our favor. But do not ever forget that each of them is double-edged. Here and there they carry disadvantages for us, so we need to assess them carefully before deciding how best to exploit them to the fullest.

There are two potential disadvantages of the process of privatization. The first is that *it does represent authentic, if limited, freedom.* Compared with the situation in the past, privatization permits more people to do more, buy more, travel more, and fulfill more of their dreams than ever before. Just think of the amazing world of information and opinion that is all a click away on the Internet. Add to that the fact that, unlike people in totalitarian societies, privatized modern people *have* a private world. Big Brother is not watching them, at least not in this part of their lives.

It is easy to caricature the results of this freedom, which are often chaotic. Do-it-yourself beliefs become as simple and as casual as online banking. Psyches can be redecorated as quickly as living rooms according to the fashions du jour. People surf convictions as easily as television channels. But be sure of this: To most people, the private world is "a world of our own," just as Facebook is all about the free expressions of a "daily me." It represents an unprecedented freedom and the chance to think and act independently as never before. So beware. The private world is a potential flash point for us, and we shall have to monitor it closely.

The second problem from our perspective is that the *private sphere serves as a form of compensation*. Many people make up in the private sphere for what they are denied in the public sphere, so the private sphere works like a safety valve or fire escape. "Out there" (in the public sphere) they may wear a uniform, whether factory overalls or a pinstriped suit, play a role and be identified by a number. "But here's one place" (in the private sphere), they say, where they can "get out of those things" and be themselves.

In the public sphere, relationships are necessarily partial, superficial and functional, but in the private sphere they can be total, deep, personal, face to face, and "authentic," as they say today. This can cut various ways. A person who is frustrated by being a small fish in a big pond at work can play the big fish in a small pond at home. Another can find the anonymity of work an escape from the problems of life at home.

The element of compensation has its advantages for us, since it acts as an opiate against public reality. But once more, the problem is that at its heart lies a dangerous core of freedom, independence and choice, which the Adversary may always tap.

These potential disadvantages of privatization are far outweighed for us by its advantages. As I lay out some of these advantages, you will see why we are able to move in on religion and drive it unsuspecting into captivity.

Limited and Limiting

The first great advantage is that privatization ultimately acts as a decisive limitation on freedom. Granted, it offers freedom, unprecedented freedom, but only within strict limits. In the end, the price of this freedom is captivity. What do people want to pursue? Yoga? Satan worship? Spouse swapping? Bridge playing? Speaking in tongues? Happy-clappy "worship experiences" (which once used to be worship "services") and touchy-feely fellowship groups? Let them feel free. The choice is theirs. Everything is permitted in the private sphere. Money, time and, to a mild extent, local sensitivities, are the only limits.

But what will they discover if they try to bring those personal commitments out into the public sphere? The same Grand Canyon, metaphorically speaking. The world of work—the world of Wall Street, Capitol Hill, Google, and NASA—is a quite different world with completely different ways. Personal preferences have no place there. Prayer breakfasts *before* work maybe, or Yoga during the lunch hour for the East-West set perhaps. But in the normal working world, faith, along with hats and coats, is to be left at the door.

Privatization thus spells freedom but only in the private sphere. In fact, far from being the arena of choice and creativity it sets itself up to be, the private sphere is really a sort of harmless play area.[4] Individuals are free to build a world of their own to their hearts' content—so long as they rock none of the boats in the real world. This means that for the religious believer, the private sphere serves as a sort of spiritual Indian reservation or Bantustan, a homeland for separate spiritual development set up obligingly by the architects of secular society's apartheid.

It is true that disastrous outbreaks of spiritual revival in history have always featured a highly personal faith. You well know of the cell groups set up by Wesley in the eighteenth-century awakening, and there are signs of such an outbreak in the developing world today, especially in places like Costa Rica and South Korea or in Chinese provinces like Henan. These are places where the fire is spreading fastest and most uncontrollably when the spiritual movement is rooted in home groups and

Pentecostal styles of worship. The last generation has even seen a decided shift in the West toward more personal, informal and home-based expressions of faith, and more contemporary styles of worship in churches.

All this I freely concede. Such evidence only illustrates why this pressure has risks and why we cannot be too careful. But remember, our sector of responsibility is the modern sphere alone, so citing pre-modern examples is beside the point. We are not concerned with the past or with the developing world where it is not yet modernized. Remember too that in the modern world the very point of using privatization is that it adds a new and unexpected catch to faith. It guarantees that personal freedom is no longer what it has been in the past.

There is therefore only one serious issue for us: Are the various movements of Western renewal still contained by the *social inhibitions* that accompany privatization, or are they marked by a *spiritual inspiration* that has the power to break out of the limits of the private sphere? Put the question that way, and you will see your answer. Look closely at the marked shift of emphasis in religion over the last generation—from institutions to individuals, from programs to people, from the formal to the casual, from the mind to the feelings, from the set-form to the freeform, from the head to the whole body, from the word to the spirit, from the local church to the home.

Would you have taken all that as a disturbing sign of authentic revival? In the past the answer would have been yes. But, thanks to privatization, that is no longer so. The outbreak of spiritual concern may be authentic, but the boa-like squeeze of privatization acts to constrict and smother any dynamic that could have culture-wide significance.

Put simply, the charismatic movement in general and your American renewal in particular are not what they seem to be, nor what they wish they were. Their weakness is not that renewal starts in the private world, but that *it ends there too*. Spiritual inspiration they may have. But social inhibitions overwhelm them in the end.

If this were not so, the renewal movement would be extremely dangerous. It has reawakened a hunger for transcendence that refuses to be satisfied with secularism. It has rediscovered how to exercise a diversity of individual gifts that threaten to by-pass professional categories. It stresses the practice of community and claims to answer the modern cry for meaning and belonging. Were it not for the grip of privatization (and of a further tactic I will introduce later), all this could become disastrous.

We have come a very long way in the last 200 years. Lord Melbourne, British prime minister in the 1830s, once listened to a pointed sermon and made the indignant remark: "Things have come to a pretty pass when religion is allowed to invade the private life!" He was a perceptive old curmudgeon. Personal faith was once seen as very demanding. In touching the personal life, it threatened to become a force that reached out into all of life and left nothing untouched. That, for a prime minister in the days of the British Empire, was a bit much.

Compare that with the present view of personal faith. In the early 1970s, an American historian commented on what he had observed of the Christian faith in California: "Socially irrelevant, even if privately engaging."[5] We could ask for no better. Lord Melbourne would be untroubled now. In much of today's world things have come to a pretty pass if religion is allowed to invade *public* life with integrity.

In terms of Christian theory, privatization means that the grand, global umbrella of faith has shrunk to the size of a plastic rain hat. Total life norms have become part-time values. In terms of Christian practice, watch your average Christian businessperson or politician. Are there family prayers at home before leaving for work? That's the private sphere. Are there Bible studies with colleagues at the office? Still the private sphere. Are there big, impressive prayer breakfasts that attract the high and mighty in the land? Still only the private sphere.

Look for a place where the Christian's faith makes a difference at work beyond the realm of purely personal things (such as witnessing to colleagues and praying for them, or *not* swearing, *not* fiddling with income tax returns, or *not* sleeping with their secretary). Look for a place where the Christian is thinking "Christianly" and critically about the substance of work (about the boardroom and not just the bedroom; about the use of profits and not just personnel; about the ethics of a multinational corporation and not just those of a small family business; about a just economic order and not just the doctrine of justification). You will look for a very long time. This or that business leader may be "into religion," but so are colleagues "into golfing" or "into theater" or a score of other hobbies.

A Christian's priorities outside the office may be God, family and business, but once inside the office that order is reversed. Such Christians are of little use to the Adversary and pose no threat to us. The fascinating thing is that their fatal deficiency is so subtle they do not see it. *The problem with modern Christians is not that they are not where they should be, but that they are not what they should be where they are.*

Do you see what an opening this is for us? We can encourage Christians to accept a damaging degree of spiritual specialization *as entirely normal.* When this happened before, in the fourth century A.D., we fostered a gap between the "advanced" believer who was truly spiritual and the "average" believer who muddled along as best he could with a less demanding rule of life. Christians even spoke admiringly of the difference between the "perfect life" and the "permitted life." It was this widening gulf that slowly brought the conversion of the Roman world to a halt.[6]

The new gulf is different—between the private and the public, rather than the average and the advanced—but our goal is the same: to create such a spiritual specialization that Christian penetration of the modern world slows to a grinding halt.

Let these four words *privately engaging, socially irrelevant* be engraved on your mind. That is what privatization does to renewal in the modern world. "Jesus is Lord," they declare (and sing and strum on their guitars to their hearts' content). But what do they demonstrate? Little better than a spare-time faith and a pocket-discipleship. The once wild animal may roar, but safely behind bars.

Fragmenting and Dislocating
I have spent time on the first advantage, since it is absolutely critical to us, but let me briefly cover some others. A second one is *that privatization*

induces a sense of fragmentation or dislocation. In the highly complex and diversified conditions of the modern world, there is not only greater freedom *within* each separate sphere but also a greater difference (and distance) *between* each sphere.

On the one hand, this fragmentation means that people today are more anonymous in more situations than ever before in history. This is important because it does not take a cynic to see that morality is often a matter of accountability through visibility. Thus, if character is who they are, and ethics is what they do *when no one sees,* character will now be trumped by image and ethics by compliance (and what they can get away with when no one is looking).

On the other hand, fragmentation means that the different worlds through which people migrate daily will all be *very* different. Worlds that are only minutes apart physically may be light years away morally and spiritually. A person's life can therefore come to resemble a nonstop process of commuting between almost completely separate, even segregated, worlds.

The net effect of these constant crossings is spiritual compartmentalism, if not ethical and psychological confusion. For some people, moving in different worlds and having to wear different hats are a source of only minor irritation. Others can be driven into a state of deep inner division, as has been said of the bureaucrat: "He lives in two worlds, and he must therefore, so to speak, have two souls."[7]

The potential here for spiritual, moral and intellectual schizophrenia is great. Christians have always been warned against the hypocrisy of double-thinking. But now that they are juggling with double-, triple- and quadruple-living, modular morality and compartmentalized convictions are becoming as interchangeable as Lego-like lifestyles.

At the very least, this fragmentation fosters the breathless, strung-out feeling characteristic of busy modern Christians. Better still, it means that modern Christians are denied the chance of a total expression of their gifts and personalities. Best of all, it makes certain that there is no Christian mind integrating all of life, only a personal faith with compartments between its various disciplines and activities—one mind for Church, another for the classroom; one for reading the Bible, another for reading the newspaper; one for the world of the family, another for the world of business. In the busy rush of life's commuting, Christian convictions are boxed-in as neatly and firmly as the commuter behind his paper in a crowded morning train.

Unstable and Unrealistic

A third advantage is *that privatization creates an inherently unstable private sphere*. Consider the difference between steering a sailboard and piloting an ocean liner. For anyone wanting the freedom to follow every caprice of the breeze, wind surfing is the obvious choice. But for crossing the Atlantic, the ocean liner is the surer bet.

From the perspective of the believer in the private sphere, much of the institutional Church—sometimes at the local level, certainly at the denominational level—appears about as maneuverable and responsive as an ocean liner. So the growing desire is to cut loose and find the freedom and exhilaration of spiritual wind surfing in the burgeoning home groups.

So, Christians and their groups today can be as free as sailboarders, and as collapsible too. There are two reasons for this instability. On the one hand, the private sphere is decidedly *understructured*.[8] The extended family (such as it was) has shrunk into the nuclear family, and religion has retreated from its previous position of influence in the public sphere. Thus the two strongest supports that traditionally undergirded people's private lives and tied them into a wider public world have been sabotaged in a stroke.

The result is a crisis in the traditional ways of setting up and running the private life, a crisis that leaves people more uncertain as well as more free. Conventional values are no longer taken for granted, and the traditional supporting web of family, friends, neighbors and community can no longer be counted on. Family members may be scattered across the world, neighbors and colleagues change with the speed of a game of musical chairs, and genuine community has died. Some sort of supporting web can certainly be rewoven and maintained, but only by a strenuous effort of will. Privatized man and woman are free to be Atlas to their own worlds, but they will always be somewhat anxious Atlases to largely do-it-yourself worlds that can collapse as suddenly as they were created.

On the other hand, the private sphere is distinctly *oversold*.[9] It has become the sphere of spending rather than earning, and of personal fulfillment rather than public obligation. Naturally then, when conspicuous consumption grafts spending into identity, appetites become insatiable and expectations unrealistic. In short, privatized man is not only an anxious Atlas but also a spoilt Narcissus. He wants more, and he wants it now. After all, to others at least, he is what he consumes. And so is she.

This combination (institutionally understructured, ideologically oversold) is a potent blend that makes the private sphere highly unstable and volatile. One moment the impression is all freedom. Do-it-yourself this, do-it-yourself that, and almost miraculously little worlds arise overnight, replete with new homes, new friends, new lifestyles, new identities. The next moment, the impression is all fragility. The neighborhood changes, separation and divorce are in the air, children drop out, sickness strikes, a job is axed, and in an instant liberty becomes anxiety, which becomes catastrophe. For every newly constructed mini-world that rises, another is collapsing.

Privatized freedom, in other words, is highly precarious. Understructured, it is the victim of outside forces pulling it apart. Oversold, it is the victim of inner forces tearing it down. What begins with Atlas ends with Humpty Dumpty, and all the king's counselors, therapists and attorneys cannot put the pieces together again.

Both aspects of this general dilemma apply to the religious world too. How privatized faith becomes under-structured is evident in many of the fringe groups in the charismatic movement—the "off-off-Broadway" of the world of the spirit. They cut themselves off from the Church of the past and from the wider Church around the world, and very often from other local churches too. In place of these, they concentrate on the private and personal, often in a form no larger than the nuclear family or a home fellowship group. Wind surfing requires a somewhat smaller crew.

Where does this lead? Such groups have a social base that is smaller, shakier and shorter-lived. They lack theology, they lack a sense of history and tradition, they lack discipline and accountability, and they lack clear boundaries as to what membership involves. As "thin" communities, built only on choice, rather than "thick" communities, built on custom and tradition, they are easier to join, but easier too to leave. Launched more easily, they capsize more easily. Viewed overnight, they seem to offer the liberation and flexibility of a highly personal and deeply authentic faith. Viewed over the course of a generation, they have all the ocean-going stability of a cockleshell.

The way in which privatized faith is oversold is equally plain. Drop into your local secular bookstore sometime and size up the amazing range of how-to and can-do publishing. Do people want to improve their memory, banish boredom, relax, cope with stress, overcome fears, brighten their love life? It is all there for them, with self-awareness the dominant theme, and success, wealth and peace of mind close behind.

Then visit a local Christian bookstore. The themes and style are precisely the same; only the gloss is different. Ninety percent of the books are about "I, myself, and me." I was recently shown a title that even I could hardly believe: *Me, Myself & I Am*—the vision of the Adversary that once terrified Moses on Mount Sinai and launched the culture-shaping power of radical monotheism now domesticated for cute Christian self-help.

As with consumerism, privatization brings out the best in "copycat Christianity." Originally, Christians mimicked the words of pop songs. Then the copying craze spread to advertizing jingles ("Jesus is the real thing," brought to you by association with Coca-Cola). Now the instant imitation is the predictable response to every fad. When dieting became fashionable, for example, Propaganda and Disinformation were ready with a line of counterfeit slogans. But they were redundant even before they were released. The Christian ones were far more fatuous. Dieting Christian-style became "Trim for Him." Then, with the stress shifting to fitness, there came *Aerobic Praise, Devotion in Motion, Praise-R-Cise,* and the most astounding so far: the album *Firm Believer* and the slimming slogan, "He must increase but I must decrease."[10] Seriously.

Even Propaganda and Disinformation were taken aback. By traditional Christian standards these slogans were nearly blasphemous. Some other dirty tricksters must be at work. But the slogans proved authentic. Normally, canny copywriters use puns to give their products a leg up, caring little for the original meanings. (The 1970s slogan "Datsun Saves," for example, takes one of the Christians' most precious slogans and lowers it to the level of fuel efficiency. "Jesus Saves" is then devalued forever, and no one can ever hear it in the same way again.) Incredible as it may seem, Christians now do the reverse: They use double meanings to sell their product, and not only devalue the original meanings but demean themselves in the process.

Firm Believer says it all. With spiritual narcissism so well advanced, "firm believer" is a matter of aerobics rather than apologetics, of human fitness rather than divine faithfulness. Shapeliness is now next to godliness, and to judge by the new "shape-up centers" in Christian stores, training righteous character has given way to trimming the right curves.

Poor old Paul. Wrong again. Bodily exercise now profiteth much—for the fitness gurus at least. Poor old John the Baptist. Decreasing, for him, meant losing his head, not shedding some pounds. But then our bandwagon believers are in danger of losing their heads as well. No wonder such privatized faith has been described as "credit card religion."[11] It takes the waiting out of wanting. It certainly takes the waiting out of waiting on God.

We are now at the stage between the setting and the springing of the trap. This is our operational moment of truth when there is no way out but forward. There remains the one major risk to which I have referred. Instead of sealing faith's captivity in the private sphere, something might trigger the reawakening of a faith that is both personal and culturally powerful at once. Faith would then elude capture and break out into the larger world again.

That is the worst-case prospect for us. So, I would urge constant vigilance on your field agents at this point. Let me illustrate the danger with two current examples that we are monitoring. At one time they each looked potentially disastrous, but both are going our way now.

The Megachurch Mirage

One of the recent movements that we are following with great care is the church-growth movement, and especially its championing of megachurches. At first sight, these churches looked extremely danger-ous, with their passion for reaching out, their determination to over-come stereotypes, and to present the Adversary in the best possible light to those outside the Church. Then, when they get their clients in—and no one disputes their success in doing that—they do an above average job in catering to their "felt needs" of every kind, felt needs that appear to be for gyms and bowling alleys as well as for guitars and PowerPoint presentations.

But we soon saw why the megachurches would be no threat to us. Critics have pointed to other weaknesses in the movement, such as the way their "seeker-sensitive" stance so often becomes a faux ver-sion of the spirit of the age. But there is a simpler reason why they do not pose a problem in the end. The megachurches do not rock the boat of privatization. They reinforce it.

There you have it. So long as the mega-booming activities remain in the private sphere and the more successful they are, the better—for us as well as them. They are just a religious equivalent of shopping malls: "Every need under the sun now under one roof." So let the competition to be "the biggest church in the world" heat up. Let all the interests catered to in the name of "felt needs" proliferate expo-nentially. Let the conferences describing the latest ministry "innova-tions" and "out-of-the-box" pastors be hotly over-subscribed. None of it will amount to a hill of beans while it remains in the private sphere. "Privately engaging, publicly irrelevant" is still the yardstick of our success.

The Political Seduction

Along with the story of the megachurches, we have followed the course of the Christian right for thirty years. It goes without saying that here, if anywhere, is a movement that could have undone privatization in one fell swoop. American Evangelicals are the ones who count in the West, and prior to the 1970s they had been privatized for most of the twentieth century. Remarkably, most had even slept through the 1960s, the most radical and influential decade of the century. The comment "privately engaging, public irrelevant" was actually made in the '60s.

The wake-up year for Evangelicals was 1973, which saw the convergence of Watergate, Roe v. Wade, and the OPEC crisis, so it could have spelled disaster for us when the Christian right emerged toward the end of the '70s. Imagine what might have happened if an army of William Wilberforces had sprung forth to engage American life. But there was no need to worry. Politicization had affected American life at large since the 1930s, both inflating politics and tempting Americans to rely on it to do more than politics can ever do, so we were relieved when Evangelical political engagement was soon politicized in the same way.

A protest in one of their own manifestos came very close to the mark: "The other error, made by both the religious left and the religious right in recent decades, is to politicize faith, using faith to express essentially political points that have lost touch with biblical truth. That way faith loses its independence, the Church becomes 'the regime at prayer,' Christians become 'useful idiots' for one party or another, and the Christian faith becomes an ideology in its purest form. Christian beliefs are used as weapons for political interest."[12]

Useful idiots? We could not have said it better as Evangelical leader after leader kowtowed to the White House and danced to the tunes of the political puppet masters. In 1870, Lord Acton said of the Roman Catholic cardinals who pronounced the Pope infallible at the First Vatican Council that "they went in as shepherds, and came out as sheep." Entering the Oval Office seems to have the same unnerving power over Evangelicals. One Christian leader defended his weakness in confronting a president by saying that he "intended to go in as Nathan, but ended up being Barnabas."

Naturally, some leaders of the Christian right huffed indignantly at being described as "useful idiots," while many outside the movement smirked in agreement. But equally naturally, no one did anything, and the protest was ignored. As these brave Evangelicals can all see now, the Christian right failed to achieve almost all its stated goals. More importantly, it so abandoned the traditional Christian maxim of "doing the Lord's work in the Lord's way" that it came to contradict the Adversary's ways altogether. Instead of his superhuman command to "love your enemies," "turn the other cheek," and "do good to those who hate you," the Christian right became so politicized that it was carried away and became all-too-human, demonizing their foes with relish and indulging in fear-mongering with abandon.

Again the result is delicious. Evangelicals (with our help) have created the most vicious backlash against the Christian faith in all American history, at least among the elites. Listen to the new atheists and their adoring admirers. When Christopher Hitchens throws his well-aimed barbs, charging that "religion poisons everything," the American elites now applaud wildly and think of the Christian right. These, after all, are the "American ayatollahs" and the "Christian fascists." Think how far we have come from the dangerously genial days of President Eisenhower and Billy Graham, and it is all progress.

Periodic outbreaks in public life such as the Christian right will never harm us. Politicization is an extreme that is the mirror image of privatization, but it compounds the work of its twin. Whereas privatization undermines the integration of faith, politicization undermines the independence of faith. And where do you think disillusioned Christians go when they give up on a politicized faith?

As always, we remain alert, though never mistake caution for hesitation. Nothing is insecure but thinking makes it so. Apart from these two tripwires I have indicated, nothing stands between our plans and their consummation. The Director calculates that if we can sustain our efforts for one more generation, victory will be ours. The trap is set. We have only to wait for one more lifetime to spring it.

The Smorgasbord Factor

FROM: DEPUTY DIRECTOR, CENTRAL SECURITY COUNCIL
TO: DIRECTOR DESIGNATE, LOS ANGELES BUREAU
CLASSIFICATION: *ULTRA SECRET*

"Nobody ever went broke underestimating the taste of the American people." H. L. Mencken might repeat his wicked remark about some of the fast food you will encounter in Los Angeles. For you, perhaps, it may not be so telling since your immediate contrast will be with the English equivalent. But I never think of his remark without recalling my time in Paris. Mercifully, French democracy did not extend to a popular leveling of taste. They know how to prepare food superlatively, and they know how to serve it.

Have you ever noticed how the way food is served affects the person dining? I remember a curious example of this when I was dining in Los Angeles some years ago. I visited your predecessor just as Sunday brunches were becoming the rage, and he took me to the opening brunch at a lavish ocean-front hotel.

The opulence and bounty of the table were magnificent, and the endless choice of dishes strained the term "smorgasbord" to the limits. But what was fascinating was people's response as they faced such an array. A few ate what I suppose they would have ordered anywhere, taking their pick without a moment's hesitation, almost as if the sumptuous range were not there. These were the minority.

Most people acted quite differently. Some treated the choice as a challenge to their capacity, an affront to their reputations for never passing up a bargain. Others were less sure of themselves. They wanted to miss nothing that was tasty or new, and probably no meal in all their lives was chosen and eaten so self-consciously. They inspected the full board, weighed the options, asked advice of those ahead, and dithered forever before finally selecting their choice, obviously aware of what they had left behind. Clearly, the surfeit of choices threatened to play havoc not only with their waistlines but also with their confidence and peace of mind.

That is a trivial incident (hardly the sort that would figure in your reports to the Council), but it captures the essence of the third pressure we are bringing to bear on the Church. It was in fact this incident that gave the third pressure its code name—the smorgasbord factor.

Before I go further, a word about your reports on the advance trips to L.A. In terms of theoretical understanding, you have clearly accomplished the switch from counter-apologetics to cultural subversion as swiftly as I hoped. But you hardly seem able to disguise your disdain for the post-secular alternatives to the Christian faith that you have come across in California.

I trust this is only a mild form of culture shock. We hardly expect you to "go native" with some of the target movements, but California is as much the womb of the gods as the dream factory of the Western world. Too great a sense of distaste will be a handicap to you. I would hate to conclude that your life in Oxford was that much of an ivory tower existence.

The Heart of the Matter

The technical term for the third pressure, the smorgasbord factor, is "pluralization," a dry term for a devastating process. By pluralization, I mean the process by which the number of options in the private sphere of modern society rapidly multiplies at all levels, especially at the level of worldviews, faiths and ideologies—decisively affecting the consciousness of what choice means and how the chooser sees it.[1] The key feature here is not just variety but such extreme variety within a single society.

This process of pluralization, unlike secularization, is neither new nor difficult to understand. The first century A.D., when the Church was born, was a period marked by a similar pluralism. The collapse of confidence in the classical gods of Greece and Rome had left a cavernous vacuum, and into it was sucked every imaginable kind of popular philosophy, esoteric cult and mystery religion (including, alas, the Adversary's).

You might think that this early experience of pluralism would have prepared Christians for resisting pluralization today. On the contrary, they have completely forgotten what it was like. Whereas pluralism once left them more sure of the truth and superiority of their faith in contrast to others, it now leaves them less sure. Indeed, their moral and intellectual caving-in resembles the notorious "failure of nerve" of the pagans that characterized the popular mood of the first century when the classical religions failed.

There are simple reasons for this different response. As the Church grew from a tiny minority to a dominant majority, its experience of being a monopoly disarmed Christians and made them forget what the challenge of pluralism was like. Besides, the experience of centuries of dominance left them with a guilty conscience about all the evils and excesses of that dominance. Most importantly, the modern brand of pluralization is a uniquely powerful one that is at the heart of globalization. And this time it comes hand in hand with both the process of secularization and the philosophy of postmodernism. The result for us has been sensational.

Pluralization, then, is not new. But it does run counter to more normal human experience, which is characterized by a desire for an underlying coherence of things. Every society in history has had differences within it, such as differences of work, rank or tradition. But at the same time, most societies have had an underlying cohesion, and usually the most cohesive force in any community has been its religion.

In Europe, for instance, despite the enormous diversity (such as the differences of language and the presence of Jews, Muslims and atheists), the underlying cohesion was provided by the Christian faith. Hence "Christendom."

That's why the traditional role of religion in society has been described as a "sacred canopy"[2] or "global umbrella."[3] It overarched all of society and culture, defining the world and determining the way of life for those who lived under its shelter. What it denied was forbidden. What it ignored did not exist. What it affirmed as true was self-evident.

Do you see the contrast, and therefore the measure of our success today? In the modern world, pluralization sees to it that there is no sacred canopy, only millions of small tents. There is no global umbrella, only a bewildering range of pocket umbrellas for those who care to hoist one. The grand overseer of life has been reduced to being one of a jostling crowd of job seekers and volunteers, all competing for the consumers' attention. The once-commanding symbol of unity has become just one more element in the abstract mosaic of diversity. Taken-for-grantedness has gone the way of the ancestors.

Roads to the Present Position

There are different roads to the present position of pluralization. One way for you to trace its rise is to study its Christian origins. By its very character, the Christian faith carries the pluralizing potential within itself.[4] "In the world, but not of it," the Christian faith stands as a permanent criticism of every given, every established institution and every rival belief. By calling for a switch of allegiances ("repentance and faith"), it unmistakably draws a line and calls for choice. Thus Christian propaganda always insists on an alternative perspective, and as such it is a constant generator of choices and dissent. This, as we have unfortunately seen in the past, is the source of the Church's disruptive and revolutionary power in history.

Today, however, we have turned this strength into a weakness. For the principle became self-destructive when what was always inherent in the Christian faith became rampant after the Protestant Reformation. It then went to seed and began to work back on itself. Protestants rejected papal authority and unwittingly began the fateful swing to the authority of personal conscience, which was soon indistinguishable from a riot of personal choice and individualism.

"Here I stand," cried Martin Luther, who in facing the Pope and the Holy Roman Emperor tackled the most powerful political forces and structures of his day. "Here I stand," cry our contemporary Christians, who use it to opt out of any and every belief, practice, and music style that does not suit their petulant preferences.

Strictly speaking, the Reformation did not introduce pluralism. Nor did it intend to. Indeed, Protestants at first tried to defend their separate Protestant realms as zealously as Catholics had defended the whole of Christendom before. But in the wake of the wars of religion, the irrepressible urge toward pluralization was born, and we have fostered it carefully ever since.

Christians may point to their more virtuous contributions (the generating of choices, the respect for freedom of conscience), but the contribution of their vices was as important. Pluralization gathered momentum through the fragmentation of Christendom and through the tolerance bred by widespread disillusionment with Christian fanaticism and bigotry.

You move much closer to the present with the invention of the denomination (as with so many things, "made in the U.S.A."). Prior to the American experience, a national Church had territorial claims and its membership was virtually established by birth. But those who came to America were not just from nonconformist groups such as the Baptists, who had rejected national churches; they were also drawn from various state churches, each of which had now lost its territorial supremacy and had arrived to find other "former state churches" already there.

The result was the modern denomination, the "ex-Church," which has been forced to bow to the permanent presence and competition of other churches within its territory. For a while, the Roman Catholic Church, as Lenny Bruce quipped, was "the only The Church left," but now it is falling nicely in line with the others as one more denomination. In the South, the Southern Baptists are "the only *the* church left."

You will appreciate that this kind of pluralization bites far more deeply than denominational differences. It eats into basic beliefs too. What modern Christian would argue against the place of the modern denomination? But then, how much can the same Christian still believe that his own denomination has the inside lane on interpretation, especially when he realizes there are some 20,000 others in the world (2,051 in the U.S. alone)?[5] But what then of the absolute truth of his own faith when there are so many other religions? If other religions are shaped by different cultures and times, could his own faith be so too? Before long the acid of doubt has eaten through to the core.

The Modern Contribution

A second way to trace the rise of pluralization is to see the forces within modernization that have accelerated the tidal wave of choice and change.[6] These are obvious and hardly need elaboration. Through the crowding growth of cities, modern people are all much closer, yet stranger, to each other. Through the explosion of knowledge, other people, other places, other periods and other psyches are accessible as never before. Through modern travel, people can go to any part of the world within twenty-four hours. Through modern media, the world and all its options can be brought to them. And so on.

Pluralization is accelerated and intensified in a hundred such ways. "Everyone is now everywhere," it is said. What then happens, the heightened awareness of *the presence of others* leads automatically to a sense of *the possibilities for ourselves*. In essence, therefore, the modern person/consumer scans the smorgasbord and says, "*Their* cuisines, *their* customs, *their* convictions are all now *my* choices, *my* options, *my* possibilities." The widest range of choice is often at the most trivial levels, but the proliferation of choice at more important levels is staggering.

Life is now a supermarket or a smorgasbord with an endless array of options, whether the choice is a question of a gender, a marriage, a

hobby, a vacation, a lifestyle, a world view or a religion. There is something for everybody—and every taste, age, sex, class and interest. The family of your choice (traditional/gay/lesbian/polyamorist/polygamist)?
The church of your choice? A liturgy to your liking? *The Good Food Guide*
has its counterpart in *The Good Church Guide*. Pass down the line. Take
your pick. Mix your own. Do your thing.

We have reached the stage in pluralization where choice is not just
a state of affairs but also a state of mind. Choice has become a value in
itself, even a priority. What matters is no longer good choice or right
choice or wise choice, but simply choice. Freedom is simply having
choice, and to be modern is to be addicted to choice and change. Choice
and change have become the very essence of life.

Driving Home the Consequences

The processes of pluralization are fascinating and the possibilities they
open up kaleidoscopic. But do not miss the wood for the trees. Our real
concern is only with consequences.

What happens when choice becomes a state of mind? Obligation
melts into option, "givenness" into choice, form into freedom, and duty
into decision. Facts of life dissolve into fashions of the moment. But the
consequence we care about most is this: *The increase in choice and change
leads to a decrease in commitment and continuity.*

Imagine someone who owned a silk handkerchief inherited from
his Victorian great-grandfather. If he lost it, he would search for it everywhere. It would be a prized possession, beautiful, old and with special
associations. He is "attached to it," he might say. Yet no one in his right
mind would become attached to a Kleenex tissue, and it would be absurd to waste time looking for one if it were lost. After all, a Kleenex is
disposable. It is made to be thrown away. Commitment and continuity
are entirely foreign to the notion of a paper handkerchief.

Another trivial illustration, you may say. Deliberately so, but never forget the sociology of knowledge. The truth about the modern world can

be learned as readily from the trivia of life as from the philosopher's essay. Most modern people have a relationship to their choices that's closer to the model of the Kleenex tissue than to that of the silk handkerchief.

There is no nostalgia in that judgment, I assure you. I hold no brief for silk handkerchiefs and no grudge against disposable ones. We are interested in the extension of this mentality to more important areas. What may be trifling at the level of handkerchiefs becomes telling at the level of relationships, societies and, above all, faiths. What happens when modern people "run through" homes like disposable handkerchiefs? Better still, when they "run through" marriages? Above all, when they "run through" beliefs?

New Partners for New Phases

An obvious place to look for the impact of pluralization is marriage. Pluralization at the level of relationships is putting a unique strain on Christian marriage, which as it disintegrates puts an added strain on the plausibility of faith and the stability of the Church. Christians often forget that the centuries-long persistence of one man/one woman marriage was not due solely to their own principles. True, for a couple to commit themselves to each other "till death us do part" was a matter of principle. But social pressures played their part too.

Traditional communities, mostly rural, were comparatively small and stable. Under such conditions, permissiveness would have led to social chaos. Christian principles were therefore silently supported by strong social pressures. And because people did not live so long in the past, "till death us do part" used to be a realistic assessment of the odds. Today it is more often wishful thinking.

Pluralization has been key in effecting this change. The modern individual lives longer and meets and knows more people than ever before, but as I said in the previous memo, is also more anonymous in more situations. The average modern Londoner meets as many people in one week as a medieval person would have met in a lifetime. A Londoner's (or New Yorker's or Washingtonian's) lifestyle is accordingly faster, freer and more flexible, just as the average relationship is briefer, more superficial and more functional.

The result? Cultural pressure and Christian principle have parted company and now work against each other. "Ring the changes!" says the one, "New phases in life. New partners in life!" "No!" says the other, "If marriage collapses, civilization does too!"

Which of the two is winning in wider society is easy to see. The wedding vow "Till death do us part" has given way to the wedding wish, "So long as love lasts." With the expressive revolution triumphant, and sex now linked to pleasure rather than procreation, love seems not to be lasting so long. Surprise, surprise.

"It is ridiculous," Clare Booth Luce remarked, "to think that you can spend your entire life with just one person. Three is about the right number. Yes, I imagine three husbands would do it."[7] And that she said as a good Catholic, and a full generation before the bewildering chaos of fragmentation that we have promoted in marriage and families since then.

The fashionable philosophy behind this is at its height. With the value of choice and change up and the value of commitment and continuity down, freedom, flexibility and convenience are everything. Courting has given way to "hooking up," and lifetime faithfulness to free sex just as formal dining has given way to fast food. Of course, do not expect most people to swing to the silly extremes that magazines trumpet to sell copies and that moralists attack. Free sex all the time—whenever, however, and with whomever—is no more pleasurable or healthy than fast food all the time.

The damage to Christian faithfulness is done at a far less advanced stage. "Creative divorce" is a little avant-garde for the average Christian, except where you are going. But once change is considered appropriate and necessary, and marriage has been boiled down to one thing only—the make-or-break achievement of emotional intimacy—faithfulness can easily be made to look constricting and hopelessly old-fashioned. Can anyone devise a surer recipe for a loveless marriage?

It is instructive to examine the expanding range of Christian rationales for change. Some spouses are quite straightforward. Their marriages no longer "fulfill" them, and they want to get out. But keep your eyes open for more sophisticated cases, particularly those infected by thinking that is the product of privatization and pluralization combined.

For instance, a Christian conservative writes that the break-up of his marriage was a sad but "healthy new beginning for each of us in our own way."[8] And he continues that he was called by faith like Abraham to leave the security of marriage to embark on a spiritual pilgrimage toward emotional authenticity.

Another Christian writes, "I hope my wife will never divorce me, because I love her with all my heart. But if one day she feels I am minimizing her or making her feel inferior or in any way standing in the light that she needs to become a person God meant her to be, I hope she'll be free to throw me out even if she's one hundred. There is something more important than our staying married, and it has to do with integrity, personhood, and purpose."[9]

The ultimate in refinement are those who claim to be *separating out of faithfulness to Christ*. Formerly, this would have meant a non-Christian husband or wife leaving the Christian partner because of the faith itself. Now it often means a Christian divorcing another Christian over a Christian issue.

Would you have thought, for example, that a commitment to a simple lifestyle could ever lead to divorce? Yes, one writer urges today, "The split finally comes when one recognizes that this kind of conscience can't be compromised. There are levels of importance and urgency in biblical morality. And Jesus' driving concern for the coming of the Kingdom, as a counter to the culture, far outweighed his concern for the maintenance of family structures. There can be as much sin involved in trying to perpetuate a dead or meaningless relationship as in accepting the brokenness, offering it to God, and going on from there."[10] Disobeying Christ out of faithfulness to Christ! The irony is exquisite, and I must say that some of our recent successes have a perfection that is sublime.

Early on, it appeared that ordinary Christian believers would be resistant to these trends, but the sluice gates have been opened. The incidence of divorce among clergy and Christian celebrities has become an epidemic, and the wider Church is going down with the same virus. Divorce is now in the air they breathe. The opinion-formers went down, and the sheep were bound to follow. "A fish decays from its head first," they say in the intelligence world. Or, as the Director puts it more pertinently, a Christian celebrity sneezes and the Church catches the cold.

Commitment-Shy Convictions

The collapse of Christian marriage is a signal of success for us, especially when we can now sit back and read polls showing that Christian marriage is worse off than the marriage of atheists. But when all is said and done, the only level of damage we really care about is the pluralization of beliefs and believing. Commitment-shy faith is a contradiction in terms, you might think, but we have achieved it in various unnoticed ways. Think of some of the side effects that pluralization has had on faith.

One side effect of pluralization is that *modern believers have an excessive degree of self-consciousness.*[11] Each choice raises questions. Might they? Could they? Should they? Will they? Won't they? What if they had? What if they hadn't? And so on. The forest of choices raised by modern options leads deeper and deeper into the dark freedom, then the even darker anxiety, of seemingly infinite possibility.

Like a hall of mirrors, the reflections recede forever. Choice is no longer simple. Choosing is never complete. The outside world becomes more questionable, the inside world more complex. What can they believe? What ought they to do? Who are they? Modern people are constant question marks to each other. Permanent self-consciousness is the price of modern choice.

"He who never visits," runs an African saying, "thinks his mother is the only cook." Today's believer does not have the excuse of such blissful ignorance, and with the wider outlook comes not only self-consciousness, but uncertainty . . . anxiety . . . doubt. We do not need to force this. Pluralization is an acid that works slowly but effectively. Modern faith is rarely as assured as it sounds, and the few remaining pockets of certainty can be driven toward defensiveness and fanaticism.

A second side effect of pluralization is that *modern believers have become conversion-prone.*[12] Just as the traditional bedrock of faith was solid and reassuring, so the traditional turn-around of conversion was complete and lasting. Indeed, it used to grate on us when Christians claimed that conversion was the most radical and complete transformation in life, but they were right. Reorientation to a new life, new world, new relationships and new ways of life was radical, and Christians did not see this as unreasonable: It was a once-in-a-lifetime requirement that was expected to last forever.

That has all changed. Under the impact of pluralization, faith has grown precarious, which leaves it prone to being converted—and reconverted—and reconverted. Or, as has been recently perfected in American Christian circles, "Born again, and again, and again, and again," ad infinitum. In today's pluralized and mobile society, the once-telling "testimony" of the great life-change is reduced to the status of a temporary visiting card, where the address is left blank to allow for constant updating.

Multiple conversions in a single life are now common, but the special conditions of periods like the 1960s step the pace up even further. The activist Jerry Rubin, for instance, was a master of spiritual "switchcraft," who claimed to have experienced 18 different "trips" in 5 years, ranging from EST to bioenergenetics.[13] Not that such fruitless exploits have any value to us. What matters is their aftertaste.

Slowly, a whole generation grows shy of commitment, embarrassed by conviction, and congenitally open to revision. For the countercultural type, the order of the day was "hang loose." Today's version is "cool," "laid back," and "undecided." For the postmodern type, the passwords are "ambiguity" (never certainty), "reflection" (never revelation), and "conversation" (never conclusion). The general result is the same. The search for meaning has shrunk to finding meaning in the search. To be on the pilgrimage is the only progress. All else is yesterday's arrogance, passing out of the reach or the desire of today's thoughtful person who can never decide for long.

A third side effect of pluralization is also to our advantage. *Pluralization reduces the necessity of choosing at all.*[14] In other words, the extension of choice leads to the evasion of choice.

The Christian faith always work best with an either/or option, or when contrast is the mother of clarity. Let them put the choice starkly, and even the air will be charged with the responsibility of decision. The choice matters. The choice must be made. The choice cannot be ducked. When told they must choose, most people respond by choosing.

But having too many choices leads either to vertigo or a yawn. Back in 1885, Pope Leo XII barked out the warning, "The equal toleration of all religions . . . is the same thing as atheism."[15] Dead right, of course, but a trifle indelicate in the modern ecumenical climate, and we can expect such archaic sentiments to be ignored. Far more likely is the continuing trend toward a multiplication of choices in which would-be competitors cancel each other out, leading toward the neutralization of values in particular and to intellectual chaos in general.

The net effect of pluralization is that it acts on faith like a non-stick coating. Christians and convictions were once inseparable. Pluralization, though, coats faith with spiritual Teflon, sealing Christian truth with a slippery surface to which commitment will not adhere. The result is a general increase in shallowness, transience and heresy. Picking, choosing and selectiveness are the order of the day. Asked about her beliefs, Marilyn Monroe replied, "I just believe in everything—a little bit."[16]

Many Christians are only slightly different. Doctrinal dilettantism and self-service spirituality are all part of the trend toward effete gourmet godliness. We are home and dry, however, when this "cafeteria spirituality" becomes so prevalent that faith loses its authority and shrivels into a preference.

Traditionally, as one of the enemy scholars put it, faith had "binding address." Faith led to obedience, belief to behavior, and "the talk" to "the walk," as they put it quaintly. All that is yesterday. Belief has been severed from behavior. Commanding truths have softened to inviting choices. In the world of the smorgasbord and supermarket, people pass down the line and choose "the church of their choice" and "the principles of their preference." It is all a matter of cafeteria convictions. "So you don't like coleslaw? Choose iceberg lettuce. And you find hell uncomfortable to believe? I prefer love, myself."

Need I say it? We have nothing to fear from such faith. A consumer-driven faith of preferences and choices will go nowhere and achieve nothing. They are nothing more than T.E. Lawrence's "dreamers of the night." Whereas people of real faith are "dreamers of the day," dangerous to us because they pursue their dreams with open eyes and bring them to fulfillment, "dreamers of the night" are fated always to wake and find their dreams were vanity.

Go for the Big Prizes

Exploiting pluralization is another of those assignments in which you will need to keep a close check on your agents. They will be all too inclined to let subtle subversion degenerate into dirty tricks. That is because pluralization works itself out so outrageously in the more extreme cases, and these are easier (and more entertaining) to imitate.

Instruct your agents that they have pushed pluralization far enough at the level of things. Our goal now is to encourage pluralization at higher levels, so that it produces side effects in relation to places, tasks, values, relationships, societies, and finally beliefs. If they devote too much energy dabbling around at the lower levels, they will miss what is important at the higher ones.

The Director, as you know, deplores the lack of economy in overkill. He has stipulated that pluralization should not be rushed. There are built-in human and social forces to reverse it if it becomes too extreme. Touch off these extremes and you chance setting in motion a counter-trend, a sort of retro-rocket that could waste much of our work.

It is well known, for instance, that it was excessive junk food that led to the health-food craze, just as fast food led to the "slow food" movement. If pluralization rebounds similarly, there would be a powerful compensating trend in religion toward moral authority and social unity. Were this to happen, we would change course and steer even that toward our ends. But it would be a pity not to ride the wave of pluralization right onto the beach.

Once you have grasped the distinctive workings of pluralization, stand back and see how secularization, privatization and pluralization all work together. When secularization and privatization have finished their task, every religion in the modern world has lost its power. When pluralization has done, each has also lost its uniqueness. Secularization is the body blow, the relentless stamina-sapping punch that leaves the Church still on its feet but finished. Privatization and pluralization are a two-punch combination that are guaranteed to knock it out for the count.

P.S. I gather that before you leave England finally, the Director is sending you down to interview the Old Fool, as he contemptuously calls him. There is much more than dismissive ridicule in that title. It is a recognition that he and people like him are among the most dangerous of Christian exceptions. Their entire stories are a living reversal of our Operation. They have virtually backed into faith through a long process of disillusionment with the very fantasies by which most Christians are enthralled. To make matters worse, the Old Fool brings to his faith a comic vision of the frailty and absurdity of life. He thinks this allows him to peep impudently around the corners of the world's mesmerizing triumphs and pronounce them laughable and less than final.

The Director is sending you, however, for an important reason. The role of the media will be central in your work in Los Angeles, and there are few people alive who understand it as well as the Old Fool. Fortunately, he is misunderstood and ignored by his own people, but you need only listen to him carefully, especially to his views on the fantasy-creating power of the media, to see how your strategy should proceed.

In this case, know your enemy and know what your enemy knows and you will know the best and worst of the Church in an afternoon. The insights their own side will not use, we will—against them.

Creating Counterfeit Religion

FROM: DEPUTY DIRECTOR, CENTRAL SECURITY COUNCIL
TO: DIRECTOR DESIGNATE, LOS ANGELES BUREAU
CLASSIFICATION: *ULTRA SECRET*

There used to be an old Cold War joke among military strategists that any conflict between China and the Soviet Union would go like this: The Soviets would take a hundred thousand prisoners on the first day, half a million on the second, and a million and a half on the third, only to surrender on the fourth day—overwhelmed by the number of their captives.

Our main approach to following up the pressures of modernization works much like that: Where religion still flourishes, we go with the flow and create such high-quality counterfeits of religion that real faith is devalued to the point of uselessness.

Needless to say, this approach is quite unnecessary in Western Europe and wherever secularization has assisted religion in its grand disappearing act—such as the university world in America. In places like that, secularity reigns supreme, the Church's spiritual and social influence have been sapped, and all we need to do is sprinkle on top a little extra confusion and controversy so that the disappearance of religion is welcomed and taken for granted. The best garnishing to the pie is to add confusion and controversy to such terms as "secularization," "secularism" and "secularity," so that even educated people become hopelessly entangled and never actually confront real faith directly. There has to be a strong dose of theory in that approach, but the goal and the gains are practical.

When religion still flourishes, however, our creation of counterfeit religions is practical from the start. The tactic works like this: In times of comparative strength, the Church makes many converts. It is then up to us to see that these converts turn out to be as embarrassingly awkward and unmanageable for the Church as a horde of Chinese captives would have been for the Soviets. This we do by multiplying counterfeits and compromising the integrity of the new converts from the outset. "The more the messier," you might say.

What do I mean by counterfeit religion? Perhaps not what many people think. Propaganda and disinformation have always encouraged Christians to limit the term to non-Christian religions, and especially to groups they despise, such as "cults," so that they do not see the counterfeits they themselves are creating and circulating. Obviously I am not limiting the term in that way. We could not care less about the other religions. Our sole goal is counterfeiting the Christian faith itself, and my main focus is not on counterfeit individual faith but on counterfeit Christian faith on a collective or social level.

Fortunately for us, clear, confident Christian attitudes toward other religions are out of fashion in today's world, and held to be "arrogant," "intolerant," and "politically incorrect." (This is why we have been able to shut down so many of our counter-apologetic divisions.) Surprisingly, alertness to counterfeit faith at an individual level has diminished at the same time. But luckily for us, what is really extraordinary is that few Christians today are alert to our counterfeiting of faith on a collective level.

As with our age-old counterfeits of individual faith—in attitudes such as pharisaism, legalism, hypocrisy, and cheap grace—our counterfeiting of collective faith pivots on the inescapable struggle between faith and religion, or as they put it, between the "new nature" and the old nature," between "the power of God" and the pull of "fallen natures" gravity. Our focus, in other words, is the point where the spiritual force of "conversion" to the Adversary's ways meets the natural forces of "reversion" to ours. We simply have to ensure that in each case the former is neutered and the latter wins. That is, that the Church conforms to the spirit and shape of today's world rather than being transformed and transforming, that Christians revert to their old ways rather than being converted to new ones.

I described in my first memo the mounting levels of worldliness involved in our overall subversion (the movement from "culture-blind" to "culture-bound" to "culture-burnt"). The trick is to keep the counterfeit so close to the real thing as the Church passes through these levels that only a trained eye could tell the difference.

Among the great advantages you have in working in the United States is the marked absence of trained eyes and the plentiful supply of empty-minded religion. In short, there will be few to detect what we are doing. American popular religion has parted company with serious thinking for so long that many believers could spot only the crudest and most careless of counterfeits. Indeed, in the climate of the present culture wars and the strident onslaught of the new atheists, even the crudest counterfeits are now defended stoutly as if the faith depended on defending all faiths. Indeed, serious discernment in American popular religion must be the most valuable commodity on earth. It is certainly the scarcest.

Be that as it may, the awkward thing about American religion is that, while vitally changed through pressures such as the private-zoo factor, it still has a disturbing degree of spiritual and social vigor—at least among the middle classes. What is left of European religion, by contrast, is hardly worth counterfeiting. We are therefore following up our initial gains in America by twisting the relative strength of faith through counterfeit religions, in order to capitalize on the weaknesses we have already exposed there. Let me highlight some of our principal counterfeiting campaigns.

Civil Religion

Civil religion is counterfeit in the sense that it is *religion shaped by the priorities and demands of the political order,* so that loyalty to Caesar once again overrides loyalty to the Adversary.

It goes without saying that we did not need to use civil religion in our European armory because we exploited the excesses of state churches to the full. After a long, 1,500-year run since Constantine, state churches are almost completely out of fashion in Europe, and the reason is obvious: religion that sold its soul to gain state support was sooner or later bound to be corrupted by the devil's bargain. The clearest example was the pre-revolutionary Catholic Church in France, and the cry of the Jacobin radicals (borrowed from Diderot) said it all: "Strangle the last king with the guts of the last priest!"

When the Bastille fell in 1789, the French Church and the French state were both corrupt and both oppressive, and the revolution blew off both at once. From then on and even today in France, the mindset holds that if you are in favor of religion, you must be reactionary; and if you are in favor of freedom, you must be secularist. This equation was set in concrete by the condition of the Church at the time of the Revolution, and as you can see from recent events in France, the mindset of *laicite* is still decisively in our favor. What could be a better partner to our overall work of secularization?

The American situation is very different, so we have worked it differently. Americans rejected the state Church solution almost from the start. Having left Europe to escape religious oppression, and arriving to find a diversity of energetic faith communities, they took both religion and religious liberty seriously and saw both as positive. Their solution was to separate Church and state institutionally but not to separate religion and public life. The result was Jefferson's celebrated "wall of separation."

Almost all American Christians, including Roman Catholics, supported and welcomed this separation (Jefferson actually used this phrase in writing sympathetically to a Baptist), and therein lay the seed of their present problems.[1] Even for Jefferson, the "wall of separation" was originally both porous and wavy—rather like his famous serpentine walls at Monticello. In other words, the relationship of the churches and the states—for in America they were always plural—was far from a strict separation and it was all a matter of nuance and trust.

Nuance and trust are rarely enduring qualities, and certainly not in this case. All we had to do was to harden the partial and institutional separation into a strict and total separation and give it the force of a legal doctrine. The two Religious Liberty clauses of the First Amendment would then work against each other, and the First Amendment itself would work against religion rather than for it. This we finally achieved in the Everson case in 1947, and deliciously, one of the main architects of the doctrine of strict separation was a Southern Baptist Justice on the Supreme Court.

Ah, the ease of seducing Christians once you know their mixed motives. Not only was the worthy justice a Southern Baptist, he was also a Ku Klux Klansman, and his intention was to protect his fellow-Baptists from the rising threat of Roman Catholicism. Little did he know that he was working with secularists to hurt Christians of all stripes. For as anyone can see half a century later, strict separation turns religious liberty from liberty *for* religion into liberty *from* religion. Irony upon irony, Christians originally intended to use the separation of Church and state to safeguard pluralism, but a tiny twist of the screw and their well-intentioned efforts have ended up establishing secularization by law. The Christian faith in America has had a slightly boxed-in character ever since, and the achievement was both voluntary and in place before many of them realized.

That is only the start of our triumph. Much of what is left of American faith in public life we have turned into our first great counterfeit: civil religion. What is civil religion? In its American form, civil religion is that somewhat vague but deeply treasured set of semi-religious, semi-political beliefs and values that are basic to America's understanding of itself.[2] You can witness civil religion at its most elegant in the speeches of any presidential inauguration, at its more homespun on any Fourth of July, or at many a point when Americans are sounding off on how they are "proud to be American."

Like nationalism, civil religion goes beyond a patriotism that the Adversary sees as legitimate. And do not fall for the folly of mistaking the apparent vagueness of civil religion for weakness. The American Creed is quite different from the Apostle's Creed. The latter is basically theological, the former political. The latter is a matter of sacred covenant, the former of social contract. The latter is highly distinct, the former deliberately vague. But the American Creed is just as deeply held as the Apostle's Creed, and even more so when the two are confused. As you can easily test for yourself, the charge "un-American" is far more likely to provoke an outcry in American hearts than the charge "heretical."

How have we succeeded in fusing the two creeds? The issue underlying civil religion is a straightforward one that is inescapable in constitutional democracies: What is the source of a nation's unity and legitimacy? For most of Western history, the accepted answer was to adopt a religion to provide the official undergirding of the national and social order, and so to ensure its unity and vitality. Each country therefore had its own established religion and its official state Church that was the spiritual and moral basis of its political order.

When Americans swept away the last vestiges of state churches, there was a reason why they did not anticipate the problems of moral justification that would arise in public life later: Christian assumptions and virtues—along with certain Enlightenment values—were taken for granted as foundational to the consensus that held the nation together. The specific beliefs of Christian denominations may have been left unmentioned, and none of the assumptions were ever given the binding force of an established religion as they had been in Europe, but the necessity and value of general Christian virtues were taken for granted, even by non-Christians.

Two hundred years later, the folly of relying on this unspoken consensus is plain. Enlightenment notions have been swept away under the onslaught of postmodernism, and the Christian consensus has been eroded beyond recognition by the increase in pluralism, the surge of strident secularism, and the general coarsening of a post-Christian culture impatient with virtue and restraint of any kind.

This is hardly what the American founders and the early American Christians bargained for, but it raises the old question with a new vengeance. What is the basis of American unity and legitimacy if there is no established religion? *E Pluribus Unum* ("out of many one") may be a stirring national motto, but it is a demanding and costly ideal to live up to. As this dawns on people (often half-consciously), the way is opened for us to promote the thrust toward civil religion. "Under God," however vague and however controversial, provides a point of potent unity that somehow transcends difference.

For seen from one angle, civil religion is a kind of halfway house. It stands between what Americans see as two extremes: on one hand the dangers of a state Church and an established religion, and on the other the dangers of a public life without any values at all (a "naked public square" as one of them put it). At first this halfway solution seems useful to both state and Church. It helps the state because, if public values are not to be imposed from above (an essentially authoritarian solution), they must be nourished from below. It helps the churches because it allows them to contribute to public life, if only in general terms. Civil religion is thus a compromise solution that allows the Church to exist as an entity that is neither established nor proscribed. Jefferson's wall is porous, as it were, and some faith seeps through. There is no national god in America, and the President is his prophet.

Like many compromises, however, the solution is unstable, and public debate demonstrates a series of restless and violent swings between these two extremes. One extreme is, sociologically speaking, *idiocy*—the idea that the social order needs no moral basis at all. This might be true if the U.S. were a totalitarian country like the former Soviet Union. But since the country is as free as it is, the outcome would be plain: a spiritual void, moral confusion, social chaos, and national decline.

Fear of that possibility rears its head in different ways at different times (the call for "law and order," the condemnation of "all these illegal aliens," and so on). Whenever it does, it automatically fosters a swing to the other extreme, the one we are really after—civil religion. For without a doubt, civil religion is indeed an extreme and not a meek and mild compromise if seen from the correct angle. Civil religion is an extreme because it is, spiritually speaking, *idolatry*.

Our achievement here is phenomenal because, as you know, the heart of the Jewish and Christian faiths is a radical monotheism—"There is one God. There is no god but God. So God alone is to be worshiped." It is this central and vital demand that civil religion undermines subtly but devastatingly.

So once you see the dynamics of the swing from idiocy to idolatry, you can see that, for American Christians, civil religion is a case of out of the melting pot and into the fire. As things proceed well, we push to make civil religion such an unholy alliance of faith and flag that Christian ideals and American interests are welded inseparably. The Adversary then becomes the court chaplain to the American status quo, and ringmaster to the American dream. A dire case of "God on their side"? That is not the half of it. Civil religion is idolatry for one reason only—in raising what unites them to the point of reverence and then worship, Americans are literally worshiping themselves. The god of civil religion is dazzling because it is wrapped in red, white, and blue, but the god of civil religion is still themselves.

Consumer Religion

Both historical and current conditions in America are ideal for breeding civil religion, and the same is true of the second counterfeit: consumer religion. This is *religion shaped by the priorities and demands of the economic order*—service of "Mammon" outstripping service of the "Master," to use the Adversary's terms again.

Have you heard the story of Samuel Goldwyn's attempt to secure the film rights to George Bernard Shaw's plays? Seeking to impress Shaw, he put exaggerated emphasis on his concern for cultural excellence and absolute artistic integrity. Shaw listened politely but finally refused.

"No," Shaw said, "there's too much difference between us. You're interested in art. I'm interested in money."

That is worth remembering when you approach the heat and din of the debate surrounding consumer religion. The lines are not always drawn where you would expect. The politics of envy or sour grapes on one side can sometimes seem as strong as the theology of affluence or egotism on the other. Even well-placed denunciations often do little more than harden the identification of the moneychanger with his wares.

Anything as elementally powerful as religion was bound to be commercialized. History is littered with examples. But what religion is supposed to be more at odds with Mammon than the Christian faith? Jesus made a big point of driving out the moneychangers. The house of prayer, he said, was not to be a warehouse for loot. Martin Luther attacked Tetzel's indulgence sale. Grace was being priced out of the market.

Yet such is our success today that consumer religion's "best practices" are best demonstrated by the very disciples of Jesus, those who would pride themselves on being the heirs of Martin Luther and the truest sons and daughters of the Reformation. Driven out of the temple 2,000 years ago, moneychangers are now resurfacing in American churches with all the latest methods of Madison Avenue and the Harvard Business School to make up for lost time.

As always, our approach is through cultural assimilation. Consumer religion is an unholy amalgam of convictions and consumption that creates a sacramental materialism in the name of God. Forget for a moment the wild and ludicrous examples—the crass theologies of "health and wealth," the laughable "prosperity doctrines," the pastors driving Cadillacs as evidence of their "success spirituality," the fraudulent offers of prayer for money, the inflated emotional hypes, the self-glorifying building projects, the "holy hardware" and the "Jesus junk." These are easy to list, but really only symptoms. What few people analyze are the forces behind them. They fail to see the powerful undertow of commercial forces in America that suck down all claims to be "good news" to the level of one more television jingle. If consumer religion had not existed already, some American entrepreneur would have lost no time inventing it.

What are the forces behind it? Where these forces are present, consumer religion seems as natural as motherhood (as you can tell by the shock when it is attacked). Where they are absent, as in the less-developed world, consumer religion can be seen from a distance for what it is—a particularly crass form of cultural captivity.

One contributing force is the same American pattern of Church-state separation that has broken up the monopoly powers of the former state churches.[3] As we have seen, representatives of what were formerly "established churches" in Europe arrived in America to find themselves "ex-Churches," and in the process they were forced to change their stance from one of coercion to one of competition. With no state sword or purse behind any of them, each church was on its own, forced to carve out its own market, win its own clientele, and beat the drum for its own appeal.

Put differently, disestablishment acted on the churches in a manner that is parallel to de-monopolization in the economy, and churches experienced a marked shift to stances very like those in the laissez-faire capitalist market. They were no longer monopolistic authorities; more and more they acted like marketing agencies. One nineteenth-century critic observed, "Our metropolitan churches are, in general, as much commercial as the shops."[4] But as Tocqueville and others noted earlier, this was neither new nor accidental.

The major force contributing to consumer religion, however, has been America's role in leading the world from an economy of production (in which things were valued according to what it took to produce them) to an economy of consumption (in which things are valued according to their capacity to satisfy consumers' needs and desires). Among a myriad of results is a marked shift from the "virtues" of the Protestant ethic to the "narcissism" of the consumerist desires, with fatal consequences in areas ranging from citizenship to faith.

One observer sums up America's consumer society acidly: "Hence, the new consumer penchant for age without dignity, dress without formality, sex without reproduction, work without discipline, play without spontaneity, acquisition without purpose, certainty without doubt, life without responsibility, and narcissism into old age and unto death without a hint of wisdom or humility. In the age in which we now live, civilization is not an ideal or an aspiration, it is a video game."[5]

For our purposes, consumerism has two main effects on religion that allow us to corrupt it entirely. One is the pivotal shift from meeting genuine "needs" to fulfilling "desires, wishes, and fantasies"—"taking the waiting out of wanting," as an early ad for credit cards put it well. The other is the unexpected outcome that is called "infantilization" or induced childishness. With the ability to produce more goods than people need, consumer capitalism has to make children into consumers earlier and keep them at it longer. Hence contemporary America, a culture of perennial adolescents.

All this represents a bonanza for us, as faith is confused with the American dream just as it is with American civil religion. Religion, you remember, has been confined increasingly to the private sphere at the very time when the private sphere has become the sphere of individual gratification and consumption. This special configuration has produced a surge of conspicuous consumption in religious guise.

You can find examples without end. "Whatever the mind can conceive and believe, it can achieve," one television preacher promised his audience in his latest variation of "possibility thinking." "Turn scars into stars," another offered from his self-help arsenal. Slogans like these are designed for plugging into the Apostles' Creed or the American Creed or both. The good news and the good life, the Christian Way and the American Way are all serviced under the same franchise: Brand Jesus. And as for the induced childishness, witness any of the "happy-clappy" "worship experiences" that Evangelicals take for worship these days.

The result is a spectacle for our eyes and ears. Theologies compete brazenly to rationalize wealth, success and material blessing. Prosperity doctrines gush forth from rallies, radio and television. ("God's got it, I can have it, and by faith I'm going to get it."[6]) Even Psalm 23 has been revised ("The Lord is my banker, my credit is good. . . . he giveth me the key to his strongbox. He restoreth my faith in riches. He guideth me in the paths of prosperity, for his namesake."[7] Gutter-to-grace testimonies have become rags-to-riches testimonials, and fantastic expenditure is poured into showcase projects that are flagships for the showman commanders of the new empires.

Without seeing why, thousands of individual Americans are flocking to this Good Life Gospel and thus doing obeisance to consumer capitalism. They "consume" faith and church memberships as they would vacations or restaurants, "surfing" churches to find better satisfaction with more congenial music and the like. They even rise socially, not only from being bank clerks to bank presidents, but from being Pentecostals to being Presbyterians or Episcopalians. (Believe it or not, a correlation has been found between denominations and the likelihood of obesity. Episcopalians, like upper-class people generally, being the leanest.[8])

A third, more recent, force contributing to consumer religion is the highly commercial nature of the American media that are shaping its Christian users. China is typical of the world's authoritarian type of communication system, just as the BBC stands for a more paternalistic type. The other main type of system is commercial, and nowhere has this been developed further than in the U.S., especially in the day of the multiple channels and blogs.[9] (The average American child, for example, sees over 20,000 commercials every year and spends more time in front of the television than in the classroom.[10])

In some ways the commercial system is unquestionably the freest. But its hidden snags lie in the remorseless logic of its economics, since first and foremost it is a marketing medium. It requires vast capital, sure results and quick returns, so it has a built-in bias against the small, the risky, the innovative and the controversial. Yes, almost anything can be said on commercial TV, *but only if someone can afford to say it and if one can say it profitably.* In other words, not everything can be said on commercial television.

What, for instance, would be the ratings appeal of one of their old prophets such as Jeremiah or Amos? Or what would be the appeal of what they used to call "the offense of the cross"? Commercial television is for profits, not prophets, and the televangelists and megachurch pastors have been quick to learn the difference. "It's not about you," they repeat like a litany now. But who is kidding whom? Even those who say it do not escape the fact that it is almost all about them.

There is also a fourth factor, a force that is carrying consumer religion right into the big league: We are seeing a new rage for "culture creation." With the perceived failures of both a privatized and politicized faith, Christians now realize they have to move out of the closet and into the culture. Many of them have all the starry-eyed naiveté of a Johnny-come-lately. They want to catch up and make up for lost time. And notice whom they ask to countersign their excesses.

"Why should the devil have all the good music/art/jobs/success/life?" they argue reasonably, before shedding the inhibitions of centuries and plunging into freedom like new converts to hedonism. Or, if you ask them how they reconcile all that talk about money with their Christian faith, "It's easy," one of them explains. "I believe God made the diamonds for his crowd, not for Satan's bunch."[11] Only a towering naiveté could think such freedom is a gain.

So we might go on but the point is sufficiently established. Examples of the brash worldliness of consumer religion will be all around you, nowhere more than in Southern California. But leave it to others to get bogged down in fascination with the particular examples. Our job is to see broad trends and isolate forces so we can analyze and exploit them. Many of the sternest critics from the other side have failed to analyze the underlying trends. This gives us a critical edge.

Christians overlook the fact that to become a significant market is as much a source of problems as a sign of power. They might have learned from the youth market in the '60s, which was the immediate forerunner of the Evangelical market in the '70s. The principle is simple: the stronger the subculture, the more powerful its commercial potential. The so-called counter-culture came to express its protest and its aspirations in the rock music and blue jeans that became the sound and style of the movement. And in the process a vast new market was created.

Once these things were on the market, however, they could be sold by anyone and bought by anyone. As a result, counter-cultural symbols lost their distinctiveness and became fashionable, then empty and open to manipulation. Who could take radicals seriously when their rhetoric was interrupted by the jingle of a million cash registers? "Every thrust at the jugular," as one of them put it, "brought forth not blood but sweet success."[12]

That was partly why the counter-culture did not succeed. It was co-opted by Madison Avenue. In the end it was not even a permanent sub-culture, only a way station for youth. We are bringing the same Midas touch to the current Evangelical renewal, so that through the amalgam of convictions and consumption a market is made out of a movement, congregations are turned into customers and the gospel is groomed to gross well.

This is proving easier than we expected, as a glance at a recent trend in advertising will show you. Bob Hope once told a story about flying across America in a plane that was hit by lightning.

"Do something religious!" shrieked a little old lady across the aisle.

"So I did," he wisecracked. "I took up a collection."

But the relationship between the Bible and the bucks is no joke today. It's big business. It's the right button to push, whether in jest or in earnest. A recent ad in *The New Yorker* ran, "After 20 years of driving Volkswagen religiously, the Reverend Dr. Gray-Smith converted. . . . Le Car has turned millions into true believers." Can you imagine Renault advertising like that in France? In secular Europe their little joke would have all the resonance of a wet cardboard bell.

In America, however, the joke is now told not only behind Christians' backs but also to their faces. You do not need market research to tell you that conservative Christians have a biblical text to justify whatever they do. So how has El Al, the Israeli national airline, advertised in a leading conservative Christian magazine? "In 10 Hours We Fly You to Where Jesus Walked," ran the headline over a shot of Lake Galilee with the text, "Come ye after me, and I will make you to become fishers of men." You've come a long way, baby, to buy that one so solemnly. But the El Al "Pilgrimage Department" winks all the way to the bank.

You can see how the course of consumer religion is Operation Gravedigger in miniature. Late American Evangelicalism is partly descended from English Puritanism, but between them are three centuries, two worlds and a complete theology. The earlier movement saw covetousness as the master sin, the essence of the lust of the spirit. Such Puritans were dangerous. They treated riches with a disciplined inner detachment and regarded poverty as infinitely preferable to prosperous worldliness.

Their heirs have neatly reversed this. They see the official master sin (if there is one at all) as the lust of the flesh, not the spirit. Unofficially, poverty and failure are even worse, whereas riches are glorified and equated with blessing. "It is the duty of every man to be a prosperous man," exclaimed a nineteenth-century trailblazer for this truth.[13] "God's will is prosperity," echoes today's telepriest as he thanks God for his "blessed Cadillac."[14] Such high buffoonery is harmless to us, though an invaluable contribution to the decline of the modern Church, if not the West itself. Late American Evangelicalism is early Puritanism in its dotage, the Protestant work ethic gone to seed. Even the "Christian Booksellers" have changed their name to "Christian Retailers," a change that is as accurate as it is revealing.

American religion has always been known for its sacramental materialism, but with television and the arrival of the megachurches, it has tools of which Tetzel never dreamed and profits to make even Chaucer's Pardoner blush. Today, what is to be escaped is poverty, not purgatory, and what is for sale is indulgence of another kind. With miracle prayer cloths now sent out by mass mailing and by Protestants, the wheel has come full circle. The co-opting of the Reformation is well advanced.

Little wonder that the market in retail religion is bullish. Spiritual renewal means business is booming for the brokers of consumer religion.

Closed Religion

America's refusal to have a state Church and her extraordinary wealth make her uniquely open to the seductive powers of civil religion and consumer religion. This, as I said, is offensively plain to outsiders, though only because they do not happen to share the same conditions. Watch almost any European program on American religion (on the megachurches, for instance, or on the religious Right), and you'll see how superior outsiders can be. Much of this is sheer hypocrisy. Superiority born of a cultural accident is hardly a moral achievement, though Propaganda and Disinformation are always able to use the caricatures it creates.

Therefore, as a third example of our counterfeits, let me take a phenomenon that is found in almost all modern countries and which only happens to be more advanced in the U.S. because the U.S. is more advanced. This is closed religion, by which I mean *religion is shaped by the priorities and demands of the social order.* The issues behind closed religion and civil religion are similar, but with closed religion the focus is not on society, it is on the interests of the individual. The issue at stake in this case is: What is the source of an individual's meaning and belonging, and how is this formed under the conditions of modern mobility, freedom and change?

Nothing is more characteristic of the modern world than the restless, sometimes desperate, search for meaning and belonging—the "shopping for selves" in modern consumer society. Sense of some kind, stability of some sort—these are prerequisites for a tolerable human life, keeping the specter of irrationality and absurdity at bay. Yet for many modern people, both meaning and belonging are in short supply because of the high degree of disintegration in advanced societies.

This lack gives rise to a simple dynamic that is natural for us to harness: *when social chaos, then religious cults.* This is not new. You can see it in the lively religion of the frontier days in nineteenth-century America, or further back in the long succession of extreme millenarian movements in Europe. The principle is the same. Periods of rapid change and social disruption create powerful needs that seek answers in new sectarian groups.

Do you know the so-called hemline indicator of economics? It is the idea that the stock market rises and falls with the hemline, looser financial controls meaning freer and more revealing clothes (and vice versa). Closed religion can be charted even more reliably than that. It was no accident, for instance, that expressions of closed religion mushroomed in the '70s as a direct reaction to the '60s. "Freedom!" was the cry of the 1960s—freedom from tradition, custom, routine, morals, authority and all that inhibited the spontaneous expression of the autonomous individual in the unbounded moment. That, as we know, led to some ridiculous things. But its value for us was that it created a vacuum that in turn built up a consuming hunger for the very things that had been discarded.

Predictably, there was a rebound from such unrestrained freedom— from openness to closure, from virtual anarchy to authoritarianism, from a tolerance of ambiguity to an intolerance of anything but buttoned-down certainty, from a make-it-up-as-you-go-along freedom to a prepackaged form. The liberated generation suddenly woke up and found itself the fatherless generation; and in the ensuing scramble for authority, community, family and home, it showed itself decidedly unparticular.

This is the context of the '70s-style surge of closed religion, which reached its twisted climax in Jonestown. But the People's Temple was not the deranged exception many people thought. It was only following to a logical extreme what a whole decade showed in milder ways—and not least the churches.

I said to you earlier that we were using two weapons to counter the potential danger of the charismatic movement. Privatization was the first, and here (in closed religion) is the second. You may have noticed the sudden somersaults of some of the fringe charismatic groups, for example. One moment they were all for freedom, and could be heard noisily rejecting "one-man ministry," "hide-bound liturgies" and "patriarchal domination"). Then hey presto, and a thousand mini-popes were strutting around telling their followers what to believe, how to behave, whom to marry, with whom not to associate, and so on.

Such swings toward micro-totalitarianism were dressed up properly, of course, sailing under the flags of respectable notions such as authority, discipleship, accountability and "shepherding." But unquestionably they were closed religion. Under the chaotic conditions of modern freedom, mobility, choice and change, the Christian faith is reaction-formation prone—vulnerable to being sucked into the black hole of today's vacuum of meaning and belonging. Few disillusionments with faith are more hurtful and harder to overcome than an experience of closed religion. Many of our most notable renegades from the Adversary's side were produced this way.

These three—civil religion, consumer religion, closed religion—are only samples of the different counterfeits on which we are working. I could mention others, such as common religion (religion shaped by the priorities and demands of populist opinions and feelings) or clan religion (religion shaped by the tribal groupings, such as the characteristic "fiefdoms" of Evangelicalism, each following its own mini-pope).

I could also mention other valuable side effects. Counterfeit religion is an easy way, for instance, of increasing prejudice against the Christian faith around the world. If American Christians cannot distinguish between the Christian faith and Americanism, how can others be expected to do so? But our aim in them all is the same: to ensure that the Church is shaped rather than shaping, reverting to the pattern of its culture rather than renewing its culture after the pattern of the Adversary.

The old, "brooding Dane" saw this beginning more than a century ago. "In every way it has come to this," Søren Kierkegaard wrote, "*that what one now calls Christianity is precisely what Christ came to abolish*. This has happened especially in Protestantism."[15] The only surprising thing about our success is how open and obvious the result has been. "He who travels in the barque of St. Peter had better not look too closely into the engine room," Ronald Knox warned earlier.[16] Our success with her Protestant sister ship is now so total that engine-room affairs have taken over the bridge and spilled out onto the decks.

This concludes my review of the strategy through which we have followed up the advantages of the three main pressures of modernization. Having seen the pressures operating full force, and our own campaigns to confuse and counterfeit going well, we can turn next time to survey the damage.

P.S. I was telling someone from the Archives Department about the holy hardware (Jesus baby bibs, Christian tea bags, fortune cookies with Scripture texts inside, Frisbees with the legend "The rapture is the only way to fly," and so on). Admittedly he is a little thick, but he simply could not believe it. Would you send him an assortment of the stuff the next time you are over? It would be useful for the archives anyway. In 50 years' time no one will believe it without seeing it.

Damage to Enemy Institutions

FROM: DEPUTY DIRECTOR, CENTRAL SECURITY COUNCIL
TO: DIRECTOR DESIGNATE, LOS ANGELES BUREAU
CLASSIFICATION: *ULTRA SECRET*

During my time in the Paris bureau, I used to dine regularly with a colonel in the French Secret Service who was famous for two things: his passion for Châteauneuf-du-Pape wines and his cold realism. In terms of the latter, he used to tell a story from World War II to make his point. When the German U-boat menace was at its height, the U.S. Defense Department was making every effort to find an effective solution. Among the dozens of suggestions considered, one was from a scientist who recommended boiling the Atlantic until the submarines rose to the surface and exploded. Highly skeptical, a Defense Department official asked the scientist how he proposed to do this.

"I'm paid to have the ideas," the scientist retorted. "You're paid to implement them."

All their proposals, the Colonel warned his staff, had to be practicable. The impractical, however imaginative, were not wanted.

Sweet realism. Would that it were branded on the tiny minds of all our Bureau directors. Intelligence work recognizes only one final law: results. I shudder when I think of the time and energy wasted on harebrained schemes with almost no return. Your former division of counter-apologetics has not been guiltless here. Even your predecessor at Oxford was ridiculously profligate in his efforts to foster a once-for-all, knock-down argument against the Christian faith.

He never achieved it, of course. There isn't one and there never will be, though doubtless he would still be trying to find it if we had not sent you to replace him. But his real folly was this: Even if he had managed to contrive the conclusive argument, it still would not have been conclusive for many people. Most people, many atheists included, are not argued out of faith any more than they were argued into it in the first place.

Operation Gravedigger takes this into account and has no such drawbacks. Let us therefore turn from examining the pressures brought to bear on the Christian faith and look at the problems they have created for the Church. I will begin by outlining the damage to Christian institutions. In later memoranda, I will look at the damage to Christian ideas and to Christian involvement in the world.

Two Reminders

As we shift our focus to the specific problems created for the Church, keep in mind two important points.

First, remember that these problems are not unique to the Christian Church. Other religions have also been affected insofar as they have been modernized too. Take the case of a movement that was so appealing to the Beatles a few years ago—Transcendental Meditation, led by the Maharishi Mahesh Yogi. What the West saw was a streamlined, export model of Hinduism, designed especially for the Western market and even masquerading as a nonreligious "science."

The numbers of Americans who practice TM are minuscule compared with those attending weekly Bible studies, so its coverage was always due to its novelty. It does sell reasonably well in the present spiritual climate, but what many of its Western clientele did not realize was the extent of the modernizing done on it, a cosmetic facelift that simultaneously disguises its worst features and abandons some of its better (not least that in India its teaching was traditionally free of charge).

What is true of the damage to other religions is true also of other institutions, ranging from the family to the state. Above all, it is true of countless millions of modern individuals (in the compounding of loneliness in modern cities, for example). The advanced modern world has indiscriminately left its mark on all sides. Almost no one and nothing is immune from its shaping power at some point.

If we can conceal this fact from Christians, they will have a picture that is both distorted and discouraging—distorted because they do not see the damage to other religions, and discouraging because they think the damage to their faith is due to its inherent weakness. The Christian faith has certainly been among the hardest hit, although not for the reasons some think. The blow seems worse to the Church, partly because she was so strong and central before, and partly because she was so influential in creating the modern world. "Those hit first are hit worst," as it is said. That, in a sense, is the closest thing to a eulogy the Christian faith will get in the modern world. But not knowing the background, some Christians think that the damage to their faith must be due to an inherent weakness in the faith itself.

Second, remember that the damage we are talking of concerns the Church's plausibility, not its credibility. It is all about whether the Christian faith *seems* true, not whether it *is* true. I do not need to tell you about the extent of the Church's credibility crisis. You instigated part of it. But as I stressed earlier, our concern is to undermine Christian plausibility, to create such a gap between its spiritual rhetoric and its social reality that, whatever Christians may say, the Christian faith is bound to seem hypocritical or untrue.

Think of it from the angle of the Church itself. The Church, you remember, is the plausibility structure of the Christian faith. In their own words, it is the so-called "pillar and bulwark of the truth." This means that subjective certainty in the Christian faith rises or falls, fluctuating according to the fortunes of the Church. When the Church is consistently and continuously strong, the Christian faith will seem true. When the Church is weak, any certainty anchored in the Church will weaken too, and the Christian faith will seem less true, even untrue.

In the early days of the Church, the issue of plausibility worked against us. The Christian faith in the Roman world grew from being a minority to a majority to a monopoly. As it did so, thousands jumped on the bandwagon, especially after the "conversion" of the Emperor Constantine in A.D. 312. The Christian faith seemed to be more true every day, or (to be more accurate) it seemed true to more people every day.

Now, however, plausibility is working for us. Once it was too easy to *believe* for the wrong reasons. Now, as Christendom has crumbled, the Church's status in many countries has slipped from a monopoly to a majority to a minority—or as in America, to a despised majority that is treated as a minority. As a result it is easy to *disbelieve* for the wrong reasons. Whether or not the Christian faith is true is now irrelevant. All that matters is that to more and more people in the modern world it no longer *seems* true.

Another way to look at it is from the angle of the Church's claims. However attractive or coherent they sound in theory, if these claims can be denied in practice, they will not seem true and neither will the Christian faith.

As I pointed out earlier, our focus in the nineteenth century was on the Church's stand on intellectual freedom and social justice. The heart of our attack was not that the Christian faith was untrue, but that it was unfree and unjust. Marxism, in particular, represented a brilliant shift in tactical offense. It by-passed any attempt to pin the charge of intellectual falsity on the Christian faith, and concentrated instead on its failure in terms of social function. Regardless of whether the Christian faith was obscurantist for the philosophers (the old charge), it was an opiate for the masses and a mask of respectability for those who exploited the masses. In the early industrial era, with its new-found indignation against social inequities, this new charge of injustice was far more damaging than a hundred clever or "conclusive" arguments about truth.

In the same way, hypocrisy is the unanswerable charge against the Church in the age of "authenticity." You can see how most of the damage caused to Christian institutions today comes from the glaring inconsistency between Christian principles and Christian practices, between the Church's spiritual rhetoric and its social reality, between the claims Christians make and their failure to carry them through consistently. Above all, you can see how the Adversary's rule (which they trumpet as "the lordship of Christ"), although supposed to be a dynamic ideal in principle, has become a dead letter in practice. The three great pressures of modernization have seen to that. They have opened a yawning chasm between Christian claims and their consequences, and so ushered in a plausibility crisis of historic proportions.

Hold in your mind, then, that if the Christian faith is to seem plausible, its claims would have to be practiced with reasonable consistency. Let us therefore look at the Church in the modern world and see how its institutions have fared, particularly in terms of the requirement to make the Adversary's rule a reality.

Evacuation from the Public Sphere

It is a generalization, but a sound one, that the unquestioned traditional place of the Christian faith in the public sphere has been called into question everywhere in the West. Sometimes this has happened because Christians themselves have retreated from the public square—as with Evangelical pietism and privatization earlier. Sometimes this has happened because different Christian traditions have become so controversial through their own failures and scandals. Think of how the Protestant mainline was sidelined by its over-identification with '60s radicalism, how the Catholic Church was tarnished because of its pedophile crisis, or how Evangelicals have been dismissed because of their uncritical alliance with the religious Right. The net result, whatever the route, is the same: The Christian faith has been decisively disconnected, uncoupled or disengaged from the public world in the very civilization it helped to create.[1] Even one of the enemy agents, a man who hotly disputes the extent of secularization, has been forced to admit: "Big Government, Big Business, Big Labor, Big Military and Big Education are not directly influenced either by religion or by the Church."[2]

This evacuation has rarely been the Church's conscious choice, except for the voluntary separation of Church and state in the United States. The obvious reason for it is secularization, just as privatization is the reason why it was not noticed. Sector after sector has been successively freed from the influence of the Christian faith, so that for all practical purposes the heartland of modern society is thoroughly secular. The steely grip of the sacred-secular distinction is now a stranglehold.

In terms of the Church's previous public influence, there are only two significant exceptions to this general evacuation. But once you examine them, both prove empty. The first is "ceremonial religion," a term to describe the remaining role of the previously powerful state churches in Europe. The second exception, which we looked at in the previous memo, is "civil religion," where an indirect and diluted Christian influence on public affairs is still possible despite the deliberate rejection of a state Church.

These are certainly exceptions. Such as they are, they still weakly limp into the public world. Religion stops at the boardroom door, the factory gate and the laboratory bench—that is taken for granted. But it is also still taken for granted that you do not solemnize a royal marriage, declare a foreign war, swear an oath in court or inaugurate a president without some traditional religious references.[3] As I write, the American airwaves are crackling with controversy over the conservative and liberal pastors asked to pray at the beginning and the end of the imminent presidential inauguration.

Such religion plays a part in public life, like icing on a cake or parsley on a steak. But who is kidding whom? European ceremonial religion is the Christian faith at its emptiest and most occasional, a pageantry machine rolled out for state occasions, an archaic, Gothic ornament-inspiring rhetoric and nostalgia in a prosaic and hard-bitten age. In England, ceremonial religion has almost lost its spiritual authority altogether. It now alternates between the lofty detachment of its national role as "the imposing west front of civic religion"[4] and its more engaged, day-to-day stance as the moral footnote of a *Guardian* editorial (with bishops conspicuous for their vagueness about the Apostles' Creed seemingly compensating with near god-like certainty in their political pronouncements).

Sweden, with even stronger secularization, has taken the process further still. There ceremonial religion keeps alive a flicker of historic nostalgia but serves mainly as a social service station—state-subsidized to see to the "hatching, matching and dispatching" of a population that otherwise lives in scant regard of its claims.

In much the same way, American civil religion is the Christian faith at its vaguest and most general, a spiritual Muzak that has become regulation accompaniment to certain public occasions. For American politicians, "Under God" carries little theological content. They are merely emphasis words to underscore seriousness, just as "God bless America" is a crescendo phrase to lift the last line of their speeches and save them the trouble of thinking of an original closing line.

Neither ceremonial religion nor civil religion is entirely valueless to Christians, but in terms of any spiritual power each is a devotional intrusion rather than a decisive influence on public affairs. Neither is a true exception to the picture of a general evacuation.

Who can take seriously a faith that claims to speak to all of life but has tamely withdrawn from the areas that are central in modern society? "Jesus is Lord," Christians say, but what do they show? He does not appear to be lord here . . . or there . . . or anywhere much where it matters. This almost total evacuation represents a rout of the first order, effectively giving the lie to Christian claims of sovereignty and lordship. Ritual and formality have a see-through flimsiness today, and certain people are falling over themselves in their eagerness to play the small boy who pronounces the emperor naked. In short, whatever is left of the Christian faith in public we can either manipulate or mock.

Restriction to the Private Sphere

There have been two broad responses to the general evacuation of the Christian faith from public life. The first is the majority response, mostly comprising Christian movements at a popular level but including many individuals from higher levels too. This response has been *to accept the restriction of religion to the private sphere.*

We have already examined the trend of privatization and seen its decisive damage to the Christian faith. Secularization has been the major force behind the evacuation of faith from public life; privatization has been the principal reason why the extent and significance of the evacuation has not been noticed. Not only is the Christian faith restricted to the private sphere, most Christians like it that way.

A natural result is that forms of faith that have flourished are those best suited to the private sphere. Thus they have been tailor-made for manipulation. In America in the '50s, for example, there was a religious revival that turned out to be little more than a suburban family boom. Spiritual indicators such as church membership, giving and education all soared, but social influence soon sagged.

Membership often turned out to be temporary, superficial and hypocritical. Why? Because parents were more committed to the idea of their children being "churched" (or better still, "Sunday-Schooled") than to the church itself. They went on their own terms, not the Adversary's. In addition, most of the churches' booming activities related to the private life rather than the public, so that the church, apart from catering to the family, was socially irrelevant—and shown to be so by the subsequent events of the '60s.

One enemy expert warned clearly that so naive and family-oriented a revival was virtually "the second Children's Crusade."[5] Fortunately, he was ignored, but the '60s proved his point. Members of the baby boom graduated from their Sunday Schools and their faith at the same time. When they took their stand in the streets of Berkeley, Columbia and Kent State, their earlier naive Christian faith had become their opponent, not their inspiration.

Decades after the 1950s boom, privatized religion is still as useful to us, though the forms have changed. It has come a long way from the innocence and intactness of the world of Eisenhower. Not only are new technologies available to it, new factors, such as the preoccupation with survival, are influencing its mood.[6] Unlike their predecessors, today's privatized parents are likely to feel increasingly under siege. Yet they are still glued to the television that simultaneously thrusts in the hostile outside world and offers the best escape from it. For some tips in catering to this present mood, listen to the televangelists. Electronic churchmanship lacks nothing in market research.

I am sure you can appreciate the invidious choice now facing modern Christians. They can opt for a faith that is a matter of public rhetoric or one of private religiosity. The choice is between embracing a faith that has wider relevance, or a faith that is personally real. To the extent that faith goes public and achieves wider relevance, it lacks reality; to the extent that faith remains private, it achieves reality but lacks public bite or social consequence. The Christian faith has lost its footing in the public square and is on the horns of a vicious dilemma.

The restriction of religion to the private sphere is so widespread that many people overlook a second response to loss of public influence: a *reduplication of the spirit of the public sphere.* In other words, Christians attempt to re-enter the public sphere by uncritically reduplicating the stances and styles of the public sphere itself. At first sight this response might appear to threaten our work, but in the long run it does not. To use their jargon, it does "the Lord's work in the world's way." It uses the tools of the public world, and does so on the public world's terms, so it ends up compromised and captive yet again.

Following the Star

A clear example of reduplicating the public sphere is *commercialization,* the Church's deliberate attempt to re-enter the public sphere by copying the principles and practices of the capitalist market. As we saw, this is how consumer religion develops and becomes an effective counterfeit. Its uncritical reduplication of the marketplace leaves it sold out to its culture. Undeniably, consumer religion is religion that has re-entered the public world—colorfully, successfully and profitably. Undeniably, too, it has done so only by working in the public world's way.

Another example is the way in which Christians are duplicating the public world's celebrity system. When Adlai Stevenson was running for the U.S. presidency in the 1950s, he was asked whether the public adulation was doing him any harm. "It's all right," Stevenson replied, "so long as you don't inhale." Today that attitude would be thought of as humility to a fault. Publicity rivals money as the mother's milk of politics. Politicians, it is now said, no longer run for office—they pose. But Christians too have become hooked, inhaling publicity like chain smokers, quite oblivious to the warning on the packet.

The context speaks for itself. Modern media offer a novel power for manufacturing fame. They create an instant fabricated famousness with none of the sweat and cost of true greatness or heroism. And in a highly anonymous society, one that is obsessed with image and impermanence, who can calmly wait for recognition? Fame is the highest of all highs, and publicity—even bad publicity—is the instant fame that by-passes the need for accomplishment or worth. As Oscar Wilde said, "There is only one thing in the world worse than being talked about, and that is not being talked about."

Hence the celebrity, the person who in Daniel Boorstin's phrase is "well known for his well-knownness," the "personality" for whom television is not for watching but for appearing on.[7] As you can see, publishing and the celebrity system overlap here. A "best seller" is becoming the celebrity among books, one that is bought more than read, yet one that sells well partly because it sells well, the essence of the successful hype.

You might think Christians would be held back by that rather awkward saying of Jesus, "Woe to you when all men speak well of you."[8] Conveniently they seem to have forgotten it, particularly in America where the access to the media is greatest. Hence the celebrity system, Christian-style ("A Star Is Born-Again"). Titans from the worlds of politics, sports, music, television and religion stride the Christian stage and screen with an authority born, not of their faith and character or their missionary exploits, but of their mass appeal. "Following the star" has become the exact opposite of what it was for the three wise men. Today it leads away from Jesus, not toward him.

As a young preacher in Indianapolis, Jim Jones (of People's Temple fame) is reported to have thrown his Bible on the floor and yelled at his associates, "Too many people are looking at this instead of looking at me!" Christian celebrities might not go that far. They would not need to. More importantly, they would not do the reverse. By definition, celebrities are to be celebrated. Therein lies our chance.

If consumer religion transforms congregations into clientele, their idolizing of celebrities produces a series of fateful switches in focus: from private identity to public image (devaluing inner life and character), from saints to stars (devaluing models of spiritual growth), from followers to fans (devaluing patterns of discipleship), from being gifted to being glamorous (devaluing leadership and spiritual authority), and from wisdom, understanding and experience to endorsements, personal glimpses and slogans (devaluing faith).

Modern men and women do not live by bread alone, but by every catchword and revelation that comes from the lips and private lives of their heroes. But since such fame is largely based on famousness, these celebrities are living tautologies and the emptiest of heroes. Thus for ordinary people, the consumption of celebrities is like psychological fast food. For Christians, it is not only non-nourishing but also a slow and deadly poison. Those who live by the image die by it too. And those who worship them are like them.

The contrast here with the Old Fool is plain, and you can see why his one-man war against fantasy would be dangerous if his lead were followed. Look back at the transcript of your interview, and you will see examples of the sort of subversive impudence I mentioned to you when you first went down to see him.

"If you imagine yourself as a pure sojourner in a world in which a great many people—some of the most influential and perhaps even gifted people—assume that this world is the full story, and you know it isn't, you can't but find their circumstances and behavior and state of mind rather ridiculous."

Even for the celebrity worshiper, such a perspective might be hard to disagree with when stated like that. This sense of incongruity and discrepancy spoils the image for good, and the celebrity can never be seen in the same light again. The small boy has cried out once more, and another embarrassed emperor must hurry home for some clothes.

Fortunately, though, the Old Fool's way of seeing is too rare to trouble us. I have pointed out before that effective subversion requires at least two things: the passive acceptance of the masses, and the positive allegiance of a ruling counter-elite. Christian reduplication of the current celebrity system makes this area an obvious tool for achieving the former.

What's Good for Microsoft...

If commercialization is what occurs when the Church uncritically employs the principles and practices of the market, the result of the Church's uncritical emulation of the public world's form of thinking and management is *rationalization*—the way everything in the modern world is reduced to reason, method, calculation, "measurable outcomes" and "best practices."

Bureaucracy was an early form of this rationalization, and fortunately for us, it has given the process a bad name. Just think of Franz Kafka's *The Castle*. That, however, is old-fashioned rationalization, which lumbered along until the swelling army of management experts and behavioral engineers moved in to streamline and update the notion. In its advanced modern form, no form of organization and administration is more rational, efficient and characteristic of the twenty-first century. Business, military affairs, science, education, and even government itself all reflect these newer rationalized ways of doing things. And now so does religion.

It goes without saying that nothing could be further from the needs and aspirations of privatized religion. But rationalization caters to a different group of Christians. It therefore complements rather than contradicts the former because it operates at a different level. Privatized religion is mostly, though not exclusively, found at the grassroots level, whereas rationalized religion is the result of the reduplication of the modern world at the level of leadership, management and organization.

Rationalization is nothing new for the Church. The hierarchy of the medieval Church was a rationally organized administrative system modeled on that of the Roman Empire. An early modern example of our success in spreading rationalized structures is the denomination. Indeed, we have made such strides that only a fool or a true believer still thinks that denominations differ from one another for decisive theological reasons. For all their different traditions, most denominations now resemble each other remarkably closely in structure.[9] They are all cast in the same organizational mold, run by the same organizational logic and confronted by the same organizational imperatives, such as public relations, fundraising and lobbying. Watch their day-to-day operations, their hierarchical chains of authority, their external dealings, and what do you see—the "Body of Christ" or a pale ecclesiastical version of a multinational corporation?

In the last generation we have helped spread the virus to a new area: the so-called parachurch ministries, those independent ministries that operate alongside the Church. Here you can see the element of reduplication with particular freshness, since many of these groups have risen only in the last generation and among people who previously had a wary suspicion for the ways of the world.

Make no mistake. The parachurch movement is a menace to us. That was why the Director singled it out for attention. He anticipated that the contemporary Church would be at its most enterprising and energetic at this point. Here can be found the Church's most potent blend of vision, enterprise, initiative and dedication. Movements such as Evangelicalism, which had lost control of the denominational institutions to the liberals and revisionists, would be weak and diffuse without the strong networks and cross-fertilization of the thousands of parachurch ministries. (There are more than 10,000 in the U.S. alone.) Today, these organizations have their people everywhere. You name it, they have a ministry for it—the Third World and the student world, sportsmen and film stars, down-and-outs and "up-and-outs."

Despite that energy, we can be confident because of the effects of rationalization. In their eagerness to break away from stale and ineffective ways of doing things, they are rushing breathlessly and mindlessly after the latest management theories, the top experts and consultants and the most effective modern insights and tools. Hang the Bible. That has nothing to say. But is there a recent insight from the American Management Association or from McKinsey & Company? A new case study from the Harvard Business School? New statistics from a public opinion survey? Fresh "innovative" methods from a fast-growing ministry we had not heard of before? The doors are open, and the rush is on. Like dollar-happy bargain hunters, they are out to streamline their organizations with the best rationalized methods and structures that money can buy.

As this trend continues, we can trap them at two places. The first is where rationalization *fails*. As the current Wall Street crisis shows, human calculation is never as wise as it thinks. Often the best and brightest prove badly wrong, and usually it is because they leave out the most crucial factor of all: the reality of human nature. So goals tend to be displaced as means and procedures become ends in themselves; relationships become depersonalized as they flatten out into roles; certain cookie-cutter personality types develop because certain characteristics such as security, loyalty and dependency are emphasized unduly; and there are always the unintended consequences. Each of these developments represents a snag for efficiency of any kind; for "the Body of Christ" they can become a denial of its truth altogether.

The second place we can trap them is where rationalization *succeeds,* but where its success will be on its own terms—terms that will militate against the Church. I have just mentioned how rationally organized structures override distinctive theological differences, such as between congregational-style government and government through bishops. We want the same thing to happen to parachurch ministries.

This is our variant on the old adage that "In matters of the spirit, nothing fails like success."

Take the current craze for "innovation" and "re-engineering" that is sweeping the Evangelicals. No self-respecting pastor today can afford not to be "innovative," "risk-taking," "edgy," "out of the box," and someone who constantly "pushes the envelope." After all, as their brave new consultants tell them, "there are two kinds of churches—those that are changing and those that are going out of business."

Needless to say, both the maxim and the slogans come from the business world, where their results have been mixed, to say the least. Many a "re-engineered" business has in fact lost profitability (except to the take-over consultants and lawyers), and many an innovation has been disastrous. Nothing in recent years was more "innovative" than sub-prime mortgages, for example, yet the innovation turned out to be toxic and disastrous.

We are making great headway with the Evangelicals. The methods of the B-School have replaced the methods of the Bible. Reliance on the computer is fast replacing reliance on the Holy Spirit. Development is a growing substitute for conversion. Modern personnel descriptions (dynamic, personable, efficient) are crowding out traditional categories, such as preacher or evangelist, and ignoring old-fashioned qualities, such as meekness or humility. Prayer letters are drowning under a deluge of slick appeals for money. "Results" and "measurable outcomes" have ousted growth in character and "fruit" as the yardstick of success, and the matrix of action is no longer worship and fellowship. Instead, a self-perpetuating series of congresses, consultations and committees is orbiting the Christian world, launched, serviced and commanded by a new elite of international consultants. These are the seasoned Christian "congressnauts"—at home in all the world except at home.

Christians have always shown a curious inability to consider things from a long-term perspective. Most have been blind to the dynamics of a parachurch movement. How else could they fail to see the natural stages of its trajectory?

Put simply, there is first a *man or woman* with a vision of something lacking in the wider Church. Next, there are people who share that vision, and gather around the pioneer to support his stand. Then, there is a *movement,* structured and organized to express that vision and thrust it on its way. Finally, after however many years, with the hallowed portrait of the founder smiling down on the boardroom of his or her successors, all there is left *is a monument.* In short, rationalization not only quenches the true Christian spirit, it helps turn the revolutionary into the routine, the insight into the institution. This trap is slower and less glamorous than the Midas touch of consumer religion, but just as deadly in the end.

An important part of our game here is bluff. Leaders of parachurch ministries are well aware that to succeed in their task they must feed their contribution back into the local churches. Their job, they say, is to put themselves out of a job. And, of course, they are right. Nothing would arrest rationalization faster. But out of many thousands who pay lip service to this principle, only a handful actually follow it. Most parachurch ministries clutter the ground long after their days of usefulness are over.

We bluff them by agreeing with them. We urge them to make "service" their motto and their theme song, knowing that *service is addictive once it becomes the source of their identity (and income).* Slowly they get hooked: At first they are needed, and they serve. Soon they both need to serve to be needed, and they need needs to serve. Before long, they become experts in service. And, because indispensable servants often become indistinguishable from masters, they finish as masters, not servants.[10] In the end, they put the local churches out of a job, not themselves.

You can see why we assign field agents only in the early stages. After a certain point the shift from ministry to movement to monument becomes automatic, and rationalization does its own work. Parachurch ministries start with service as their motto and end with it as their epitaph. We cannot have too many such movements. There are a few exceptions to this, but these are extremely rare.

Throughout this section I have referred to *reduplication*. But don't forget that copying itself has advanced light years. Therein lies a latter-day parable. Gone is the poor quality and slavish imitation of the carbon copy. In its place the modern copy is highly customized, pseudo-personal and deceptive. (Prayer letters, in some cases, are processed by machines that put the stamps on crookedly to give the appearance of a human touch.) This is the auspicious stage at which Christians have taken to cultural copying.

This concludes my survey of the damage done by modernization to Christian institutions. The damage can be placed in two main categories: first, the general evacuation from the public sphere; second, the unenviable choice, either to follow the majority and accept the restriction to the private sphere or to side with the minority and attempt to re-enter the public sphere by reduplicating its structures and styles. The Christian plausibility crisis is deepening. There is nothing like two false alternatives for puzzling the mind and demoralizing the spirit.

Damage to Enemy Ideas

FROM: DEPUTY DIRECTOR, CENTRAL SECURITY COUNCIL
TO: DIRECTOR DESIGNATE, LOS ANGELES BUREAU
CLASSIFICATION: *ULTRA SECRET*

President Ford was once reported to have said, "Whenever I can I always watch the Detroit Tigers on radio." Faux pas apart, radio would be a tame way to tune in to the Electronic Church for the first time. I wish I could have seen your first reactions to some of the more exotic species of *Ecclesia Electronica*. As you say, even *The Harvard Lampoon* in its prime could not have scripted some of that stuff. Truth here is indeed stranger than fiction. Even satire must humbly bow to reality. The last time I visited your new post I watched one of their talk shows while changing for dinner. The customary parade of celebrities was passing across the screen, quick-tongued as ever, each one endorsing the Christian gospel with all the sincerity of a toothpaste commercial.

The mood suddenly changed, however, when an African-American singer sang an old spiritual in a way that threatened to inject reality into the proceedings. I must have actually stopped dressing for a moment, instinctively alerted to something that might be serious. I need not have worried. The show's hostess clapped her dainty, bejeweled hands, rolled her eyes heavenward and cooed: "Fantastic, brother! Fantastic! Christianity is so fantastic, who cares whether or not it's true!"

These little inanities signify nothing, you say. Perhaps not if judged by your academic criteria. But forget for a moment your fastidious preoccupation with intellectual things and what qualifies as *proven* knowledge. We are dealing with people where they are, and where most people are, *what passes* for knowledge is all that matters. Besides, in a day when common religion and cultured religion have parted company, the average talk-show host has immeasurably more influence than the average theologian.

Empty-headed religion is hardly new or unique to the Christian faith. (As one EST—Erhard Seminar Training—graduate said once, "I don't care how much of this is crap. It changed my life."[1]) But what is new in the talk-show-hostess's remark is the degree to which the Christian faith has lost its intrinsic value and taken on an almost purely instrumental value. It is prized for what it does rather than what it is. No longer does it work because it's true; it's not even true because it works. It works and that's all there is to it.

Such faith is little better than magic, the fine art of manipulating God. I heard a guest on a Christian radio program asked whether he felt there was a lesson to be learned from the life of Eric Liddell in the Oscar-winning film *Chariots of Fire*. "Certainly," he replied. "Blessed are the pure in consciousness for they shall win."

These are excellent illustrations of what modernization has done, not only to Christian institutions but also to Christian ideas. I would not, of course, deny that the major damage to Christian ideas has come from other ideas. This is manifestly obvious, and I do not need to dwell on it to a counter-apologist like yourself. Dismissals such as those of Marx and Nietzsche, counter-explanations such as Freud's and frontal attacks such as those you have worked on have devastated the Christian faith. To the educated and the "couth," what is left of its former intellectual integrity is as shattered and dazed as the survivor of a nuclear blast.

Having said that, most Christians are untouched, since they live outside the range of an intellectual strike. They have seen the results of such strikes, so they warily avoid entering the danger zone of thinking and debate. This means that there is always a risk for us. Once the fallout has lessened, popular religion may supply the grass roots faith that arms a new movement of resistance.

This is where we have promoted modernization to form the perfect complement to skepticism. Christian ideas have been devastated by other ideas, thanks to skepticism. At the same time, secularizations, privatization and pluralization have provided an atmosphere designed to intensify the problem, deepening the damage caused by intellectual skepticism and extending it into areas where skepticism alone would never reach. Thus, in the age of video games, Middle-town-wherever will always be closer to Mars than Athens to Jerusalem.

There are three main areas where you can see the impact of modernization on Christian ideas. As with the impact on Christian institutions, our objective in each case is to widen the gap between Christian claims and consequences, spiritual rhetoric and social reality, so that the Christian faith appears neither credible nor plausible. Once this is achieved, we create the situation where, for those who put stock in argument, skepticism leads to the conclusion that the Christian faith is not true; while for those who do not, secularization means that it does not *seem* true anyway.

Loss of Certainty

The first main point of damage is that Christian ideas have lost their former certainty. Under the impact of the modern world, there has been a definite melting down of the assurance of faith. Secularization makes the Christian faith seem less real, privatization makes it seem merely a private preference, and pluralization makes it seem just one among many. We are now reaching the point where the content of faith bears an uncanny resemblance to its context. Christian certainty is being diminished and distorted in the process.

Faith has always been pivotal for Christians (as it is not, for example, to Jews who stress right living or Buddhists who stress right-mindedness), so the traditional sense of the certainty of faith has been a key to their survival and their victories—their armor plating against doubt, their steel will in adversity or persecution, their trump card in evangelism, their Archimedean lever with which to move the world.

At the same time, Christian certainty has always been multidimensional. It was never purely intellectual nor purely spiritual, but a many-stranded combination of spiritual, intellectual, social and emotional threads woven together to form a tough, anchoring assurance.

This multi-stranded character of certainty was its strength. If one or more threads snapped, the others could be counted on to hold the strain until repairs were complete. But given enough carelessness, this many-sidedness could be turned into weakness, since often people were not sure which strand had gone and which needed repair.

Today's casual attitudes about truth and thinking are a tremendous advantage. The vague foreboding that something somewhere has given way is usually quickly dispelled with, "Never mind. The rest will hold." The result has been a climate of ignorance and neglect in which we have seen to it that the vital strands of faith have gone for good, and those that remain are too weak to stand any real test.

I am not suggesting that certainty and assurance have disappeared altogether, although you might think so to listen to some of the Young Guns of the Emergent movement. Their talk is peppered with professed candor about doubts, or (more respectably) rationalized by notions such as "humility," "ambiguity," "nuance" or the "confession of triumphalism" (or "ethnocentrism," "cognitive imperialism" or "generational blindness"). All such notions serve as a protective theological solution to mask the deepening erosion of convictions once as fresh-cut as Gothic carvings.

In most places, however, certainty has not so much collapsed as changed. Much of the certainty that remains is either a subjective certainty (rooted in subjective experience rather than in objective facts) or a sectarian certainty (rooted in membership in a tight-knit group and lasting only as long as the membership). This, of course, is a fatal change from the traditional Christian certainty of faith.

You can observe this collapse or change at various points. One is where Christians refer to their own faith. In the talk of many Christian liberals and revisionists, certainty is as elusive as the Loch Ness monster. Occasional sightings are reported, but no confirmation is ever possible. Dogma is now dubious and doubt dogmatic. Ambiguity covers everything like a Scottish mist, and in the end a suspicion arises naturally in the minds of others, if not their own: As with Nessie, so perhaps with God: if faith is that ambiguous and that elusive, is there really anything there at all?

Many Christian conservatives, on the other hand, exhibit the kind of certainty that has changed rather than collapsed. They sound as certain as before, but the source of certainty has shifted. With some, the new source is faith in faith itself. Listen to their positive mental attitudes and their possibility thinking. Such faith needs neither facts nor God, only itself. "I'm such an optimist," boasts one such motivational salesman, "I'd go after Moby Dick in a rowboat and take the tartar sauce with me."[2] A sure recipe for selling seminars and books, perhaps, though not quite what the writer of Hebrews 11 had in mind. Assertiveness has stolen the show from conviction.

With other conservatives, the new source of certainty is faith in feeling and experience. Listen to their songs and testimonies, and you will hear how knowledge words have given way to belief words, which in turn are giving way to feeling words. The faith that remains is beginning to sound like something bordering on an adrenal condition. Its certainty is little better than a "god of the gut," no deeper than its latest experience, no firmer than its current fellowship, and no stronger than the findings of the latest opinion poll. (Though, of course, if we are to take a current Christian record company seriously, "firm believers" are no longer to be measured by their theology but by their thighs.)

Yet another place to observe the erosion of certainty is in the changing way Christians identify themselves. Not long ago, traditional denominations were glacier-like in their massive historical "givenness." Now they are melting into fast-flowing rivers of choice. Obligations are turning into options; traditions are breaking up and becoming matters of taste. And as all this happens, ways of identification are changing too. For a Swede to be Lutheran, for example, was once synonymous with being Swedish, as it was for a Spaniard to be Catholic. Today, "I am a Lutheran" (or Anglican or Quaker) melts into "I'm part of the Lutheran tradition," which melts further and begins to evaporate into "We go to the church around the corner, which happens to be Lutheran."

This shift, by itself, is neither here nor there to us. But notice what it represents. Christians were, once, as obstinately attached to their denominational distinctives as to their fundamental convictions. Now they are as casual about the latter as the former. Far more than ecumenical motives are at work. These only serve to divert attention from the important process of social mixing and doctrinal leveling through which spiritual content comes to reflect social context. The glacial mass of traditional orthodoxy has been caught in the great thaw and is now easily siphoned off to fill the shallow hot tubs of contemporary religious experience. Human selection, rather than divine election, is likely to be the ground of Christian certainty today. Modern believers may not be "chosen," but at least they can feel they have chosen well.

A final place for you to observe the loss of certainty is in the confusion of theological authorities and ethical applications aggravated by pluralism. As the disarray spreads, authority is dissolving into ambiguity and its central question, *Who says?* is being replaced by the common answer cum-anxiety, *Who knows?*

The trick here is to raise questions that recede in infinite regress into the mists of doubt. Is there really a biblical message, or is the Bible only a library of contradictory views? If there were such a message, whose interpretation would be right, and who is to say? Even if an interpretation could be agreed on, whose application of it would be the true one? And so on, and so on, with an infinite regress. In the postmodern jargon, all issues of knowledge and truth are finally "undecidable." Or as one Christian said with weary resignation, "We are all agnostics now."

Put differently, the question "Who knows?" can be answered equally by saying "no one" or "anyone." The result is a melee of uncertainty and diversity that borders on chaos. Traditional boundaries between insiders and outsiders, orthodox and heretical, believers and unbelievers are vanishing before their eyes. The rules of the game are unclear and both sides seem confused. (Are "the lost" really "saved," or are "the saved" merely lost?) Once vital links are systematically being broken (the so-called "binding address" of the authority of belief over behavior, for example, is kept alive not by Christians, but by the sects).

Mother God? The deity of Jesus a myth? Practicing homosexual ministers? Christian atheism? You raise it. Someone will run with it. Almost anything passes for Christian belief these days, and almost anything is permitted as Christian behavior. Modern Christian discourse is punctuated only with question marks. Like Sam Goldwyn, it will give you "a definite maybe." A clear answer would spoil everything.

Loss of Comprehensiveness

The second main point of damage is that Christian ideas have lost their former comprehensiveness. Under the impact of the modern world—particularly of secularization and privatization—there has been a distinct miniaturizing of the faith. Its relevance is restricted to the private sphere or to highly limited spheres elsewhere, so faith seems real only when people are dealing with private or partial matters. Elsewhere faith is silent or only a faintly Christianized echo of the views of others.

There was a time when the comprehensiveness of faith was as important to Christians as its certainty. It was the secret of their mustard-seed growth and their restless expansionism. Christian truth, as they saw it, was total. It was meant to cover everything, or it meant nothing.

Comprehensiveness was also the sting in their challenge to other faiths. "All truth is God's truth" was the genial face of their claim to the totality of truth. But there was also a darker side: what the Christian faith disagreed with was simply not true. In other words, truth was total. It not only covered everything for those who believed, it challenged everything for those who did not.

Old Pharaoh, stubborn fool that he was, found that out to his cost. "Let my people go!" said Moses. And what did he mean? Not just the men, and not just for worship, as Pharaoh was willing to grant. But every last person and everything they possessed, right down to the last of the livestock ("Not a hoof must be left behind").[3]

You cannot negotiate with spiritual totalitarianism like that. Its creeping comprehensiveness is insatiable. Either you beat it at its own game, or you subvert it from within as we have done.

Many religions would have no problem with such a drastic shrinkage of faith. They are preshrunk anyway, as it were. Religions such as the New Age Movement make no claim to being anything other than privately engaging and socially irrelevant. But the Christian faith is not like that, any more than Judaism, Islam and Marxism are. Each of them demands a holistic integration—Jews under the Torah, Muslims under the Qu'ran and Marxists under the leadership of the Party. In the same way, Christian integration was once "under the lordship of Christ," and was therefore supposed to cover the whole of life. After all, such claims were said to be a matter of life or death, all or nothing.

So, for the Christian faith to lose its character and capacity as a comprehensive worldview is highly significant. How are the mighty fallen indeed! No wonder the infamous Muslim radical Sayyid Qutb was so shocked when he encountered mid-Western churches in 1949 (long before the 1960s and the ravages of the decade of "drugs, sex, rock and roll"). Their faith, he wrote in *Milestones,* the book that inspired Osama bin Laden and many Islamic extremists, was a form of "hideous schizophrenia." It had accepted a "desolate separation between this Church and society." "God's existence is not denied, but his domain is restricted to the heavens, and his rule on earth is suspended."[4] We could not have put it better ourselves.

This lethal miniaturizing of faith can sometimes be seen best in trivial incidents. An illuminating example from a few years ago was the *Reader's Digest Bible,* a svelte new version advertised as "40 percent slimmer" than the more rotund *King James Version* or *Revised Standard Version,* with 50 percent shed from around the Old Testament and 25 percent from the New.

And why not? Isn't all good preaching a form of abridgment? Isn't the original 66-book edition a trifle long for the busy reader of single-evening condensed classics? It was only a matter of time before the twentieth-century's publishing phenomenon would turn its attention to the world's no. 1 bestseller and extract from it "the nub of the matter."

Examine the record of modern digests, and you will see that abridging and digesting are not what they once were, devices to lead readers to an original that would give them what they really wanted.[5] In today's world, with its excess of information and its dearth of time, the digest is all they want. The abridgment is therefore no longer a bridge to the original. The shadow now overshadows the substance.

The unintended effect of these Holy-but-not-wholly Scriptures was sheer magic. What price biblical authority now that the Bible's own stern warning against its being cut down has itself been cut out—and by Christians? What old King Jehoiakim got into trouble for doing with his penknife and brazier, what Martin Luther only contemplated doing with the "right strawy" sections, what they have always attacked liberals for doing with their scholarly scissors and paste, certain Christian conservatives are now doing cheerfully and enthusiastically—and all for the sake of better sales and their own convenience.

There you have it: the triumph of consumerism and convenience over canon, of timesaving over truth. The spirit of the modern reader has spoken, and even the divine author is cut down to size, his "essence" distinguished from his "embellishments" like anyone else's. A small step for the *Reader's Digest*, perhaps, but a revealing step for the Christian community.

The very notion of "convenient Christianity" would once have been anathema to those old Christians who held the hard wood of the executioner's cross close to their hearts. Today, however, the reach of faith is shrinking, "convenience" and "relevance" have transformed the cross into a fashion accessory, and all that is awkward and angular in faith is consigned to the realm of the purist, the fanatic, and the crank. Philosophers, theologians, and ethicists can all be declared redundant. Today the condensed Bible and the comic-strip version. Tomorrow the complete Scriptures in a single bumper-sticker slogan.

Another, more widespread, example is the critical notion of *sin*, a notion central to the Christian view of human nature. Sin once had a collective dimension. It was never a purely individual matter, and among its wider, practical consequences were those that concerned nature and ecology and justice in the economic order.

But what does sin now mean to the average conservative believer? Here is a good litmus test. Whenever you hear an evangelist thundering about specific sins, notice what he names. Nine times out of ten, I'll wager, the sin is a personal one. Adultery? Drunkenness? Drugs? Gambling? Swearing? Those, no doubt, and more, but they are all characteristically personal and individual. Certain conservatives actually seem obsessed with the idea of sin, but their view of it is so shrunken that they are blind to its original significance.

Try another simple test of this miniaturizing process. Go to your local Christian bookstore (in round-the-clock commercial America, conveniently open on the "Sabbath") and see which books are stocked and which sell best. The topics will be revealing, as will the titles and blurbs. Most of what you could think of for the devotional life will be there—though not the old classics. Anything you could desire for the people who watch their feelings as they watch the bathroom scales. Everything for the family, too, and all in the how-to, can-do, self-help style pioneered in the secular market.

But as one Christian leader acknowledges, 90 percent of the books are about "I, myself, and me." Where are the books to help the scientist in her discipline, the politician in his decisions, business people in their deals? These are conspicuously absent, and for the Christian to be relevant in public life without them is as hopeless a task as brick making without straw.

Such examples demonstrate how the silken noose of privatization constricts Christian ideas as well as institutions. In fact, the spiritual content of faith sometimes reflects its social context so closely that it is almost farcical. I passed a church in San Francisco last year, and this was the solemn message on its notice board: "There is a place for duty in work, but not in love." (I confess I couldn't resist stopping to ask if it was a joke and was met with high indignation, which was my answer.) Sociologically, so thoroughly contextual; theologically, so totally contradictory. No wonder divorce is increasing among Christians. With teaching like that, who needs temptation?

At the lowest level, this miniaturizing of faith is one of two impulses behind the proliferation of so-called Jesus junk: bumper stickers, buttons and religious trivia of all kinds. As one lapel button summed it up, "Let your Jesus Button so shine before men that they may see your good graphics and glorify your P.R. man who lives on Long Island." Such trivializing is a direct consequence of the loss of comprehensiveness in faith.

My favorite recent example of spiritual "mellowspeak" is a belated birthday card I was shown recently by the Director. The greeting ran: "God's timing is so perfect I cannot feel I'm late, for wishing you God's best is never out of date." What pleasure it would give me to show that to Augustine or John Calvin: The once-towering doctrine of divine sovereignty reduced to the salable size of a handy excuse for having forgotten a birthday.

All these examples are diverting, and they provide a certain comic relief for the Council, but what matters is the principle and its consequence. One of the major consequences is the way these forces interrelate and aggravate each other. Loss of comprehensiveness in the Christian faith is a boon to civil religion and consumer religion, for instance. Many Christians have so personal a theology and so private a morality that they lack the criteria by which to judge society from a Christian perspective. Their miniaturized faith could "never" create any friction with the status quo. In fact, it acts like spiritual lubrication for the smooth running of the social system, the Christian "service with a smile" to assist society.

A recently converted vice president of NBC who was interviewed in the *Washington Post* went out of his way to stress that his new Christian outlook would lead to no new moral standards around NBC. "All it does is give me peace of mind in my personal life," he said. "But whether it will affect my programming, it doesn't. It just makes me think clearer, but that just means that I probably think more commercially than I did before."[6]

In some fringe circles, there is an obsession today with identifying "antichrists." But it is worth remembering that in most periods, short of the final conflict, one mini-Christ is worth more to us than a legion of antichrists.

Loss of Compelling Power

The third main point of damage is that Christian ideas have lost compelling power. Under the impact of the modern world, there has been a growing drive to market the faith.

The general thrust should be obvious to you by now. Social context shapes spiritual content. Why the loss of compelling power? Secularization and privatization. Why the new emphasis on marketing? The nearest modern equivalent to the gospel's dynamic, as they see it, is the sales drive. In other words, the commercialization of Christian institutions has its counterpart in the realm of Christian ideas.

The theoretical symmetry of the Director's plan is so exquisite that it is vital not to miss how it has worked in practice. But, first, be sure you appreciate the compelling power the Christian faith once had. It has always had its points of weakness, but that is not the same thing as the condition of settled mediocrity in which it finds itself today.

Only a simpleton could mistake the modern Western Church for the entity it used to be. At times in history the Christian faith had an almost irresistible attraction. Even more, it was able to command uncoerced obedience. We have never been able to get to the bottom of why this was so. Nor have we ever been able to fully explain the mysterious magnetism of the person of Jesus. But judging from the evidence of those drawn into its orbit, the compelling power of the Christian gospel lay in at least three central points: its stark claim to be absolute truth, the strange drawing power of the cross, and the subversive notion of divine wisdom wrapped up in human folly.

Explain such compelling power any way you will. Fortunately, the issue is only academic now, since the original dynamic has been replaced by something far easier to explain and exploit. Let me give you an example. A few years ago I was meeting a contact in Madrid during Holy Week. More out of curiosity than anything else, I kept half an eye on the Catholics' week-long commemoration of the final days of Jesus. Each day had its appropriate services and processions, building up with a heavy accent on suffering and agony to the final Friday. Saturday was dead quiet, and Sunday I expected the usual Easter folderol. But oddly there was almost nothing.

I was intrigued and made a mental note to do some research. Clearly the cultural climate of medieval Spain, untouched by the Reformation, had shaped the Church, exaggerating the cross and minimizing the resurrection. I suspect there was some late-medieval operation of cultural subversion similar to our own.

The incident flooded back into my mind a year later by force of contrast with an Easter special that I viewed during some investigations in California. It was Good Friday, and I steeled myself for the inevitable hour-long meditation on the crucifixion. I need not have bothered. It may have been Good Friday, but there were no references to blood, pain, suffering or death. The cross was not even mentioned—not once. Instead, there were images of surf pounding on rocks, lilies bursting up through the ground and the sun breaking through clouds. The dialogue was a kind of Hallmark card theology, spiritual sentiments supplying wings for human dreams.

I sat through it enchanted. "Lotus-land Christianity, California style." Never before had I seen a whole program with so skillful a blend of saccharine spirituality and consumer religion. And on such a day.

Most cases are less ripe than that, but the trend is unmistakable. The old compelling power of Christian truth has diminished, and its dynamic has been taken over by the current drive for relevance and customer satisfaction. As we saw earlier with Christian institutions, so here with ideas. The Christian gospel is being modified to become a consumer product. Its proclamation is becoming a matter of packaging, and its reception a question of consumer preference. Preparation through prayer and study is giving way to market research, opinion surveys, and focus groups. And a new type of minister is emerging, half talk-show host and half salesperson. That little L.A. cathedral actually boasts of being a "22-acre shopping center for Jesus Christ."

In a famous description, G. K. Chesterton called America "a nation with the soul of a church."[7] Yes, agreed Alistair Cooke, but also "a nation with the soul of a whorehouse."[8]

Our real triumph, however, is not in the blatant and the bizarre, but in the quiet, ordinary ways this is happening—with the injection of "sale-speak" into the testimony over the garden fence, of "relevance" into the small-town sermon that could never hope to draw a television audience, and of "innovation" into the daily anxiety of the pastor. Equally, our real goal is neither the financial scandals of the Church nor the bitter jokes about Christian rip-offs. Our goal is simply to add link after link after link to the ever-lengthening chain that shackles the gospel.

What are the practical gains? First, the Christian faith is badly presented. It becomes one product among many, with sales pitches that sound phony at best and crass or fraudulent at worst. You can imagine the panic if a truth-in-religion law were enacted in the U.S. Who believes propaganda in a Communist country? But then who believes commercials in a capitalist society? Let the Church apply marketing attitudes and assumptions uncritically to its communication. Christian claims and Christian experiences will be toothpaste-bright and deodorant-fresh, with all the gravity and depth of a catchy jingle and a 30-second spot.

Second, the Christian convert is badly prepared. Compare the spiritual training and diet of today with the gospel originally offered. For all our obvious disdain, we have to say that Jesus was a forbidding and unsparing leader. He issued an invitation, but made clear his demands.

He supplied needs, but required sacrifice. He made promises, but emphasized costs. He was as offensive as he was appealing. No one who chose to follow him could have done so with their eyes closed.

Today's spiritual diet, by contrast, has undergone remarkable improvements. It is refined and processed. All the cost, sacrifice and demand are removed. (One of your more progressive, local megachurch pastors has even dropped the tactless word "sinner" as being too offensive.) Today's diet is also enriched with a full range of additives from modern psychology. The formidable diet for the great race of faith has now become little more than an easy-to-take supplement for boosting spiritual blood sugar.

Notice particularly how anything sacrificial, prophetic, controversial or unpopular (but true) is diluted more and more. Stretching further and further for an ever-expanding clientele, Christian salesmen are out-offering everybody, but only by thinning down their truth. Soon, the last traces of truth will be negligible. What was once the "scandal of the cross" is unrecognizable. It has become not only respectable but all the rage, and all the weaker for it—history's encore to the Palm Sunday crowd scene. Jesus again has multitudes who clamor about his kingdom, but few who carry his cross.

Stop for a moment and survey the whole breathtaking scene: the three pressures of modernization, the two strategies for follow-up, the damage to Christian institutions and now the damage to Christian ideas. All this with barely a voice that can break into the Church's final sleep.

Undoubtedly you were deeply excited by some of the devastating counter-Christian arguments you were working on in Oxford. But even in your most ambitious moments, did you ever dream there could be a strategy of such sweeping scope and utter simplicity? I salute the Director. The plan's the measure of his genius.

Fossils and Fanatics

FROM: DEPUTY DIRECTOR, CENTRAL SECURITY COUNCIL
TO: DIRECTOR DESIGNATE, LOS ANGELES BUREAU
CLASSIFICATION: *ULTRA SECRET*

A few years ago I heard a prominent and controversial bishop of the Church of England regaling an audience with a story about the demise of an equally prominent and even more controversial Presbyterian minister and Ulster politician.

The Ulsterman had arrived at the gates of heaven only to be stiffly redirected to "lower regions." Later, in the middle of the night, there was an enormous commotion and banging at the gates.

"Oh, no," St. Peter muttered. "Not that Ulsterman back."

"No," said the gatekeeper, "It's the Devil—asking for political asylum."

The audience greatly enjoyed the joke, and so did I, though not for the reason the bishop intended. For behind the jest was a revealing gulf, not between Englishman and Irishman or Anglican and Presbyterian, but between far more serious rivals: conservative and liberal churchmanship.

Nothing better illustrates and introduces the third main area in which we have inflicted serious damage on the Church: damage to its involvement in the modern world. All sorts of labels have been attached to the different sides of this gulf—orthodox versus revisionists, reactionary versus progressive, right wing versus left wing, "fundies" versus "trendies"—but all are a revealing admission that in almost every department of the Christian faith there is now a bitter division over how to engage the modern world.

Earlier, Western citizens were well aware of their deep divisions in facing the challenge of the Soviet bloc. Were they hawks or doves? Supporters of cold war or of détente? But Christians have generally failed to appreciate how the far greater challenge of modernity has left them just as hopelessly divided. This fatally compromises their integrity and effectiveness. Ecumenism, as the bishop shows, often stops at home. Thanks to the overwhelming challenge of modernity and the chronically divided Christian response, a credible, united Christian Church is no longer possible.

This grand polarization is far more important to us than the divisions between denominations. Indeed, we have reached the place where an orthodox Baptist or Presbyterian is closer to an orthodox Anglican or Lutheran than they are to revisionists in their own denomination—and vice versa. Ecumenism is thought to be a tremendous gain for the Church. But if our research findings are accurate, it will not be in the long run. Whatever the gain, it is comparatively trivial. Trends such as secularization and rationalization have already eroded the foundations of the once-impregnable denominational walls, so all that the "ecumaniac" is achieving is the dismantling of crumbling masonry.

More importantly, Christians have become so excited about the din and drama of demolition that they have not noticed the even greater wall of division rising nearby. What is left of old partitions between denominations is nothing compared with what is now dividing different Christian stances toward the modern world.

Civil war has always been the most refined and the most cruel of wars—the two sides know each other so well. Similarly, conservative Christians and liberal Christians confront each other implacably, like pope and anti-pope in the medieval world. Each lays claim to the truth and accuses the other of being in error. But each undermines its own claim by failing to see that it feeds on the other and uses the other as one side uses the opposing team in tug of war. If the tension between them were severed, both would fall flat.

The best way to appreciate this polarization is to view it as a continuum stretched between the two poles of extreme conservatism and extreme liberalism.[1] But before we look at this in detail, let me make some preliminary points.

First, our interest in describing the polarization is to survey the broad trends and tendencies that we can use. We are not obsessed with individual people or schools (although you will notice that the polarization has greatly increased the vice of "naming names" and has therefore given a lot of mileage to Propaganda and Disinformation). Reality, of course, is often a little messier and more complicated than the broad types, which I have deliberately simplified to make a point and to help us discriminate in labeling real cases.

Also, be sure never to allow the question of sincerity to creep into your assessments. Sincerity is one of the strongest drives in the whole movement of polarization. Passionate sincerity fuels the polarization and makes it extreme and bitter (each side, being sincere, regards the other's position as not wholly honest). This becomes useful in allowing us to egg them on and compound the damage. But our first task is to understand the polarization and the extent of the damage it is causing. For that task, the issue of sincerity only muddies the water. Both sides are sincere. The question is, in which direction and to what extent?

Finally, notice the distinction between our use of the terms "conservative" and "liberal" and the common religious usage that is restricted to theology. The common usage refers only to the way Christians relate to the modern world "theoretically" (conservatism resisting modern thought and liberalism adapting to it). Our distinctive use is important. In line with our whole operation and its goal of subversion through worldliness, we regard theology as only *one part* of the Church's involvement in the modern world. Our categories of conservative and liberal, therefore, cover practical as well as theoretical involvement. We are as much concerned to foster worldliness of institutions, which they seldom consider, as worldliness of ideas, a far more common preoccupation.

This is crucial strategically. Although conservatism, defined theologically, often coincides with conservatism, defined culturally, at other times it may be extremely liberal when defined culturally *and yet not know it because of its lack of a wider category by which to judge.* As we shall see of the Evangelicals and the fundamentalists, this fact allows us to turn Christians who are the most world denying in theory into those who are the most worldly in practice. Their language masks their lifestyle from themselves.

THE GREAT POLARIZATION

	CONSERVATIVE TENDENCY	LIBERAL TENDENCY
Ideal	Resistance	Relevance
Characteristic posture	Defiance	Bargaining
Self-image	Speaking (proclamation)	Listening (dialogue)
Political tendency	Rightward (conserving society)	Leftward (changing society)
Common problem	Containment (stifling the truth)	Compromise (squandering the truth)
End result	Sectarianism	Secularism
Image of theology presented	Queen of the Sciences in exile	Fashion model
Basic problem	How strong are the defenses?	How far should one go?

I am not trying to set out a comprehensive overview of Christian conservatism and liberalism, but only to analyze the polarization between the conservative and liberal stances toward the modern world. I have jotted down a short outline of the main contrasts between them. As I stressed, this is highly simplified, yet it serves as a rule of thumb with which to make preliminary assessments. Stand back and look at the broad strokes and you will see the real pattern emerge.

In this memo, I will examine the conservative tendency, leaving the liberal tendency to the next one. Notice that on either side they are in an invidious position and neither represents a real solution. The track record of both extremes makes rather shabby reading. Unable to maintain a balanced third way, Christians have found themselves pulled irresistibly toward one pole or the other.

Émigrés from a Lost World

Has the clock of history ever been turned back after a broadly based revolution has succeeded? In fact it has, and two of the greatest movements in Western history were just such a "return to the past"—the Renaissance and the Reformation. But such is today's thoughtless, pell-mell rush to the future, and such is the instinctive denigration of the past ("so yesterday"), that this awkward fact is quite forgotten. In today's climate, supporters of any *ancien régime* may try ceaselessly to turn back the clock, but all they do is consign themselves to the scrap heap of history.

Ponder this point, and you will see why today's Christian conservative is the spiritual *émigré* from a lost world. The *ancien régime* of the spiritual has been overturned in the secular uprising, and the once taken for granted solidity of yesterday's religious certainties are shattered into a thousand fragments. Or to change the picture, Christian conservatives are like the scattered embers of a once-blazing fire, extinguished in the grate, which still smolder and spit in the corners to which they have been flung. Fierce loyalties, long memories, forlorn causes, splintering factions, fading dreams—conservatives are refugees from yesterday and show all the marks of the *émigré* mentality.

To see the heart of the conservative dilemma, start from the two problems at its core and then trace the inevitable weaknesses that follow. The first problem is one that has confronted conservatism in every age, not just in the modern world: *It is impossible to be absolutely conservative.* The reason is simply that time does not stand still. So even if an individual or group manages to preserve something from one generation to the next, it may come to have a different meaning (or perhaps no meaning) because it has a different setting.

What is true of communication across languages is also true of communication across generations. An idea or intention can mean the same thing in another tongue or in a different time only if its form is changed when necessary. "Thank you" in English means "thank you" in French only when it is translated to *"merci."* In the same way, if there is to be authentic communication from one generation to the next, what is assumed naturally in fluency between languages would have to be paralleled by flexibility between generations.

Here, then, is the nub of the conservative dilemma: passing time. Only the eternal does not eternally change. So the less eternal a reality, the more ephemeral it will be. Absolute conservatism is therefore self-defeating: the ideal of changelessness is an illusion. Nothing changes more inevitably than that which refuses to change.

The second problem is peculiar to the modern world. *The central thrust in modernization toward change and choice puts an unprecedented strain on conservatism.* As impossible as absolute conservatism has always been, most pre-modern cultures naturally bred a high degree of conservatism, sometimes even creating the illusion that time was stationary and society static. In such periods it was change, not conservatism, which needed justifying. For most people conservatism has traditionally been a state of affairs, not a conscious philosophy.

Like a new broom or a revolutionary government, modernization swept all that away. Gone is the sense of the taken-for-granted givenness of things. Choice and change are now the state of affairs. No longer is there anything automatic or assured about tradition, so to be conservative is to be defensive *self-consciously.* The result is a new nervousness, insecurity, and anger. Genuine conservatism in a fast-changing world is a threatened species, and the aggressiveness with which it defends itself betrays its underlying insecurity. The old assurance has gone for good.

We have therefore forced modern conservatives into a vicious quandary. To defend conservatism well, they must do it in a progressive way; to fight for tradition, they must use weapons that are modern. This is why fundamentalism has become *a modern reaction to the modern world.*

Like democrats condemned to become illiberal in the process of defending pluralism, or humanitarians who become inhuman in defense of humanity, modern conservatives are caught in a double bind. They must sup with the devil, but the long spoon is in short supply. They will resist change to the death, but in the struggle for tradition not a single feature of their familiar world will be left unchanged.

Small wonder field agents find conservative-baiting such good sport. These two core problems are inescapable for conservatism in the modern world and explain its air of inherent instability. Traditional conservatism was like a pyramid—massive, solid, stable and almost impossible to overturn. Modern conservatism, by contrast, is like a top—unless it keeps spinning, it falls.

Driving Them Toward the Traps

Once you understand this *émigré* status of conservatism and the problems at its heart, you will no longer be surprised at its precariousness and its proneness to fall into traps. There are seven main pitfalls in the path of the modern conservative. Not even a buffoon with boundless energy could succeed in stumbling into all of them. But it is surprisingly easy to drive conservatives from one pitfall to another, and thus to weaken their otherwise considerable energy.

The first three pitfalls can be engineered as a result of a conservative impulse to resist modernity by withdrawing from culture (hence "fossils"). The other four are related to the alternative impulse to resist modernity by engaging with culture, although in a distinctly conservative, sometimes belligerent way (hence "fanatics").

Pitfall 1: Elimination

The first pitfall concerns *the vulnerability of extreme conservatism to elimination by force.*[2] This is the rarest pitfall, one that is inoperable in the West today, but I include it for the sake of completeness since it illustrates the dynamics of conservatism so well. The problem for the conservative here is clearly not internal. Quite the opposite. Sensing a menacing degree of corruption or compromise in the wider Church or society, a conservative community may determine to be radically different. It may even achieve a level of consistency and purity that contrasts dramatically with the rest of the Church.

But if it does this by almost completely disengaging from the surrounding culture, it will achieve its victory at the price of becoming not only dramatically different but also totally defenseless. It can then be eliminated by political decision or, as in the past, through mob violence.

This is what happened in Russia around the time of the revolution. Prior to 1917 there were various Utopian religious communities that even the Marxists regarded as progressive. But once the Marxists came to power, the story changed. These communities were suddenly seen as reactionary. They were threats, centers of a different way of doing things in a society that could not tolerate such deviance. In order to be consistent, they had become detached; being detached, they had become defenseless. As such they were easily eliminated.

By contrast, the Russian Orthodox Church proved impossible to eliminate. What it lacked in the Orthodoxy of its very name, it made up for in Russianness, and therefore became so intertwined with Russian thought and life that it was ineradicable. Marxists, wishing to eliminate Russian Orthodoxy completely, would have had to break with the best and greatest part of their own past. Pushkin, Dostoevsky, Tolstoy and countless others would have had to be pitched out too.

This pre-revolutionary story in Russia illustrates the sort of dilemma with which we can confront conservatives. Are they committed to culture? Then they become contaminated and compromised (more Russian than Orthodox, more tares than wheat). Are they different from culture? Then they grow detached and become defenseless. Because they are separate, they become small; and because they are small, they are easily suppressed. Once set apart from the tares, the Russian wheat was harvested with a single swing of the Soviet sickle.

Pitfall 2: Ossification

The second pitfall is also rare today, at least in its more advanced versions: *the tendency of extreme conservatism to harden slowly into rigid and inflexible forms, whether of beliefs or habits.*[3] Here again, the primary problem for the conservative community is not internal. As with the first pitfall, conservatives may be astute in recognizing trends in the wider culture that present a danger, and they may resist them effectively while demonstrating a more consistently Christian alternative.

Nor in this case is the problem external in the sense that there is any threat of outside force. The problem lies instead in the way conservatives achieve their goals. If they achieve and maintain their purity by cutting off contact with the outside world and building a closed world of their own (especially a closed world of the mind), then the lack of challenge and interchange sets off a hardening process.

Communities that do this may be relatively successful in achieving their goals, but only at the expense of stiffening into a permanently defensive posture. Loyalty may still be high and nostalgia will run deep. But over the course of time such communities begin to resemble living antiques, Disneyesque reconstructions of a previous age. Inescapable problems then arise: How do they win new converts? How do they make sense to a new generation? How do they keep their own children?

You can see advanced forms of this in some of the old Amish settlements, or the more extreme Orthodox Jewish communities in New York. Milder versions were once commonplace among Christian conservatives of all kinds—that is, until the social earthquake of the '60s jolted many Christian groups out of the sleep of decades and into cultural awareness. Genuine otherworldliness is rarely a feature of conservatives today. Their problem is worldliness—though from time to time separatist tendencies (such as the Christian Yellow Pages movement and the extremes of the Christian Schools movement) have allowed us to revive this possibility.

Our simplest way of speeding up the hardening process is to perpetuate any success beyond the point of usefulness. Was Christian abstention from alcohol a striking stance in the gin-sodden world of the eighteenth century? Then harden it into the arbitrary absolute of prohibition, and it will do nearly as much havoc to the faith as the original drink. Is this new music something they will borrow for worship? Then put it in the deep-freeze of tradition, and over the centuries the dances of Calvin's Geneva will become the dirges of the Scottish isles. Is a new way of doing things successful? Then let it be done again and again and again, forever and ever. Amen.

Remember that what is "best" and "highest" for one generation can be made dreary and deadly for the next. Time has moved on, but the old are stuck and the young are stumbled. There is only one tactic that rivals the old trick of turning the Adversary's absolutes into relatives—turning the Adversary's relatives into absolutes. Achieve this, and ossification sets in at once.

Pitfall 3: Domestication

The third pitfall is less drastic, but likely to catch many who sidestep the previous one. It concerns *the tendency of conservatism to become docile in the demonstration of its differences.* On the surface this pitfall resembles the previous one. Once again the problem is not primarily internal; the conservative community or group maintains its distinctiveness successfully. Nor is it external in an obvious way; there is neither the threat of force (as in pitfall one), nor any need to erect a moat and drawbridge of the mind (as in pitfall two).

There is the rub. Without an external threat, the conservative community is neither troubled—nor troubling. It is tolerated, perhaps even applauded and adopted by the world outside, but only so long as it poses no challenge to that world.

I do not need to reiterate the pressures that make this pitfall so prevalent today. Privatization in particular is ideal for helping us to produce this effect. Nothing is more domesticated than the "household gods" and the "spiritual playground" faith of the private sphere. Counterfeit forms of faith fit in nicely here too. Ceremonial religion and civil religion, for example, are not only tolerated and applauded, but they are actually subsidized. They are as endearing and compliant as a regimental mascot on parade.

This pitfall has become invaluable to us as the desire to create alternatives has grown more fashionable. "Alternative" is the adjective in vogue—alternative communities, alternative lifestyles, alternative education, and so on. The list is endless and the idea sounds radical enough. But "alternative" is often merely the term by which small communities parade their distinctiveness and aspire to be a counter-culture rather than the subculture they really are.

Rhetoric and reality must part company in the end, of course. Without any effective opposition to the dominant system, conservative communities may be different, but they are also domesticated. They form a bastion against the world, rather than a bridgehead into it. You can test this social tameness by examining conservative preaching. In particular, listen for any prophetic diagnosis of culture in their sermons and, therefore, for any sign of tension between their Christian faith and their cultural fortunes. The gospel, so conservatives assure themselves, is "the power of God." If preached, they claim, it will be a force for revolutionary change. Like an old ad for Heineken beer, Christian "salt and light" are supposed to refresh society where other reforms cannot reach.

But in fact, even when the gospel Christians preach is orthodox and has strong personal impact, it often makes little social impact. The short circuit is this: However orthodox and forceful Christian doctrine is, *if it is preached in a cultural vacuum it will eventually come to rationalize the status quo.*

You can see this effect in the burgeoning Christian rock festivals, in the gap between the explosive terminology of their language and the essential tameness of their lives. Talk of "dangerous discipleship" and "Jesus the true revolutionary" usually amounts to that—talk. It does for some young Christians what drugs do for their secular peers or the portraits of gurus do for devotees in the ashrams. And when the weekend high is over, they all troop tamely back to the same "real world." Even the most revolutionary spiritual principles are quite harmless unless they are consciously brought into tension with social pressures. Therefore, so long as we can keep correct doctrine insulated from cultural diagnosis, our interests are secure.

Pitfall 4: Infiltration

The fourth pitfall is a favorite of mine. It has the elements of surprise and irony and can apply equally to conservatives who seek to withdraw and to those who seek to engage more offensively. It concerns *the tendency of conservatism to be so preoccupied with its defense at certain points that it becomes wide open to infiltration at other points.*

Modern conservatism, like a top that needs to keep on spinning, is a movement in need of a cause. Traditional conservatism was self-assured, with almost everything on its side. Modern conservatism is ever-anxious, with almost everything against it. But give it a cause to concentrate its mind and absorb its energies, and its insecurities will be forgotten in a flash. If they can just rally to where the "real battle" is, conservatives think, all may yet be saved. With such "single-issue" concerns comes single-minded determination.

That determination, you might think, would lead to feats of heroism. Occasionally it does. But in the long-term struggle, it invariably means that, being so well defended at one point, conservatives are carelessly undefended at others. They arm themselves to the teeth at the front door while we slip in at the back.

Even if all-round vigilance were possible in the modern world, it is beyond most people, so the risk of contamination from modernization is always high. But for the conservatives, with their floating anxiety and their constant need for a cause, all-round vigilance is virtually out of the question from the start. Do an end-run around "the cause," and you'll be amazed at the unguarded flank.

A current example of this is the American Evangelical alarm over "secular humanism" and their touching blindness to their own secularization. It is true to say that science, technology, politics, wealth and all the great secularizing forces are doing their work behind this generation's back.

This openness to infiltration sometimes results in absurd situations. Certain Christian colleges in the U.S., for example, require a student to sign a pledge not to attend films, while allowing television sets in every dormitory. If you examine this kind of mentality at a deeper level, you will discover how we turn the world-denying into the worldly.

Take a typical fundamentalist. He has a sharper nose for certain things than a hunting hound, and can pick up the scent of heresy or modernism a mile away. Yet you will not find anyone more insensible to back-door worldliness of all kinds, which has crept in under his nose. Thus, safely ensconced in their untainted orthodoxy, many conservative Christians have distinguished themselves in this century by a catalog of profane virtues—racism, class-consciousness, materialism and nationalism, to name a few.

As a Baptist leader put it to some fellow-ministers in a flash of rare perceptiveness, "If a man is drunk on wine, you'll throw him out. But if he's drunk on money, you'll make him a deacon."

The result we are after as always is a damning disparity between what the conservatives preach and what they practice. Kipling once remarked about King James I, "He wrote that monarchs were divine, and left a son who proved they weren't." Conservatives today are much the same. Take their support for authority of the Bible, for example. Beliefs about it have rarely been stricter; behavior under it has rarely been looser.

Conservatives claim to be a massive movement of resistance to the culture of today. But as we have seen from their uncritical use of modern methods (such as television and political action committees), and their unquestioning adherence to current values (such as personal peace and prosperity), no one is more modern. Not even the much-despised liberal is more liberal.

Our most shining success is with fundamentalism. When the movement started, its concern was a "return to the fundamentals," a laudable aim that no self-respecting sports coach could disagree with. But as fundamentalism spread throughout the twentieth century, it morphed into something different: *fundamentalism has become a modern reaction to the modern world.* Today, there are fundamentalist variations in all the world's religions, mostly obviously in Islam. There is even a secularist strain—the New Atheists are rightly called "fundamentalist secularists" even by their own side.

Needless to say, our prime target is Christian fundamentalism, and this is how we proceed. When fundamentalists get all fired up to fight the "real battle" that their leaders identify, they slip easily into a "whatever it takes" mentality. The evil they fight is so awful, and its triumph so unthinkable, that their ends can justify any and all means. That was easy with Islamic, Hindu, and Buddhist terrorists, who passionately justify the slaughter of the innocents. But don't overlook the Christian right. The Adversary's strict injunction to his side to "love your enemies" has routinely been thrown out the window. Certain pro-life campaigners even became so inflamed by the righteousness of their own cause that they trashed the Ten Commandments and justified the murder of an abortionist. Back to the fundamentals? Hardly.

Pitfall 5: Oscillation
The fifth pitfall is fascinating. It mostly ensnares those conservatives who attempt to resist the surrounding culture actively. This pitfall concerns *the tendency of conservatism to produce individuals who swing violently from one extreme to another.*[4]

"If you can't beat 'em, join 'em" runs the familiar maxim, and this pitfall is its religious equivalent. Do I need to name names? You must have seen its effects. Yesterday's conservative fundamentalist suddenly becomes the Pied Piper for today's Emergent doubters, yesterday's Bible College student the leading skeptic about the Bible's authority, yesterday's student Christian group leader today's radical theological revisionist, yesterday's conservative Catholic today's revolutionary Marxist, yesterday's advocate of "theistic proofs" today's enthusiast for encounter groups, yesterday's son of a Christian leader today's sharpest tongued attacker of his father's faith—and so on. Modern conservatives are oscillation-prone—and having swung from one side to the other, the rest of his or her life is spent in a series of compulsive attempts to purge a new-found liberal soul of its immature conservative past.

Again it is the permanent precariousness of conservatism in today's world that sets the swing in motion. Conducting a ceaseless defense is intellectually and psychologically demanding, which puts it beyond the capacity of most. This paves the way for the old secret service technique of turning and playing back an enemy's agents, which is called "coat-trailing." We simply apply consistent pressure until the inherent insecurity of extreme conservatism shows through. The sheer attrition of the modern scene is often enough to do it, and the temptation then is to join the other side. As you will discover, it is not that *even* enthusiasts are defection prone, but that enthusiasts are especially.

This susceptibility reaches its height at times when the icebergs of traditional certainty begin to melt and break up, particularly among those who speak out for the faith. More exposed, they are more aware of the precariousness of their position and therefore more tempted to jump.

In the eighteenth century, it was the iceberg of mainstream Protestant orthodoxy that broke up first. Now, following the second Vatican Council it is the Catholics' turn, and the air is blue with the radical rhetoric of ex-priests, former nuns and one-time altar boys scrambling for the safety of new causes. Evangelicalism has been touched by this susceptibility in the past, although sporadically and in random ways. Soon we will make it the focus of a concentrated campaign.

Pitfall 6: Assimilation

The sixth pitfall has snared conservatism for centuries, but now comes in a distinctive modern form. It concerns *the tendency of conservatism to be absorbed into a culture until its Christian identity is lost complelety.*[5]

This danger was obviously greater in the past when traditional society and conservative religion were natural allies. When those two joined hands you could barely tell one from the other. Together they had the power to block all processes of change and stifle any channels of dissent, creating a monolithic Christian civilization. In short, Christendom and the Constantinian solution.

We invariably gained from such a liaison because the fruit of the union was the secularization of the Church rather than the sanctification of the culture. This assimilation occurred through the mixing of the bloodlines. Gradually the culture absorbed the Church until identification became equation. The Church then doubled for culture. Eventually it *was* the culture with almost nothing left over.

You may think this is impossible for us to repeat today. Modern conservatism, after all, now defines itself in terms of its *resistance* to mainstream modern culture. How then can it be assimilated?

The answer is that conservatism can still be assimilated, although less easily, because modern culture is neither uniform nor monolithic. Because of choice and change, diversity is the essence of modern culture. It is therefore quite possible that conservatism may stoutly resist what it perceives as the central drive and danger of the modern world and be oblivious to assimilation at other points. In this sense, the pitfall of assimilation lies in line with the pitfall of infiltration, but just a little further on.

One clear example occurs where conservative religion is used to bolster cultures that are under stress in the modern world (as we saw earlier in apartheid South Africa and in hyper-Protestant Ulster, and to a lesser extent in the South of the United States). Such conservatives are clear about the dangers they are fighting ("Communism," "popery" and "secular humanism," or whatever). But the force of their attacks blinds them to the extent of their own assimilation to their own cultures or subcultures. The fact that these cultures at times show an evil face is a bonus to us, but our gains begin much earlier, just as soon as the assimilation begins.

Pitfall 7: Exploitation and/or Rejection
This last pitfall is a logical extension of the sixth, and it is another that has existed for centuries. It concerns *the tendency of conservatism to be exploited because of its usefulness and—sooner or later—to be rejected because of this exploitation.*

Exploitation is merely putting the process of assimilation to work. To get along with the culture, the Church must go along with what the culture wants. Becoming one with the culture is what qualifies the Church for bonding the culture. Acting as spiritual halo and as social glue are two parts of the same role.

Don't always expect a nation's leaders to exploit the Christian faith consciously and deliberately. Machiavellianism of that sort is rare, though certainly present today. It happened, for example, in several recent U.S. presidential elections, when the attitudes of many conservative Christians made them an obvious target. Confusing Christian principles and conservative politics, romanticizing American history and relying on single-issue politics, they were ripe for the designs of skillful manipulators. Our experience, however, is that conservative religion is best exploited when used unconsciously. Each attack on the national or tribal interest it serves is then perceived—and answered—as an attack on the faith itself. The truth and the tribe are one.

This turns conservative Christian faith into ideology in its purest religious form—that is, spiritual ideas that serve as weapons for social interests. (It also turns the Adversary into judge.)

You can see why we prefer to keep the exploitation unconscious. The Christian faith turned into ideology involves self-deception, which is a very different thing from a lie. Both lies and ideologies are concerned with untruth, but while the liar knows he is lying, the ideologist believes he is telling the truth. The ideologist misleads others, but does so unknowingly, a victim of his own propaganda.[6]

Our first gain is this: In deceiving themselves without knowing it, conservatives bring to their ideology a passion of sincerity that even a brazen and experienced liar could never match. Our second gain is more obvious. Ideology is a dirty word today (and far worse to many people than lying). It therefore springs readily to the lips of the critics of conservatism, and when it sinks into the minds of conservatives themselves, it either devastates them or makes them twice as mad as they might have been.

As a counter-apologist, you know that criticism of an opponent's position as "only an ideology" is much abused today. Any argument can be dismissed as ideology—the "moral rhetoric" being distinguished from the "real motives"—once an alternative standard of judgment is imposed. The trouble is that such criticism is itself double-edged. If Communists can accuse capitalists of being victims of their ideology (judged from the Communist perspective), capitalists can return the compliment. The one possibility includes the other. The boomerang can always return.

Christians, however, cannot escape the charge of ideology so easily. Their ideology can be exposed as such without having to go any further than applying their own Christian criteria. Which are the spiritual ideas? Which are the social interests? Was the Christian faith being exploited, wittingly or unwittingly, in, say, South Africa or Ulster or the American South, or, more recently, by the Republican Party (and soon, perhaps, by the Democrats)?

The answer is manifestly yes. Any serious discussion in which Christian principles were distinguished from cultural practices would reveal that. But is this likely to be recognized? The answer, I am equally certain, is no. Assimilation, you see, occurs prior to exploitation. Thus, once it is confused with a culture, the Christian faith can be used by the culture. Exploitation is the price of equation.

In addition, this movement toward assimilation and exploitation builds up powerful pressures that can be channeled toward the rejection of the Christian faith. "Who among us would be a free thinker," asked Nietzsche, "were it not for the Church?"[7] But is not the same often true today of the African guerilla raging against Christians-gone-racist? Or of the I.R.A. supporter hardened by Protestantism-turned-intolerant? Or of the cultured agnostic disdaining the crassness of knee-jerk Christian opinions? "Christianity-turned-anything" is like meat that has turned bad. At its worst, the stench of Christian worldliness is intolerable.

Usually, the more worldly and corrupt the Christian faith becomes, the stronger the backlash against it. Yet Christians caught in the backlash often do not examine its significance. (Is this persecution because of faithfulness, or rejection because of worldliness?) Even if they do try to detect worldliness, they tend to measure it solely by the yardstick of Christian origins (judging it as a decline from, or distortion of, the original faith). What they fail to do is measure it also in terms of its outcome, the sort of backlash it is producing.

We can almost always count on this backlash. Some reaction is likely, if in a limited way, even at the preliminary state of assimilation. By the final stages of exploitation, the reaction is virtually inevitable and probably widespread. The trick is to ensure that cultural assimilation is a long slow process of fermentation. With the elapse of enough time it will be impossible for the Church to disengage from the culture without being disillusioned itself. Its strength of will and independence of mind will have long since gone.

Look at the collusion of the Church and the political right in France after 1789 (the so-called alliance of saber and font), or at Anglican political conservatism in nineteenth-century England—that old jibe about the Church of England being "the Tory party on its knees" (today it's the liberal conscience piously reflecting).[8] How accurate these pictures are doesn't concern us. What matters is that they *were felt* to be the situation, and that is a key to understanding the anti-Christian forces in both periods. At the heart of some of the most militant and effective anti-Christian attacks in history is disappointed faith. Worldly Christian faith, especially in its conservative form, brings about its own rejection.

The Sport of Fools

A word of advice. The bulging files that cover years of operations against the recurring phenomenon of conservatism are all eloquent about one thing: suppress the temptation to indulge in conservative-baiting.

Conservative-baiting, or "fundy-bashing," as it's known in certain circles, is the sport of fools. There is enormous value in the skilled teasing that arouses conservatives to a passion of nostalgia for some lost era. Equally, there are times when a short, sharp prod in the midriff catches conservatism off guard and produces a reaction of maddened and uptight impotence.

Fundy-bashing, however, is different. It says more about the baiter than the baited. It is entirely appropriate when used by the Christian liberal or, better still, by the ex-conservative. Nothing widens the polarization so sharply. But your field agents should not resort to it out of laziness. Far better for them to learn the skills to make the most of the pitfalls.

Consider the record of extreme Christian conservatives over the last 200 years in light of these pitfalls. On the one hand, you can hear the ringing rhetoric, the stirring summons to vigilance and loyalty, the proclamations of authority and manifestoes of concern, the recounting of heroic deeds, the verbal gauntlets thrown at the feet of sundry foes, the muffled tread of millions marching to their meetings.

On the other hand, consider how much these pitfalls account for the reality: the easily eliminated smallness, the calcifying defensiveness, the tame subservience, the carelessly unguarded flank, the pendulum-like swings, the creeping compromises and the flagrant hypocrisies.

Christian conservatives stumble unwarily into all the traps laid for them. There is only one thought with which they can comfort themselves. They have fared no worse than their brothers and sisters at the liberal end of the spectrum.

P.S. Your response to my two recent memos has just come up on the screen. Frankly, I am mystified by several of your questions and by the general tone of your reply. This time your jousting has rather gone over the top.

It has been my experience that such attitudes in an agent usually indicate either a state of carelessness, a result of the deceiver's contempt for the deceived, or soft-headedness that comes from involuntary identification with the target people. Both are signs of a sort of mental fatigue in field agents. But that can hardly be true of you. Nor, to put it mildly, is it worthy of a member of the Council. So I am not sure precisely how to read you.

Please explain yourself in much greater detail. Surely you have not become addicted after all these years to the chronic seminar style (all questions, no conclusions; all discussion, no decision). Nor, I trust, has it anything to do with the Old Fool. There were some raised eyebrows here when you took the initiative to arrange a second and then a third meeting. (Surely you haven't let his cranky jokes get under your skin. I am told that he telegraphs them with a mischievous look in his eye and rolls them around his mouth before delivering them, as if savoring a delicacy.)

What the Director will make of your remarks, I do not know. I should warn you, he is not known for kid gloves when it comes to dealing with hesitations among the higher echelons. He is a grand master of the plausible denial in public, but with our own people his art of the utterly deniable compliment has become most refined. And he is merciless on his own protégés. Only the most ruthlessly tested and proven are trusted. All others are mere agents, strictly there to be handled and run, not known. I look forward to your explanation without delay.

Trendies and Traitors

FROM: DEPUTY DIRECTOR, CENTRAL SECURITY COUNCIL
TO: DIRECTOR DESIGNATE, LOS ANGELES BUREAU
CLASSIFICATION: *ULTRA SECRET*

I was gratified by your prompt response, and I, for my part, am willing to accept your explanation. As you say, the best covers are never a complete fabrication, merely a plausible extension of the truth. You have played the role of a philosophy don with considerable distinction for many years, so the sort of tenacious questioning that characterized your last memo is perhaps second nature to you by now. Perhaps. It is also true that it is the rare agent who never has a single flicker of doubt. But do not make a creed of such questions. If you wish to pursue your philosophical reflections or to carry on your offensive against the Christian faith in obscure, "free thinking" journals, I have greatly misjudged you. Cover or not, our task is too urgent for such indulgence.

The Director, however, would like to question you himself and has ordered a change in plans. Instead of flying direct to Los Angeles at the end of the month, you are to fly to Washington, D.C., within 24 hours of receiving my final memorandum. You will be met at Dulles Airport and taken to a rendezvous with the Director before continuing to L.A. In the meantime the Director wishes it to be clear that under no circumstances are you to meet with or contact the Old Fool again. You have already exceeded your brief. This is straight from the top, so there is no question of altering it. And now let me resume what I was describing before this unfortunate hiccup in our communication.

Assessment of "Agent Potential"

Just prior to leaving France in the early 1950s, I heard an interview with a former leader of the French resistance. At the insistence of the interviewer he had recounted several of his own daring exploits, and he was asked finally how he explained the heroism and farsightedness of his men.

"Heroism?" he replied. "No. We weren't heroes. Nor were we particularly far-sighted. We were simply maladjusted enough to be able to see that something was wrong."

I knew this wry, self-deprecating realism all too well. It had been almost impossible to corrupt. While in the Left Bank Bureau, I had made it my own personal interest to discover and understand the parallels between the so-called treason of the European intellectuals in relation to the Soviet Union before the war and the same tendency in the Church in relation to the modern world. I had a hunch it would open up a new line of thinking for us.

Cynicism and opportunism among European intellectuals had been easy to trade on, but there was always a risk with such easy virtue. They could be exploited by either side and were as likely to create double agents as true partisans. I saw that by far the best conditions for fostering treachery were those that combined idealism (for some cause) and impatience (with one's country or contemporaries). This was what was behind much of the seemingly unexpected infatuation with Moscow of many European intellectuals during the 1930s, whether in Cambridge or in Paris.

I realized that the combination of idealism and impatience was fateful because of the world conditions of that time. Throughout the greater part of the 1930s, none of the Western democracies showed any sign of readiness to confront the rising power of Hitler and Mussolini—

not in Central Europe, not in Abyssinia, not in Spain. Impatient with the complacency of their contemporaries, many intellectuals saw Stalin as the sole leader pledged to resist fascism. They were not aware that their idealism was foolishly naive.

"Treason," charge their critics today. "No," say their friends. "It was not a question of treachery and dishonor, but only of gross misjudgment."

Listen to that discussion for a while, take out the specific names and issues, and you might be listening to a heated argument between the two sides of our grand polarization. In many ways the conditions found on the Christian liberal side (the idealism-cum-impatience) and the charges flung from the Christian conservative side (treachery to the faith) bear an uncanny resemblance to the pre-war political alignments. But what I could not see in Paris in the '50s was how much the following decade was going to complete the likeness. For if the '30s is the key to understanding the infatuation with Stalin, the decade essential for understanding current Christian infatuation with the modern world is the '60s.

Seducing the Liberal

Traitors are made, not born. Find the Achilles' heel, spot the chink in his armor, feel the old scar, and before long the experienced secret agent will have a candidate for turning. At some point even the professional spy has to come in from the cold; even the illusionless have a last illusion. The ordinary citizen is an easier target still. Dissatisfaction with job prospects, over-indulgence in alcohol, excessive ambition, constantly critical attitude toward the political system, fondness for the opposite sex—the factors that make people conducive to recruitment are endless. Nations, classes, flags and loyalties may vary, but there is an extraordinary similarity in the dynamics by which traitors are made.

The particular challenge we faced in exploiting the liberal tendency was this: Where were the liberals open to seduction at a point that would lead them to unfaithfulness? How could we draw them from a passing flirtation with relevance into a compromising situation with the spirit of modernity? The tactic was not new. "Apostasy as adultery" was how their own prophet Hosea inveighed against an earlier version of it.

I outlined the dilemma of extreme conservatism in terms of its core problems and their practical consequences. Similarly, let me deal with extreme liberalism by pointing out the steps by which it moves toward a compromising situation and then showing the practical problems this creates for liberal Christianity.

You will remember that "liberal," as we are using the term, is not a matter of theology only. It is an index of cultural involvement and therefore of the degree of worldliness, so it refers to practice as well as theory and includes institutions as well as ideas. The professing conservative (defined theologically) may therefore be a practicing liberal (defined culturally).

Let me re-emphasize the difference between the *ideal* and the *extremes*. Obviously we gain advantage only from the extremes. At the point of their respective ideals ("resistance" for the conservative, "relevance" for the liberal), each side supports a principle that is essential to the proper functioning of faith as a whole. The faithfulness principle (of the conservative) and the flexibility principle (of the liberal) are two sides of the same coin. They are both necessary if Christians are to follow their instructions and remain simultaneously "in" the world but not "of" it.

We gain only when we isolate and then exaggerate the insight of each extreme until it becomes self-defeating. In other words, when conservatism stresses faithfulness without flexibility, it ends by stifling the truth; when liberalism stresses flexibility without faithfulness, it ends by squandering the truth. "Divide and rule" has never been improved upon.

We are playing here on a deep tension as old as the Christian faith itself. But there are two facts in the current situation that tilt the balance (or to be more accurate, the imbalance) decisively in our favor. The first is that modern Christians are extraordinarily ignorant about the art of engaging in culture, whether in words or deeds.

You know the crisis in conventions that surrounds sexuality today. With no accepted moral standards and etiquette, the distance between shaking hands and sexual relations is shorter than ever before. Indeed, for many people progress from one to the other is as swift and unexpected as the movement in a high-speed elevator with no red lights to indicate the passing floors. They have hardly pressed the button before they arrive.

Our approach in seducing liberals is the spiritual equivalent of this sexual state of affairs. Modern Christians rarely notice the fateful shift from changing tactics (a matter of adapting to the style and language of the other side) to changing truth (a matter of adopting the substance of the other side's beliefs). Before they know it, we have them in bed, and apostasy is adultery all over again.

This cluelessness and the absence of conventions give us a lot of room in which to operate. For instead of "being all things to all people" in order to "win them to Christ," as they are instructed, modern Christians tend to become all things to all people—and then stay there and move in with them. They "spoil the Egyptians," as the Israelites were instructed to do, and then—like the Israelites—create from the spoils a forbidden golden calf.

There is a second point in our favor. The modern world is overwhelmingly forceful and seductive, so the struggle is unequal. Christians put their toes into the world gingerly and in an instant are out of their depth. They gamble with it cautiously, but lose their shirts as well as their chips. They argue with it passionately, but they might as well be talking to an avalanche. Casual flirting with modernity is an automatic invitation to "becoming involved." Here are the steps by which they become compromised.

Step 1: Assumption
The first step in the seduction is the crucial one. At the outset, nothing is further from the Christian's mind than compromise, but like the Chinese journey of a thousand miles, the liberal road to compromise must begin somewhere. This step is taken when some aspect of modern life or thought is entertained as not only significant, and therefore worth

acknowledging, but superior to what Christians now know or do, and therefore worth assuming as true.[1]

You can see this step most readily in the area of thought. I am sure you heard of theologian Rudolf Bultmann's famous remark that modern people cannot use electric light and radio, or call upon medicine in the case of illness, and at the same time believe in the New Testament world of spirits and miracles? That is a clear example of the sort of assumption made in the first step.

Without stopping to think what they are doing, Christians pass from a *description* that is proper ("The scientific world view has tended to increase secularism") to a *judgment* that does not follow at all ("The scientific world view makes the New Testament world of spirits and miracles incredible").

Notice the confusion between description and judgment. Judgments like Bultmann's dress themselves up in a borrowed authority that really belongs to descriptions. Everyone can see the accuracy of the description, so how can anyone disagree with the authority of the judgment? All we need do to reinforce the confusion is to circulate the judgment with a growing chorus of conviction ("Today it is no longer possible to believe *x, y* or *z* . . ."), and it will soon seem self-evident and unquestionable.

What Christians also overlook is that this leap from description to judgment, or from analysis to assumption, is theologically decisive too. It imports a new source of authority into Christian thinking. Whatever is assumed is then used as the Christian's new yardstick. It is no longer weighed and measured; it weighs and measures all else. It becomes the Christian's criterion rather than the object of his critique. Once the golden calf is in place, it displaces the old altar as the center of the dance.

Only rarely does this happen consciously and deliberately. Most people do it without realizing it. This lack of consciousness is how we can take theological conservatives and turn them into cultural liberals, and how we can move theological liberals toward revisionism and heresy.

The megachurch movement and the Christian Right are good examples of the former. What stroke of luck, you might ask, could make them distort so many of their own Christian principles? Not luck at all, but logic, is the answer—once you see what they take for granted uncritically. Assumptions about television, for instance, or marketing or relevance or innovation or the place of celebrities in modern society—assumptions from the surrounding culture are all swallowed whole.

Talk about swallowing a camel. Ostensible conservatives can be encouraged to make bitter attacks upon liberals of the theological variety and then buy up the world's value system without a second thought. They labor away at forming their own golden calves while thundering against the golden calves of others. They may idolize conservative politics rather than secular thought, unfettered capitalism rather than Marxism. But the effect is the same. Some aspect of modern experience is assumed uncritically, so that it is made authoritative in practice. In the process, the authority of modernity replaces the authority of the Adversary. A defiant "Thus says the Lord" is as passé as a bishop's gaiters.

Step 2: Abandonment

The next step in the seduction follows logically from the first. Everything that does not fit in with the new assumption (made in step one) is either cut out deliberately or slowly abandoned to a limbo of neglect.[2] One infatuated glance at a "new woman" and the "old wife" is seen in a new and unflattering light.

What is involved in this step is not merely a matter of altering tactics, but of altering truth itself. They might excuse their little flirtations by saying they are becoming "all things to all people." But consider the old renegade they cite in support of their position. It is true that as Saul-turned-Paul debated on Mars Hill or spoke to the gullible crowd in Lystra, he did not work from his Jewish Scriptures as he did in the synagogues. But this was a tactical device. He reduced the differences between himself and his audience almost to a vanishing point, but only so as to stress his distinctiveness more clearly once they had seen his point.[3]

With the modern Christian, however, the removal or modification of offending assumptions is permanent. They may begin as a matter of tactics, but they quickly escalate to what is a question of truth. They assume that something modern is true and proper. Therefore anything in the tradition that no longer fits must go. Is it unfashionable, politically incorrect, or just superfluous? Whatever the case, whether summarily dismissed or politely discarded to collect dust in some creedal attic, it has to go.

In effect, what we achieve in this step is "anti-revelation," revelation recycled in line with the size and shape of modern assumptions. And the dividend for counter-apologetics is reductionism, the voluntary abdication of Christian truth by a thousand qualifications.

You can see it clearly in the so-called "secular theology" of the '60s (an oxymoron if ever there was one). Had newly adopted assumptions about secularity made transcendence embarrassing and immanence all-important? Then it was time to discard old images and replace old practices, each one buried in its regulation shroud of caricature. God, they said, was not "a grandfather in the sky," but "the ground of being." Prayer was not a matter of "celestial shopping lists," but of meditation.

Liberalism of this sort is refreshing to work with. It is unblushingly frank compared with the closet liberalism of the self-proclaimed conservatives. The conservatives have lost the objectivity of Christian truth as surely as if they had abandoned it publicly once and for all. Their Christian message has been cut down to size too. Not dramatically and deliberately as with the proclaimed liberals, but no less decisively. (They have a special place for blessing, prosperity and success. But what of suffering, discipline or simple lifestyles?) In each case the overall movement is inexorable: Something modern is assumed; something traditional must be abandoned.

Step 3: Adaptation

The third step in the seduction follows as logically from the second as the second from the first. *Something new is assumed, something old is abandoned, and everything else is adapted.*[4] In other words, what remains of traditional beliefs and practices is altered to fit with the new assumption.

The new assumption, after all, has become authoritative. It has entered the mind or the lifestyle like a new boss, and everything must smartly change to suit its preferences and its perspectives. What is not abandoned does not stay the same; it is adapted.

The direction in which adaptations are made depends, of course, on the new boss. Is he a workaholic? Weekends are likely to be shorter. Is he tightfisted? Expense accounts are likely to be trimmed. The same is true of the new assumptions. If the liberals uncritically assume certain postmodern premises, the adaptation will come out one way. If they assume premises from Marxism, existentialism, pantheism, psychotherapy, capitalism, feminism, or the homosexual agenda, the results will be as varied and distinctive as these philosophies.

We take our cue from the assumption, so there is no surprise in the result. Assumptions produce conclusions as seeds produce fruit. The only surprise in this part of the Operation is in the ingenuity with which each assumption is pursued and the solemnity with which each conclusion is announced.

Christian beliefs or Christian behavior can equally be adapted, and we can concentrate on one or the other as strategy dictates. A simple example is the way traditional words are redefined so that what was once prohibited is now permitted. Take the case of marriage vows. Conventional marriage, certain Christian liberals say, is for conventional people. For all others, marriage is conditional. But what, gasps the conservative, of the clear Christian vow, "till death us do part"?

"Ah," they reply. "You're interpreting it in a wooden, flat-earth way. It means not only physical death but psychological and emotional death. In other words, it is talking of the breakdown of authentic relationship. Divorce is right and proper for a Christian if the marriage relationship dies. Once you see it that way, in fact, you can say that a person was never truly married in the first place, so the problems of divorce and remarriage need never arise."

If the direction of the adaptation depends on the nature of the assumption, remember that the lengths to which it is taken will depend partly on the assumption and partly on the character of the adapter. A middle-aged Englishman is likely to be somewhat milder in manner than a youthful German, and his new theology or new ethic will probably reflect this.

We must always work particularly to encourage positions that sound moderate but are radical in implication. Take the current epidemic of "theologies of the genitive" (a theology of sex, a theology of psychology, a theology of politics and so on). At first sight, nothing looks more admirable from their point of view. Here, they claim, is an attempt to think "Christianly" and develop a Christian perspective on a particular subject.

But thinking "Christianly" is still no more than a mushy notion to many of them. Most Christians are more aware of what it does not mean than what it does (what it does not mean is often the only topic on which they agree). As a result, the current rash of theologies of the genitive is largely an outbreak of secularism. Far from being "the Christian mind" on sex or world development or art or whatever, nine times out of ten it is a warmed-over version of the contemporary mind with a Christian rationale tacked on.

As with the second step, this third step cannot be faulted, logically or theologically, if considered on its own. Adaptability, it cannot be denied, is a prerequisite of any cross-cultural communication. Christians were counseled not to put old wine into new wineskins, and the Christian faith has shown an unrivaled genius for adaptability. Obviously, there is some risk of distortion in any adaptation or translation, but the alternative to taking risks is ossification, which to the liberally minded is a fate worse than death. But once an uncritical and un-Christian assumption has been made, any adaptation will be a betrayal—by definition.

Step 4: Assimilation

The fourth step in the seduction is the logical culmination of the first three. Something modern is assumed (step one). As a consequence, something traditional is abandoned (step two), and everything else is adapted (step three). If this is exploited well, we can then drive the liberal stance toward the point where the leftover Christian assumptions are not only adapted to but absorbed by the modern ones.[5] This is the fourth step (assimilation), where the original half-truth of liberalism (flexibility) develops into full-blown compromise or worldliness, and the Christian faith capitulates to some aspect of the culture of its day.

This worldliness is the culmination of the seduction of the liberal just as it is the central goal of our entire Operation. Previous memos are strewn with examples that illustrate this step, especially the various counterfeit religions. Every example simultaneously discredits the power of spiritual conversion and demonstrates the pull of social reversion. Who is impressed by Christian thought or Christian life that has been absorbed by and assimilated into its culture with no distinctive remainder?

Christians who take this fourth step are more accurately described as *revisionists* rather than liberals. They have revised the faith to the point at which it is essentially different and even unrecognizable—what cranky old Paul complained about as "another gospel." In extreme cases we can pull off a degree of assimilation that is not only clear but deliberate, giving the impression of a kind of "kamikaze Christianity" bent on its own destruction.

Take the example of the Marxist Christian Movement founded in France in the 1970s.[6] One of my former agents worked on this, so I have followed it closely (and have recommended him for promotion on the strength on it). When the debates among the members of the Movement became bogged down, they agreed that the point of unity should no longer be Christian commitment but political action (step one achieved). This then led to a shift in thinking. No longer were political opinion and action to be viewed as a necessary consequence of Christian commitment (step two achieved). Instead, whatever attention was given to the Christian faith was considered to be just a part of the wider political commitment (step three achieved).

Not surprisingly, Christian commitment was eventually devoured whole by political commitment (step four achieved). Although the title *Marxist Christians* originally meant Christians (subject) who are Marxists (predicate), the order virtually came to be reversed. The predicate got the best of it, and many who still wanted to be Christian withdrew from the Movement, bewildered. Marxism was *obligatoire,* Christianity optional. Marxist theory had seized possession of Christian meaning as effectively as any group of workers taking over a factory floor.

Christians are often blind to this sort of quicksand because of the profusion of Christian words and references in the modern world. Little do they realize that the Christian faith is like the majestic ruins of an ancient cathedral from which stones are plundered for the construction of countless other buildings. Politicians quarry from its vocabulary, psychiatrists dip into its treasury of practices and symbols, and advertisers mimic the resonance of its acoustics. Each pillager uses just what he finds convenient, but the decisiveness of any distinctive Christian truth has gone.

There are two main forms of assimilation toward which we should pilot liberal Christians. One is assimilation to *modern ideas,* as the Christian faith surrenders to an ostensibly superior frame of reference in its pursuit of meaning. The other is assimilation to *modern institutions,* as the Christian faith surrenders to an ostensibly superior cause or group in its pursuit of belonging.

The clearest example of the first surrender is theological liberalism. Its history since its rise in Germany in the eighteenth century is virtually the history of the passing philosophical and cultural presuppositions of its day, for liberal theology follows the spirit of the day as predictably as a tail follows a dog. Many liberals would dispute this indignantly, but the best evidence is found in the liberal theologians' criticism of their own predecessors. And what do they criticize? Their predecessors' uncritical adherence to the philosophical and cultural presuppositions of their day.

Look, for example, at a real liberal's liberal—Adolf von Harnack. How was his "liberal Protestant Jesus" dismissed? "The Christ that Harnack sees," said one critic famously, "is only the reflection of a Liberal Protestant face seen at the bottom of a deep well."[7] Modern theology, as another of his critics puts it, "mixes history with everything and ends by being proud of the skill with which it finds its own thoughts."[8]

There you have it. Study today's philosophy, and tomorrow's new theology will come as no surprise. The former Queen of the Sciences has lost her throne and is now earning her living as a fashion model. Scientific positivism? Existentialism? Process philosophy? Feminism? Postmodernism? The dictates and whims of the best European houses determine each season's new lines, although in this case the fashionable designers are usually German rather than French.

The second form of surrender—institutional—is less immediately obvious, but its general dynamic is plain. Christians need to make sense of their world and therefore search for new forms of meaning when traditional certainty is shaken. But they also need to find stability for their lives and therefore search for new forms of belonging when their traditional communities are challenged. Such times provide us with a golden opportunity.

Take the case of young American conservatives woken up by the 1960s. Suddenly and rudely awakened by the earthquake of the counterculture, they rubbed their eyes in disbelief at what they saw of their country and their class. After Vietnam and Watergate, the country for many of them was "Amerika," and their class was the hollow, hypocritical and uncaring "bourgeoisie."

Regardless of whether this was true, it was traumatic. They were not only radicalized, they were suddenly dislocated from their traditions and dispossessed of their emotional and psychological homes. So the search was on for new homes, new forms of belonging, and new flags of identification. The results you know well: The passionate pursuit of new causes and the intense identification with new groups (Blacks, women, the Third World, the Left and so on).

Sincere as this search may have been, it was also insecure. It was therefore natural for us to push them into taking positions for psychological and sociological reasons and not only theological ones. What do you see as you look back? A good part of it was an ideology of disaffection, as spiritual ideas served as weapons for the social interests of a generation feeling betrayed by its country and its class. Of course, they bred a reaction to themselves that contributed to the rise of the Christian right. But as that fails in its turn, we will see the '60s trends recycled again.

The advantage to us remains the same. In each case, all they do is exchange an uncritical attachment to one group for an equally uncritical attachment to another. Whether their concern is the comforts of the middle class or any polar opposite is a matter of indifference to us. Our sole concern is that the adherence be uncritical and the assimilation complete.

Exposing the Liberal

The liberal road toward compromise is rarely taken knowingly. Nor, regrettably, is it always traveled completely. Simple factors like character and time sometimes frustrate our best efforts and keep some Christians from going the whole way. (This is part of the difference between the mild liberal, the "trendy," and the extreme revisionist, the "traitor.") But the further liberalism and revisionism go, and the more extreme they become, and the more disloyal and damaging they are to the Christian faith.

Our tactics at this point hinge on a carefully executed about-turn. Having seduced extreme revisionists into a compromising situation, we suddenly turn and confront them with its consequences. In other words, we drop the slow and deliberate coaxing tactics and switch to a sudden and dramatic confrontation. The result is often shattering. The cruel exposure of extreme revisionists always has repercussions—sometimes on the revisionists themselves, but always on Christian conservatives and on complete outsiders.

Here are some of the main problems for us to exploit in the full-blown liberal/revisionist stance toward the modern world.

1. Inconsistency

The first problem is purely theoretical, so it will matter only to a minority of observers, although with them it may be crucial. The problem is this: In stark contrast to its claims to be sharp, critical and tough-minded, extreme liberalism is often theoretically inconsistent and quite unself-critical. The reason is that extreme liberals adopt their assumptions in an inconsistent and unself-critical way, although the subsequent steps they take may be logically proper and unquestionable.[9]

How does this happen? In the first place, they fail to make a Christian critique of the assumption, so that it is not adopted "Christianly"—instead it is assumed before it is assessed in the light of any Christian belief. The usual passage from description to evaluation or from analysis to assumption is concertinaed carelessly. The new truth is assumed not only un-Christianly (in a narrow sense proper to Christians) but uncritically (in a broader sense common to all thinkers). Finally, the new and unexamined modern assumption is invited to sit in judgment on all previous assumptions.

What liberals do not see until too late is that they have indulged in a sort of favoritism with a hidden double standard, adding insult to injury. They reject and abandon traditional Christian assumptions and criticize them for being "products of their time." And by what criteria? By those of modern assumptions, which are no less a product of their time and assumed with even less criticism.

I am not suggesting that, if Christians were more rigorous, they would reject all modern assumptions and practices (though doubtless some conservatives might try). Obviously it would be in their interest to accept some and reject others after examining all of them critically and from their Christian perspective. Take postmodernism (or any modern belief). The fact that postmodernism happens to be one of the languages of the day means that Christians would have to know it and work with it. But to make the Christian faith postmodern uncritically would be both stupid and unnecessary to their cause.

The mistake of the extreme liberal and the revisionist might be called the idolatry of relevance and the fallacy of "the-newer-the-truer" and the "latest is greatest." The obsession with change and with the future, which are at the heart of modern "fast-life," seems to have gone to their heads, and they are acting like moonstruck, teen-age groupies. Liberal re-visionism is far from the tough-minded exercise it claims to be, and its repercussions all play into our hands. Seeing such folly, the conserva-tive is scandalized, the outsider is amused, and (if he ever admits what he has done) the revisionist is embarrassed. The pity is that this inconsis-tency is seen by so few. Extreme revisionism is the perfect twin to ex-treme conservatism. The poor thinking is simply in a different place.

2. Timidity

The second problem of liberal revisionism again concerns the gap be-tween its promise and its performance. In its early stages, liberalism gives the appearance of relentless honesty, courageous enterprise and daring investigation. Not for the liberal the drawbridge defensiveness of the conservative and the old, worn paths. The modern world is a brave new world, a world for the open-minded to explore and for the adventurous to exploit. Liberalism, according to its own press release, is bold and spectacular, and it also knows how to make the news.

So we encourage them to think in the early stages. But study the later stages of liberalism-turned-revisionism. What of the record beyond the rhetoric? What about the repeated unwillingness to negotiate on Chris-tian terms rather than on those of modernity? Why is it always the faith-ful who are scandalized and not, even occasionally, the world? Why do the liberals' open encounters always seem to end in the world's bed? Why is it always liberalism and not modernity that runs up the white flag?

Ask questions like that, and you see that for all its purported daring, liberalism is surprisingly timid, remarkably diffident about speaking or acting unless covered by some redeeming "relevance." This is part of the answer to your concern about the Operation's being threatened because the cultural tide is changing. To some extent you are correct: many of the toughest beliefs of the Christian faith could be ideas whose time has come again. As you say, the Christian notion of love may come perilously close to curing the disillusionments of commercialized romance. Or the Christian concept of evil might be rediscovered as radical and realistic as they struggle with the unspeakable horror and senselessness of terrorism and genocide.

You have read the cultural climate well, but your fears are groundless. Consider these brave liberals. They are afraid to challenge conventional wisdom at point after point, and embarrassed to question current optimism about human nature. Ideas whose time has come they discard as opinions whose day is done. Like the well-known "buy high, sell low" of the stock-market simpleton, they buy into modern ideas at the peak of their influences and sell out on Christian ideas just when modern thinkers are about to rediscover them.

Progress in human thinking is always "resistance thinking." It is always made in the teeth of the most troublesome issues. Resistance itself is the best avenue to fresh discovery. Through tenacity to creativity, as it were. Christian apologists once followed their own version of this. Face up to those elements in the faith that are obscure or difficult, they said, and you will break through to new understanding. Today's liberals have reversed this. Quick to alter faith as soon as it puzzles or repels anyone, they become susceptible to the special silliness and subservience to fashion of the easily swayed thinker.

Far from being pioneers of change, liberal revisionists are remarkably peer-conscious. Scrambling to keep up with the cultural and philosophical Joneses, they are fearful above all of being caught in postures that to modern people might look absurd. Just let the modern world look askance at a liberal and, like a chronically nervous strip-poker player, he takes off another layer of clothes without even looking at his cards.

3. Transience

A third problem we can expose is the transience of liberal revisionism. By working frantically for an up-to-the-minute relevance to one age or group, the liberal automatically risks being irrelevant to another, and therefore gives the impression of transience and impermanence.[10]

Relevance in itself is not the problem. As they have correctly deduced, relevance is a legitimate and necessary prerequisite for any communication. To be relevant to a person, any truth must be related to where he or she is. No one would dispute that.

The relevance-seeking of the liberal, however, becomes a problem for two reasons. On the one hand, it has lost touch with its own original Christian assumptions, and on the other hand it has been assimilated wholesale by certain modern assumptions. Relevance of this kind is no more use to them than working hard to catch someone's attention and forgetting what you wanted to say. More to the point, it is like being so overpowered by other people's conversation that you express their idea in your words and add nothing to what they think already.

This basic problem of relevance-cum-subservience has been given an added twist in the modern world, where relevance has become not only hollow but fragile and short-lived. A wider range of choices, a deeper uncertainty of events, a more pressing need for new styles—all this makes for an accelerating turnover of issues, concerns and fads. Nothing tires like a trend or ages faster than a fashion. Today's bold headline is tomorrow's yellowing newsprint.

Thus the relevance-hungry liberals achieve relevance, but their victory is Pyrrhic. It is precisely as they win that they lose. As they become relevant to one group or movement, they become irrelevant to another and find themselves rudely dismissed. Far from being in the avant-garde, Christian liberals trot smartly behind the times. Far from being genuinely new or radical, they catch up and announce their discoveries breathlessly, only to see the vanguard disappearing down the road on the trail of a different pursuit.

"He who marries the spirit of an age," said Dean Inge, "soon finds himself a widower." *Trendier than thou* has eclipsed *holier than thou,* and our gain is evident. The pursuit of relevance in the liberal mode is a cast-iron guarantee that, by definition, the Church will always lag behind the world and run at the rear of the pack. The world changes its agenda constantly, and the Church goes around in circles.

There was a time when follies like these were found almost exclusively in Protestant liberal circles. Now, I am delighted to report, we have many

Evangelicals chasing hard to catch up, though 200 years in the rear. Lusting after "relevance," passionate about "innovation," addicted to constant "re-engineering," assessing everything according to its "seeker sensitivity," "audience appeal," and "measurable outcomes," such Evangelicals are the "new liberals" and our prospects are bright.

4. Destructiveness

The fourth problem of liberal revisionism is the decisive one, and for our purposes the jackpot. Revisionism finally becomes destructive for the Church because, in their own words, it is in "another gospel" and no longer the Adversary's "good news."

First, revisionism is destructive because *it loses the distinctive content of the Christian faith.* The Christian faith has had many expressions over the centuries, with numerous new spiritual movements, theological developments, social adaptations and institutional experiments. Regrettably, many of these new expressions have been stubborn in sticking to Christian rules and remaining within bounds, so we have been unable to exploit them. But the worldliness we achieved in the past was hard-won compared with the easy success made possible by revisionism today.

Today's liberal revisionism collaborates with naïve eagerness. It is appeasement-minded and surrender-prone at heart. Take the state of the Episcopal Church in the United States. Prior to this generation, the most extreme worldliness we ever induced in history was the faith of the Renaissance popes, such as Alexander VI. Incest, murder, bribery, corruption—these great "princes of the Church" became almost entirely secular princes, with no Christian remainder, and the Vatican descended to an orgy of worldliness and decadence. Yet amazingly, these same popes never denied a single article of the Apostles' Creed, whereas our brave new revisionist Episcopal bishops deny almost every article in turn, or say them with their fingers crossed, and they still stay on proudly as "progressive Christian leaders."

These shining progressives, such as Episcopal Bishop John Shelby Spong, say the Apostles' Creed with most of the major articles turned upside down and inside out. Absolutely nothing in traditional belief or practice is sacrosanct. There are no higher or central truths by which the Church will stand or fall. Heresy is orthodoxy; skepticism is faith; no paganism is too wild and no ethical practice too abnormal to be turned away from their inclusive embrace. Everything is negotiable, the kernel as well as the husk, the baby as well as the bath water. Indeed, you might wonder whether any conceivable crisis of faith is still possible for American liberal revisionists. Like someone intent on hara-kiri, nothing short of suicide is enough. Not surprisingly their churches are declining by the week, and wonderful to say, several of the other Protestant denominations are hot on their heels.

Second, liberal revisionism is destructive because *it creates a gap between ordinary believers and the intellectual and bureaucratic elite in the churches.* This is no accident. To adapt George Orwell, we might say that it is a strange fact, but unquestionably true, that almost any extreme liberal would feel more ashamed of affirming the Apostles' Creed than of refusing to support the liberal cause du jour. The result is that, just as the pitfall of "oscillation" propels a conservative toward the liberal extreme, so the extremes of revisionism leave ordinary believers so confused and angry that they harden into the concrete attitudes of extreme conservatism. Three cheers for all Christian extremes! A toast to the revisionists who beget the fundamentalists, and to the fundamentalists who beget the revisionists!

After all, what are ordinary believers to make of these agile theological gymnasts, or their much-heralded "new theologies," situational morals and "prophetically radical" (read "liberal-Left") political stances? Aren't these suspiciously like the beliefs and practices Christians were once taught to identify as sin and unbelief? Not surprisingly, there starts to be grumbling in the camp. Why send missionaries overseas if unbelief is alive and well in the pulpit at home? Why put money in the collection plate if it goes to self-professed enemies of the Church? Why go to church at all?

So the faithful vote with their feet, and as the dismay and defections mount, a strange fact becomes apparent. While in most institutions the leadership is more committed to the goals of the institution than the rank and file, the opposite is true of the liberal Protestant Church. Its members are more loyal than its leaders. The liberal revisionist elite have got themselves into a position where it is impossible for ordinary believers either to understand them or to take them seriously. With leaders like that, small wonder that as convictions fly out of the window, congregations flow out of the door. Happily for us, liberal churches decline with almost mathematical certainty.

Third, liberal revisionism is destructive because *it is inherently weak in attracting outsiders.* Yet another superb irony. The very raison d'être of liberalism began with Friedrich Schleiermacher's concern for the "cultured despisers" of the gospel. Highly laudable on the face of it, but what has this concern achieved after 200 years? Where are the cultured despisers who have been culturally disarmed? The intellectual prodigals brought back from the far country of doubt and despair?

Confront liberals with such questions and their discomfiture is plain. Things seem to have changed a little since those early days. The item is no longer on the agenda. The cultured despisers most on their minds now are themselves. Few doubters are more doubting than the revisionist believer. Our brave Presiding Bishop of the Episcopal Church now says that personal salvation is a "heresy."

And what does the record show? It is embarrassingly clear that of those intellectuals and artists who have been converted in the last two centuries, the great majority have been attracted to traditional and more conservative churches. Take T. S. Eliot, W. H. Auden, C. S. Lewis, Dorothy Sayers or the Old Fool himself. Why they took the road to faith will always remain a mystery and a rebuke to us, but no one can deny that they had undeniably keen minds and a strong intestinal fortitude. They took their faith neat and could not stomach the tepid and diluted offerings of liberalism.

Who knows? Perhaps liberal revisionism faces one further crisis of faith after all—its unquestioned belief in the dogma that "modern man and woman" find traditional belief incredible.

To make matters worse for the revisionists, there is also clear evidence that when intellectuals reject their liberal Christian faith, they do so for a reason basic to its revisionism: When the most radical liberal revisions are complete, the result is little different from what the outsider believed anyway. "At that point," as one former atheist put it succinctly, "the creed becomes a way of saying what the infidel next door believes too."[11] Thus, since extreme liberal revisionism always ends in intellectual surrender, its carefully worded, fashionable statements have an oddly familiar ring. The secular thinker can always respond with Oscar Wilde's quip to a trendy cleric of his day: "I not only follow you, I *precede* you."

From the perspective of the outsider, the revisionist enterprise is a waste of time. The very extremity of the revisionism only confirms the skeptic's criticism of the faith. As one of the enemy agents sympathizes, "Why should one buy psychotherapy or radical liberalism in a 'Christian' package, when the same commodities are available under purely secular and for that very reason even more modernistic labels?"[12]

After seeing the report of a recent Christian commission on morality, an atheist wrote, "It is now announcing to the secular world, as though by way of a discovery, what the secular world has been announcing to it for a rather long time."[13] Agnostic intellectuals may respect the liberal stand of extreme revisionist, but rarely do they take their Christian faith seriously. One secular thinker even goes so far as to call them "kissing Judases" (following Kierkegaard). "To be sure," he adds, "it is not literally with a kiss that Christ is betrayed in the present age: today one betrays with an interpretation."[14]

Fourth, revisionism is destructive because *it actually undercuts itself.* This is the best effect of all. Just as absolute conservatism is a contradiction in terms, so absolute liberal revisionism defeats itself. When taken undiluted, it kills. No one could find a surer method for spiritual suicide.

You do not need to look further than the startled responses that extreme revisionism has drawn from inside the Church and outside. "Symptoms of the very disease for which they profess to be the cure," comments one non-Christian of such extreme liberals.[15] A "self-destructive outburst" is the surprised and amused reaction of other non-Christians.[16] And from within the Church? The comments of one intelligence expert are enough. Extreme liberal revisionism, he says, becomes a *reductio ad absurdum*, a "theological self-disembowelment," a "self-liquidation . . . undertaken with an enthusiasm which verges on the bizarre."[17] To any outsider, the practical results might well appear "a bizarre manifestation of intellectual derangement or institutional suicide."[18]

Evidence to substantiate this is easy to find. As the last generation shows beyond doubt, conservative churches are growing while revisionist churches are in serious decline. Once again, the Episcopal Church is a clear example, but take a lesser-known case, the collapse of the Student Christian Movement on many British campuses after the 1960s. There, if ever, was a clear case of organizational suicide, for the S.C.M. fell victim to its own pathological open-mindedness. As research showed, the open-minded trend was trumpeted as a beacon of "tolerant," "inclusive," "all-embracing" liberal virtues. No group could have been more open, more humble, more eager to engage in dialogue with anyone and everyone, and more zealous to build bridges to all and sundry. And bridges were built—to Marxism, pacifism, psychoanalysis, alternative communities, group therapy.

But then what happened? The conversations in the dialogue and the traffic on the bridges became one-way. S.C.M. members flowed across to become bona fide activists or to join bona fide communes. Their original S.C.M. groups did not survive, and there was no distinctive Christian reason why they should. Their minds had become so open that they were vacant. Diluted beliefs led to defections and betrayals.

Beyond Treason

Kissing Judases, defectors, collaborators, fellow travelers, fifth columnists, quislings, turncoats, traitors—these are little throwaway words, but like small fuses they run off to powerful incendiary passions that are capable of blowing apart people and nations and faiths. Our interest, of course, is not in concentrating our effort more on the conservative or the liberal side, except as a short-term tactic to divide them further. Our real objective is to push the liberals toward revisionism, and then eventually the whole Church to a state beyond treachery, to a point at which *treason itself loses its meaning.*

Treason, like heresy, is an achievement that marks an important milestone in manipulation. Significant individuals or groups in a victimized nation come to re-evaluate their country's traditional foreign-policy interests so that the policies come to be aligned with those of the aggressor. Whether they do so out of conviction or are merely rationalizing (or even bought) is neither here nor there. Subversion is well under way, and that is what matters.

The final destination, however, is a state beyond treason. When the individuals or groups in question are so committed to accepting outside influence and help that they reject the criteria by which *loyalty* and *treachery* have traditionally been defined, then treason itself loses meaning. And when treason loses meaning, no nation can effectively resist an outside aggressor for long.

The symmetry with heresy is perfect. Do you see where we are with the extreme revisionist wing of the American Church—again represented with such touching naivete by the Episcopal Church? Their initial *loss of authority* (with the spirit of the age now in the driver's seat) leads to a fateful *loss of continuity* (with the rest of the Church across the centuries and the continents), which becomes a serious *loss of credibility* (with unbelievers who already believe what the revisionist believes), which leads at the end to a total *loss of identity* (as faith is no longer recognizably Christian). At that point, with no loyalty to define treachery and no orthodoxy to define heresy, full-blown liberal revisionists are reaching a state beyond treason that presages the capitulation of the Church itself.

Such liberal revisionists have crossed cognitive and ethical boundaries so often that they have forgotten where they are, and whose side they are on. Such diehard liberals are really "fundamentalist revisionists" who have become like the agents-turned-double-agents of the espionage world—the gray no-men of the twilight no-man's land. They are the stateless ones of the modern intellectual world, the wandering Jews of the realm of the spirit, nomads in a desert of abandoned faith. Winning a single Judas was one thing; being able to rely on a whole counter-elite of Judases is quite another.

The Last Christian in the Modern World

FROM: Deputy Director, Central Security Council
TO: Director Designate, Los Angeles Bureau
CLASSIFICATION: *ULTRA SECRET*

This is the last of my memoranda briefing you on Operation Gravedigger. It is not so much a separate memo as a short tailpiece to the others. I am also enclosing your ticket for Saturday's flight to Washington, D.C., via BA 189. As you can see, check-in is only 45 minutes before the 11:45 departure, unless you wish to indulge in the perks of the first class lounge.

As things stand now, I am planning to be with the Director when he interviews you on your arrival in D.C. I trust I have adequately impressed on you the need to be concise and convincing. He regards philosophical digressions as a waste of time and a sign of uncertainty. Both are cardinal sins in his book and could become an irremediable blot in yours.

You did not know this, but before being assigned to Los Angeles you were slated to succeed the retiring Bureau chief in Moscow. The suggestion that you should go to Los Angeles instead was mine. I have watched your progress closely and have an interest in your success. If you have kept up with the activity of the Moscow Bureau, you will know that they have contributed very little after the fall of the Soviet Union. So I have saved your career from a cul-de-sac, and I expect you to clear the shadow hanging over you, to get yourself out of the imbroglio this weekend and to produce results in L.A.

Beware Third Ways

You asked me which was the most significant of the three major areas of damage (damage to the Church's institutions, ideas or involvement in the world). I would have to say the last one. Nothing else calls into question the integrity of Christian truth like the grand polarization, and nothing more weakens the Church's capacity to respond to the modern challenge. And the added advantage for us is that it is the area where Christians are least aware of the damage being done.

In the grand polarization, each extreme is acutely aware of the danger of the other, as I have said. Conservatives feed off fears of the slippery slope that leads to revisionism, just as liberals grow more dogmatically liberal to avoid the horrors of conservatism. But seldom do they consider the problem as a whole; and it is unimaginable that they should mobilize to work for a solution that overcomes the polarization altogether.

As always, the one thing we must guard against is recklessness. The worst thing that could happen is this: The increasingly apparent weakness and captivity of the Church might jolt Christians into seeing the force of the extremes, and then spur a movement to recover a coherent and balanced, ruthlessly biblical "third way." If you like, a resistance movement content to be neither *émigrés* nor collaborators. The time for such a movement is ripe, for if the '60s began to illustrate the absurdities of extreme liberalism, then the late '70s onward has done the same for extreme conservatism. The cry "A plague on both your houses!" would be a fitting tribute to our work, but it could also spell trouble for us. Nostalgia for a golden age is harmless; the desire for a golden mean is not.

Fortunately, the polarization is so powerful that no counter-movement is likely to get underway, and the odds against building such a third way are impossibly long. For one thing, the whole notion smells of the dreaded word "compromise," as if each side had to admit it was not fully right in the first place and the other side is perhaps right after all. That would be inadmissible to them. More importantly, the forces within the grand polarization are so strong that no movement could hope to hold the middle ground for long.

Having said that, we can expect to see recurring attempts to solve the problem, most probably from a combination of chastened Evangelicals and chastened Catholics, though perhaps with the support of certain more moderate liberals too. We are ready for this. The Council has made no formal decision yet, but in my judgment we would be wise to adopt the following approach.

On the one hand, we should do everything possible to *prevent the chastened conservatives from escaping the constrictions of modernity*. Since the 1960s, the general movement of conservatives has been out of the closet and into the culture, sometimes even out of the backwoods and into the limelight. This should be heady enough for them, without any radical talk of a third way. ("It is charming to totter into vogue," as Horace Walpole put it.) Their new cultural involvement should blind them to the constrictions of modernity: secularization, pluralization and privatization. Unless they break these chains, conservative Christians will never amount to more than a harmless, if commercially interesting, folk religion.

On the other hand, if chastened conservatives do succeed in escaping the constrictions, we should do everything possible to *push them to refuel the liberal cycle*. If they were harmless when they were inside the cultural closet, we can make them harmless again by pushing them toward the opposite extreme and launching them on the liberal merry-go-round. That is not as difficult as it sounds. Emerging from the stuffy darkness of their ghettoes, conservatives are now basking in the light of cultural attention. Once a generation or two behind the times, they are making up for lost time with zest and abandon. Nothing is further from their minds now than their old, instinctive fear of worldliness. So who better than these erstwhile conservatives to refuel the cycle of the old liberals?

The Last Christian in the Modern World

When you arrive in California, you will begin receiving detailed instructions from the Council on how Los Angeles is to proceed in this final stage of the Operation. But before meeting the Director on Saturday, make sure that your grasp of Operation Gravedigger is both comprehensive and meticulous.

In closing, let me describe to you an aspect of the Director's plan that has always fascinated me: the cultivation of the last Christian in the modern world.

This is not literal, of course. Nothing could be further from our plans than a pogrom. As I have stressed, even so important a tactic as secularization is not directed at faith's disappearing, but it's distortion. You may remember the secret revolutionary cell in Dostoevsky's *The Possessed*. The aim of this group was systematically to destroy society and the fabric that held it together, with the object of throwing everyone into a state of hopeless confusion and despair mixed with an intense yearning for self-preservation and some guiding ideal. Then it could suddenly seize power.

The final stages of our operation will be remarkably similar. We are working slowly and steadily to demoralize the Church and discredit it in the eyes of the watching world. In particular, to see that what is left of the Church becomes shallow, trivial, vulgar, bizarre and consistently hypocritical in a myriad of ways, but always so that its confusion and compromise are matched by at least one thing—its complacency.

You can see how far we have advanced toward this end. At the beginning of the last century, more than 150 years after the launch of the Operation, the odds still seemed stacked heavily against us. The rich and powerful nations were still Christian, while the non-Christian ones were poor and seemingly backward, their religions dormant and their cultures moribund. The Christian faith still seemed synonymous with civilization, and zealous evangelizing and high-minded civilizing went hand in hand.

No one in 1900 had heard of Lenin, Stalin, Hitler and Mao Tse-Tung, let alone dreamed of an Islamic resurgence, an East Asian economic miracle or the rise of "multiple modernities" and the decline of the West. That the coming century would be so turbulent and be marked by such horror and violence, and that so many of the worst crimes should have come from "Christian nations," would have been unthinkable.

Today, by contrast, the odds are stacked against the Church. In terms of the burden of her past, she will soon, like the builders of Babel, be buried under the rubble of her own towering achievements; while in terms of the seductions of today, she is about to be drowned, Narcissus-like, in the deceptions created by her own undisciplined brilliance, wealth and enterprise.

The great survivor of the centuries, the proud tamer of empires, nations, faiths and ideologies, is being savaged by modernity. Soon all that will remain is a little philosophy, a little morality, a little architecture and a little experience.

The Director now regards the American Christian Church as the decisive arena for the closing stage of the Operation, which he views as a movement with three phases leading toward the denouement.

First, comes *the push* phase, well underway at the moment. American Christians have been forced to face the extent, not of their captivity, but of their impotence. Now, in a desperate push for power, many of them are attempting to seize such power levers as political action, legislation, education and the mass media. But, since the drive for power is born of social impotence rather than spiritual authority, the final result will be compromise and disillusionment. Christians in this first phase are falling for the delusion of power without authority.

As this phase peaks, it leads naturally to the second. This is the *pull* phase, when Christians will be jerked back and reminded of their need, not for power, but for principles and purity, even at the expense of powerlessness. The gears will be suddenly thrown into reverse, and the drive for power will be switched to a call for "disentanglement from the powers." Power without authority, power born of the shame of impotence, will be renounced for the sake of authority without power, powerlessness born of the shame of impurity. But—and here the calculations have been precise—since this will happen when traditional theologies of cultural transformation (such as the Reformed) have become a minority taste, leadership in this phase will pass to theologies stressing prophetic detachment, not constructive involvement.

By the end of the second phase, the effect will be vicious. Uncritical pietism and uncritical politicization will be succeeded by hypercritical separatism. Being essentially worldly, the former is rapidly fueling reactions to itself that will put new life into flagging secular ideologies; being essentially otherworldly, the latter will tend to withdraw from society and create a vacuum that these ideologies will speedily fill. And the last state of the house of American culture will be worse than the first.

Then comes the third phase, *press,* the Director's own signature to the finale. Individual Christians of integrity will view these hapless alternatives and be incited to frustration, anger or grief. There will then be a fleeting moment when they feel so isolated in their inner judgments that they wonder if they are the last Christian left—"I, only I, am the only one not to have bowed the knee." This movement from insight to isolation does not last long, but when the moment passes and the emotion drains away, it leaves a residue of part self-pity, part discouragement, and part shame that unnerves the best of them.

This is how we pick off the caring, one by one. Ashamed by their secret arrogance, they sink back disheartened to the general level, their spirits sagging and their vision dimmed. Ashamed to be different, they assent to be demoralized. They thus produce the state they fear. The "last Christian" comes one person closer each time.

All this, of course, is the minority dilemma (the dilemma of the concerned) and the American version at that. The way we deal with the complacent majority is far easier: We simply keep them asleep. As I said in the first memo, the only thing that matches my satisfaction at the Church's deepening captivity is my amazement at Christian credulity. I sometimes wonder if they think they are immortal, or that they can summon revival through the click of a computer button.

The day will come when millions and millions of Westerners will still be Christians, but what they believe and how they live will be unrecognizable by the standards of the one whose name they claim to bear. Let the Adversary then return to the earth, as he promised. What he finds will not be a faith to his liking.

Do they consider themselves exempt from the normal rules of human experience and spiritual life? They believe their faith can give birth to renewal. Do they not also believe that it can die? They remind me of a tale of Nasreddin Hodja, the celebrated Turkish holy man. He once borrowed a large cauldron from his neighbor. When some time had passed, he placed a small metal coffee can in it and took it back to its owner.

"What is that?" said the latter, pointing to the small can.

"Oh," said the Hodja, "Your cauldron gave birth to that while it was in my possession."

The neighbor was delighted and took both the cauldron and the coffee can. Some days later, the Hodja again asked his neighbor to lend him his cauldron, which he did. This time a few weeks passed, and when the neighbor felt he could not do without his cauldron any longer, he went to the Hodja and asked him to return it.

"I cannot," replied the Hodja. "Your cauldron has died."

"Died?" cried the neighbor. "How can a cauldron die?"

"Where is the difficulty?" said the Hodja. "You were glad to believe it could give birth. Why will you not believe it can die?"

When the time comes, even the Adversary will put it no more clearly than that. Until then, Operation Gravedigger proceeds. Let them dig on, not knowing it is their own grave that they dig.

On Remembering the Third Fool and the Devil's Mousetrap

To be honest, no part of my involvement in the publication of these papers puts me in a greater quandary than writing this afterword. Who on earth can rouse the Church from such a grand "Babylonian captivity" but the Lord himself? Yet my source was adamant. The papers by themselves could lead to a bleak and pessimistic conclusion, which would be the exact opposite of what he intended. Nor would they give more than the slenderest clue as to why he himself was defecting to the Christian side.

On the other hand, my source was emphatic that nothing could serve the papers worse than a fairy-tale ending. Pious romanticism, a simple reiteration of truisms or a facile claim to a silver bullet answer would gloss over the stark problems and convince no one. Smart secular people, he said, do not like books that preach at the end. And those orthodox believers who do not like having their brains stretched could use the afterword to take refuge from the burden of the papers.

My dilemma, then, has been to do justice to my source's urging, and at the same time to make sense of what was no more than a lightning explanation of the thinking behind his disillusionment and defection. A quarter of an hour was all too brief for him to give me more than the ends of some threads of thought that I have since unraveled on my own. If and when his own full account of the defection is published, you may judge whether my grasp of his points has been developed in the right direction.

The Turner Turned

It appears that for some time, even before his nomination as Director of the L.A. Bureau, my source had been disillusioned with the direction of their strategy. It was becoming, as he put it, a "Vietnam war of the spirit," a war they could not win but would not dare abandon. His sense of uneasiness only increased as each post-Christian alternative proved more dreary and insubstantial than the Christian position it had been designed to replace. Curiously, these doubts were magnified even further as the Operation Gravedigger memoranda started to flow across his desk, especially as he turned from the chess playing of counter-apologetics to the realities of cultural subversion.

The switch itself had been easy enough, and the prospect of California was not uninviting. What unsettled him was something else. The Deputy Director had been half right in his barb about the ivory tower. But the ivory tower for my source was not the academic world. It was his confidence in the viability of secularism.

He found himself caught uncomfortably between the opposing stratagems of an elitist secularism and an exotic spirituality; the one unpopular with most people, the other unpalatable to him. His mind was plagued by an old saying that kept returning to him like an unthinkable thought, that while nothing is worse than bad religion, nothing is more necessary than true religion. Were even his best agents merely "cheerless atheists, religious fanatics turned inside out"?[1]

All this cast a different light on Operation Gravedigger itself. The entire strategy pivoted on a monumental irony, yet as he had once written to the Deputy Director, irony was not a monopoly of either side. Only the side with the ultimate truth could be sure of having the last laugh.

In the end it was laughter that triggered the breakthrough in his thinking. The moment came when he was interviewing the Old Fool (as they refer to the distinguished writer) for the last time. The latter, sharing what he described as his "operational orders" as a Christian convert late in life, had added a maxim of his own: "Love laughter, which sounds loudly as heaven's gates swing open, and dies away as they shut."[2]

Nietzsche had raised the right question, my source said ("Who is wise enough for this moment in history?"), but Nietzsche had no answer to his own question. As he talked and laughed with the Old Fool, he suddenly saw an alternative to the impossible ideal of the Superman and the all-too-possible madman. The way out was through the fool. A note of exhilaration entered his voice that night in Radcliffe Square. "The fool!" he exclaimed. "The answer is the fool. We'd been dealing all along with the *third* fool."

Talk of a third fool was Greek to me, and my source barely enlarged on it, apart from stating the kernel of what it meant to him and telling me where to follow it up. If I have developed it correctly, the gist of his point was this. The first fool is the *fool proper*, the person who by heaven's standards is called a fool and deserves to be. This is the fool who litters history with the vast carelessness of his intellectual and moral stupidity, the sort of fool who appears frequently in the pages of the Old Testament and who fills the passenger list of Sebastian Brant's great satire of medieval folly, *The Ship of Fools*. This, he said, is the sort of fool the Christian should never be, but the Christian worldling becomes.

The second fool is the *fool bearer*, the person who is ridiculed but resilient, a comic who is the butt of the slaps but is none the worse for the slapping. In Christian terms, the second fool is the one who is called a fool by the world, but who neither deserves it nor is destroyed by it.

What is important, since it links the second fool to the third, is the secret of this resilience. The quicksilver spirit of the second fool springs from the Christian vision of the discrepancy between the apparent and the real, between the way things are and the way things will be. Knowing this discrepancy, the fool bearer is always able to bounce back, and his laughter is neither bitter nor escapist but an expression of faith. It is the kind of laughter that absorbs pain and adversity and, seeing beyond them, in situations of despair becomes a sign of hope.

The second fool is the "fool for Christ." From the apostle Paul to Francis of Assisi and Sister Clare, to Thomas à Kempis, to the "holy fools" of Ireland and Russia, down to the countless despised and persecuted believers of the last century, the great tradition of "fools for Christ" has never lacked an heir and will play its part here too. As Reinhold Schneider wrote from his experience as a courageous poet in the

Christian resistance movement in Germany in the 1930s, "Anyone who goes against the spirit of the age in the name of the Lord must expect that spirit to take its revenge."[3] Wherever the gospel has been in contention they have stood like lightning rods in the storm. But seizing the initiative and turning the tables were never meant to be their brief.

Table-turning is the forte of the third fool. This is the person who appears a fool but is actually the *fool maker,* the one who in being ridiculous reveals. The third fool is the jester; building up expectations in one direction, he shatters them with his punch line, reversing the original meaning and revealing an entirely different one. Masquerading perhaps as the comic butt, he turns the tables on the tyranny of names and labels and strikes a blow for freedom and for truth. From the apostle Paul (again) to Nicholas of Cusa to Erasmus to G. K. Chesterton and the Old Fool himself, this strain of brilliant Christian fooling has never quite died out, yet it has never been as common as the first fool nor as understood and honored as the second.

"Who then is wise enough for this moment in history?" my source said, gripping my arm. "The one who has always been wise enough to play the fool. For when the wise are foolish, the wealthy poor and the godly worldly, it takes a special folly to subvert such foolishness, a special wit to teach true wisdom." The Christian faith is an "upside down gospel," but only because the world has put things upside down and only a grand reversal can put them back to rights. When the significance of this great secret of history dawned on him, he said it was as if he was caught off guard and catapulted toward the one conclusion he was resisting: All along it had been he who had played the fool while the fool maker had been "the Adversary."

It had been one thing to realize, he continued, that the last laugh and the ultimate truth belonged together. The inner story of his journey and his search was evidence for that. Chinese box after Chinese box, Russian doll after Russian doll, had all been opened and had been discarded as he searched for the one that was solid and would not open, the kernel beneath the husks, the pearl of supreme price.

But suddenly my source came face to face with truth itself, and it was calling into question every lie and half-truth short of itself—and doing so, not just abstractly and in general, but concretely, specifically *and in person.*

It was this that cornered him and forced him to the turn-around. He who had been skilled at turning others had been turned himself. That night in Radcliffe Square he talked about the prophetic fool-making of the Adversary as the divine subversive. He talked about conversion as the supreme turn-around. He talked about the Incarnation as history's greatest double-entendre. And then he was gone, but clearly changed forever.

Fool's-Eye View

Precisely how this helps us face the challenge of the Operation Gravedigger papers, he did not have time to elaborate. So I have struggled with what to say and to say quickly as the urgency required. Wholesale problems are rarely amenable to wholesale solutions, and seeking to offer mass medicines for a mass malaise is usually a form of illusion mongering. The real answer to the papers will be in lives lived out, not books.

But having noted this caution, what can we say in the face of the papers? One thing is perfectly clear. Their main thrust is quite obvious and can be appreciated without my help, his understanding of fools or any other intermediary. It is frequently said that in time of war it is as foolish to believe everything that comes from the other side as it is not to believe anything. The same applies here. Those on the other side are also victims of their own premises and propaganda. In any case, no one can claim to have modernity by the scruff of the neck.

"If the shoe fits, wear it" must therefore be as applicable to the fight of faith in the modern world as anywhere else. The evidence of which the other side speaks is there for any one of us to observe and verify. We are each as free (and responsible) to draw our own conclusions as they have theirs. We must therefore begin by asking: What are they saying? Is it true? What of it?

Undoubtedly there is one central question that cannot be escaped by any of us who confess that Jesus Christ is Lord. Is the Church in the Western world culturally captive, more shortsighted and worldlier than she realizes? Are we ourselves? If so, what will be the outcome, and what is to be done?

What is historically certain is that cultural conformity is never the end of the story for the Church, any more than it was for the nation of Israel. To both, God has said: When you want to become like other nations, "you are thinking of *something that can never be.*"[4] Worldliness, or cultural conformity, is only a stop on the line. That line either doubles back through grace to renewal and reformation, or it continues straight on down to judgment and destruction.

The renewal and reformation of the Western Church, or judgment and destruction? In our advanced modern setting, this choice constitutes an awesome challenge, and the outcome will depend partly on each of us. For the fact is that our real enemy today is not secularism, not humanism, not Marxism, and not postmodernism. It is not Islam, or any of the great religious rivals to the Christian gospel. It is not even modernization. It is ourselves. We who are Western Christians are simply a special case of a universal human condition to which Pascal pointed earlier. "Jesus Christ comes to tell men that they have no enemies but themselves."[5] Or as it has been put more recently: "We have met the enemy and it is us."[6]

Fortunately, we do not know the outcome of our story and whether the Church in the West will be revived, and take its place alongside the vibrant churches of Asia, Africa and South America. But for myself, having pondered these papers, I agree with my source that bleak pessimism must not be the end. Just as he said, as soon as we turn from the present to the future and from the central problem to its possible remedies, the fool's-eye view shows the way through.

Facing the Facts

First, the fool's-eye view helps us to face the situation. It enables us to assess the facts realistically and yet to see that the apparently pessimistic picture must not be taken entirely at face value. To be sure, the European believer is likely to be unduly discouraged about the state of the faith, and the American believer to be overly enthusiastic, simply because of their different spiritual surroundings. In the same way, many of us who have been suddenly forced to expand our horizons and take a broad view of the Western Church in the modern world may feel overwhelmed. The picture appears to close in like an unbroken panorama of pessimism.

But without minimizing the gravity of our situation, the fool's-eye view provides a double corrective, because on at least two accounts the pessimism may be rooted more in impressions than facts. To begin with, part of the discouragement may be rooted in the feelings that inevitably follow a switch from the bits-and-pieces thinking (to which many of us are accustomed) to a more comprehensive view of the whole. Like an inactive, middle-aged man who is suddenly forced to run, the bits-and-pieces thinkers are compelled to exert themselves at a level they are not used to, and they feel pain in muscles of which they were not previously aware. But like the runner's, this pain passes with exercise, leaving us ready to "think globally but act locally," a basic requirement of contemporary discipleship.

Another part of the discouragement may be rooted in the discomfort of being forced to see things from the other side's point of view. Inside-out, back-to-front thinking can be dizzying at first. But it can also train us in the mental and spiritual agility that eventually allows us to join the subversive table-turning of the fool maker and refuse to bow to the tyranny and finality of the here and now.

I have to be honest. The condition of the Western Church is very troubling, not least because so many refuse to face it. Things are truly in bad shape. But the fool maker's sense of discrepancy between the real and the apparent is crucial here. The current facts are not all the facts.

Some of the bleakness of the papers is simply because theirs is a perspective on the Church "under the sun." Ancient Ecclesiastes and modern ecclesiastics come around to the same conclusion: Leave out God and the high demands of his ways, and we soon find we have exchanged the "holy of holies" for "vanity of vanities." That so much of what we are doing today can be explained so adequately by categories "under the sun" is a measure of our worldliness. "Under the sun" the Church amounts to little. Under the Son she can aspire to and achieve much.

In addition, for all the comprehensiveness of their sorry catalog of worldliness and failure, what is striking in the papers is the arrogance behind all they overlook. Yet it is not surprising that in a world of the big, the powerful and the well known, most of the staggering victories and the true Christian heroes are unnoticed and unsung. These Christians are the hidden resistance fighters of our generation, the ones whose quiet faith, solid character, simple lives, and prevailing prayers have a worth more substantial than fame, a greatness surpassing any conferred by stardom. Topsy-turvily, they remain unsung, but they are the true "just ones." Known only to God, they are those without whom no church, no community, no country can long endure.

Thus the challenge of the present facts is neither harder nor easier for us than it was for the earliest believers who had to say Yes to Christ and No to Caesar. What matters finally is faith, the stance from which the discrepancy is seen, from which the facts are best assessed and from which action most effectively proceeds. God, after all, is sovereign over the wider picture and not just over our own small part.

Playing the Rebound

Second, the fool's-eye view helps us to assess the rivals to the Christian faith and to answer them. There is every reason to believe that the major alternatives to the gospel are in worse condition than the Church. In the case of secularism, for example, the plainest fact about the secular world is its disillusionment with secularism. Heralded so recently as progressive and irreversible, secularism (the philosophy) has failed conspicuously to consolidate the advantages offered to it by secularization (the process). There are more atheistic and nonreligious people in the world than ever before, as the papers attest, but there is a ferment of new spiritual movements which grows straight from the heart of the problems with secularism.

People in the secular world have too much to live with, too little to live for. Once growth and prosperity cease to be their reason for existence, they ask questions about the purpose and meaning of their lives: Whence? Whither? Why? To such questions secularism has no answer, or—more accurately—the answers it has given have not satisfied in practice. Secularism in its sophisticated humanist form is too erudite at times, too banal at others; it flourishes only in intellectual centers. In its repressive Marxist form, it creaks.

In the long term, there is no lasting substitute for religion. Sometimes for better, usually for worse, religion is the only substitute for religion. As playwright Peter Shaffer put the problem, "Without worship you shrink; it's as brutal as that."[7]

It is possible that our generation is standing on the threshold of a spiritual rebound of historic proportions in the West. The modern West has come of age and rejected the outgrown tutelage of faith. But its prodigal descent has been swift. In the same vein as the papers, we could list our own ironies. Modern cities make people closer yet stranger at once; modern weapons bring their users to the point of impotence and destruction simultaneously; modern media promise facts but deliver fantasies; modern education introduces mass schooling but fosters subliteracy; modern technologies of communication encourage people to speak more and say less and to hear more and listen less; modern lifestyles offer do-it-yourself freedom but slavishly follow fads; modern styles of relationships make people hungry for intimacy and authenticity but more fearful than ever of phoniness, manipulation and power games. And so on.

If this is so, we may be poised on the brink of the *reductio ad absurdum* of modern secularism. But then the question is this: How will people be turned, like the source of these papers, not only from secularism but from the post-Christian religious alternatives as well? How do we speak to an age made spiritually deaf by its skepticism and morally colorblind by its relativism? The prosaic sermon and the labored apology have proved ineffective, as stolid and single-visioned as the flat-earth literalism of the secularized mind itself. One contribution must surely come from a wide rediscovery of the prophetic fool-making of the divine subversive, but only once the tables have been turned on us.

The West Is Not the World

Third, the fool's-eye view reminds us that our talk of the modern Church needs balancing, for the modern Church is not all the Church. Indeed, it is the smaller as well as the spiritually poorer part. Beyond it stirs the youthful energy and expanding vision of the Church in the global South, and all around the less-developed world. Less modernized, the Church around the world is less worldly. Less sophisticated, it is less secular. Lagging behind in modernization, it is already beginning to lead in its ministry, mission, dedication, sacrifice and joy. As such, it can be a transfusion of life to the withered churches in Europe and the shallow, worldly-wise faith in America.

After centuries limited largely to Europe, the Christian faith has become the first truly global religion, the Bible the most translated and translatable book in the world, and the Church the largest and most diverse community on earth.

These facts contain their own illusions. Expressed unguardedly, they create the false impression that the only Christians who truly flourish are the less educated or the most persecuted, those who are not exposed to the tempting power and prosperity of the modern world.

How our brothers and sisters from the Global South will fare when the blandishments of modernity come their way is another question, and one they will face in their own time. But for the moment, the greater illusion is that of the indispensability of the Church in the modern world. The Western Church is not the whole Church. It is only the older Church, a Church that providentially handed on its torch just as it was taken captive by the world it had helped to create. But what if that torch were handed back to the old Church by the new, burning more brightly than when it was given? The challenge of modernity would still have to be faced, but with all the lessons of our experience and all the life of theirs.

No Fear for the Faith

Fourth, the fool's-eye view sees that the faith will endure, because of the faith itself. Even if the modern world proved to be the greatest challenge the Church has faced, or if the alternatives to the gospel were powerful and menacing rather than weak, or if the Church in the rest of the world were nonexistent or as weak as we are, the faith would still endure. Its currency is truth; its source an unconquerable kingdom.

The Christian Church may be in poor shape in the modern world, but this is not the first time, nor will it be the last. As always, when the Church is compromised by its cultural alliances, it suffers along with the culture to which it conforms. It may thus suffer doubly, once as the price of its compromise, and once as the price of its identification with a culture under judgment by God. This double judgment could be the fate of the Western Church.

Yet the kingdom of God can never be totally absorbed into any cultural system. There will always be part of it that does not fit, which cannot be squeezed into any social or cultural mold. Christian truth is finally irreducible and intractable, and it is here, in the inescapable tension of its being "in" but not "of" the world, that the possibility of some future judgment or liberation lies.

Marxism, by contrast, lacks such resilience because it lacks such transcendence. As social scientist David Martin points out, "It is a paradox that a system which claimed that the beginning of all criticism was the criticism of religion should have ended up with a form of religion which was the end of criticism."[8] *Pravda* in Russian means "truth," but truth in the Soviet Union was mastered by *Pravda*.

What is the secret of the Christian faith's capacity to survive repeated periods of cultural captivity? On the one hand, it has in God's Word *an authority that stands higher than history,* a judgment that is ultimately irreducible to any generation and culture. On the other hand, it has in its notion of sin and repentance *a doctrine of its own failure,* which can be the wellspring of its ongoing self-criticism and renewal.

Like an eternal jack-in-the-box, Christian truth will always spring back. No power on earth can finally keep it down, not even the power of Babylonian confusion and captivity. "At least five times," noted G. K. Chesterton, "the Faith has to all appearances gone to the dogs. In each of these five cases, it was the dog that died."[9]

To write these things is not to whistle in the dark. Nor is it to dredge up arguments to bolster the defenses of a sagging optimism. Rather, since the Gravedigger thesis turns on the monumental irony with which the papers began, it is apt to finish with another: There is no one like the other side for overplaying their hand.

Out of corruption came Reformation. This was the story of their sixteenth-century overbalance. But what of an earlier day still, a day when they planned another grave and held another body captive?

That day witnessed the greatest irony of all. It was, as John Donne said, "the day death died."[10] Because, as Augustine had said before him, the cross of the Lord was "the devil's mousetrap."[11]

In spite of all the forces arrayed against the Christian Church, whether seen or unseen, grave-digging has been a somewhat less than certain business for the Evil One ever since the resurrection. Therefore, in the words of the most constant refrain in all the Scriptures, "Have faith in God. Have no fear." God is greater than all, and he may be trusted in all situations.

An Evangelical Manifesto

A Declaration of Evangelical Identity and Public Commitment

MAY 7, 2008, WASHINGTON, DC

The following declaration, "An Evangelical Manifesto," was published on May 7, 2008, as a call to Evangelical renewal and reformation—very much in line with the analysis of this book. It is included here as a spur to reflection, study, and prayer for Evangelicals concerned for the state of the Church.

Keenly aware of the hour of history in which we live, and of the momentous challenges that face our fellow humans on the earth and our fellow Christians around the world, we who sign this declaration do so as American leaders and members of one of the world's largest and fastest growing movements of the Christian faith: the Evangelicals.

Evangelicals have no supreme leader or official spokesperson, so no one speaks for all Evangelicals, least of all those who claim to. We speak for ourselves, but as a representative group of Evangelicals in America. We gratefully appreciate that our spiritual and historical roots lie outside this country, that the great majority of our fellow Evangelicals are in the Global South rather than the North, and that we have recently had a fresh infusion of Evangelicals from Latin America, Africa, and Asia. We are therefore a small part of a far greater worldwide movement that is both forward looking and outward reaching. Together with them, we are committed to being true to our faith and thoughtful about our calling in today's world.

The two-fold purpose of this declaration is first to address the confusions and corruptions that attend the term "Evangelical" in the United States and much of the Western world today, and second to clarify where we stand on issues that have caused consternation over Evangelicals in public life.

As followers of "the narrow way," our concern is not for approval and popular esteem. Nor do we regard it as accurate or faithful to pose as victims, or to protest at discrimination. We certainly do not face persecution like our fellow-believers elsewhere in the world. Too many of the problems we face as Evangelicals in the United States are those of our own making. If we protest, our protest has to begin with ourselves.

Rather, we are troubled by the fact that the confusions and corruptions surrounding the term "Evangelical" have grown so deep that the character of what it means has been obscured and its importance lost. Many people outside the movement now doubt that "Evangelical" is ever positive, and many inside now wonder whether the term serves a useful purpose any longer.

In contrast to such doubts, we boldly declare that, if we make clear what we mean by the term, we are unashamed to be Evangelical and Evangelicals. We believe that the term is important because the truth it conveys is all-important. A proper understanding of "Evangelical" and the "Evangelicals" has its own contribution to make, not only to the Church but also to the wider world, and especially to the plight of many who are poor, vulnerable, or without a voice in their communities.

Here We Stand, and Why It Matters

This manifesto is a public declaration, addressed both to our fellow believers and to the wider world. To affirm who we are and where we stand in public is important because we Evangelicals in America, along with people of all faiths and ideologies, represent one of the greatest challenges of the global era: living with our deepest differences. This challenge is especially sharp when religious and ideological differences are ultimate and irreducible, and when the differences are not just between personal worldviews but between entire ways of life co-existing in the same society.

The place of religion in human life is deeply consequential. Nothing is more natural and necessary than the human search for meaning and belonging, for making sense of the world and finding security in life. When this search is accompanied by the right of freedom of conscience, it issues in a freely chosen diversity of faiths and ways of life, some religious and transcendent, and some secular and naturalistic.

Nevertheless, the different faiths and the different families of faith provide very different answers to life, and these differences are decisive not only for individuals, but for societies and entire civilizations. Learning to live with our deepest differences is therefore of great consequence both for individuals and nations. Debate, deliberation, and decisions about what this means for our common life are crucial and unavoidable. The alternative—the coercions of tyranny or the terrible convulsions of Nietzsche's "wars of spirit"—would be unthinkable.

We ourselves are those who have come to believe that Jesus of Nazareth is "the way, the truth, and the life," and that the great change required of those who follow him entails a radically new view of human life and a decisively different way of living, thinking, and acting.

Our purpose here is to make a clear statement to our fellow-citizens and our fellow believers alike, whether they see themselves as our friends, bystanders, skeptics, or enemies. We wish to state what we mean by "Evangelical," and what being Evangelicals means for our life alongside our fellow citizens in public life and our fellow humans on the earth today. We see three major mandates for Evangelicals.

1. We Must Reaffirm Our Identity

Our first task is to reaffirm who we are. *Evangelicals are Christians who define themselves, their faith, and their lives according to the good news of Jesus of Nazareth. (Evangelical comes from the Greek word for "good news," or "gospel.")* Believing that the gospel of Jesus is God's good news for the whole world, we affirm with the apostle Paul that we are "not ashamed of the gospel of Jesus Christ, for it is the power of God unto salvation." Contrary to widespread misunderstanding today, we Evangelicals should be defined theologically, and not politically, socially, or culturally.

Behind this affirmation is the awareness that identity is powerful and precious to groups as well as to individuals. Identity is central to a classically liberal understanding of freedom. There are grave dangers in identity politics, but we insist that we ourselves, and not scholars, the press, or public opinion, have the right to say who we understand ourselves to be. We are who we say we are, and we resist all attempts to explain us in terms of our "true" motives and our "real" agenda.

Defined and understood in this way, Evangelicals form one of the great traditions that have developed within the Christian Church over the centuries. We fully appreciate the defining principles of other major traditions, and we stand and work with them on many ethical and social issues of common concern. Like them, we are whole-heartedly committed to the priority of "right belief and right worship," to the "universality" of the Christian Church across the centuries, continents, and cultures, and therefore to the central axioms of Christian faith expressed in the Trinitarian and Christological consensus of the Early Church. Yet we hold to Evangelical beliefs that are distinct from the other traditions in important ways—distinctions that we affirm because we see them as biblical truths that were recovered by the Protestant Reformation, sustained in many subsequent movements of revival and renewal, and vital for a sure and saving knowledge of God—in short, beliefs that are true to the good news of Jesus.

Evangelicals are therefore followers of Jesus Christ, plain ordinary Christians in the classic and historic sense over the last 2,000 years. Evangelicals are committed to thinking, acting and living as Jesus lived and taught, and so to embody this truth and his good news for the world that we may be recognizably his disciples. The heart of the matter for us as Evangelicals is our desire and commitment, in the words of Richard of Chichester and as Scripture teaches, to "see him more clearly, to love him more dearly, and to follow him more nearly."

We do not claim that the Evangelical principle—to define our faith and our life by the good news of Jesus—is unique to us. Our purpose is not to attack or to exclude but to remind and to reaffirm, and so to rally and to reform. For us it is the defining imperative and supreme goal of all who would follow the way of Jesus.

Equally, we do not typically lead with the name "Evangelical" in public. We are simply Christians or followers of Jesus or adherents of "mere Christianity," but the Evangelical principle is at the heart of how we see and live our faith.

This is easy to say but challenging to live by. To be Evangelical, and to define our faith and our lives by the good news of Jesus as taught in Scripture, is to submit our lives entirely to the lordship of Jesus and to the truths and the way of life that he requires of his followers, in order that they might become like him, live the way he taught, and believe as he believed. As Evangelicals have pursued this vision over the centuries, they have prized above all certain beliefs that we consider to be at the heart of the message of Jesus and therefore foundational for us—the following seven above all:

First, we believe that Jesus Christ is fully God become fully human, the unique, sure and sufficient revelation of the very being, character and purposes of God, beside whom there is no other god and beside whom there is no other name by which we must be saved.

Second, we believe that the only ground for our acceptance by God is what Jesus Christ did on the cross and what he is now doing through his risen life, whereby he exposed and reversed the course of human sin and violence, bore the penalty for our sins, credited us with his righteousness, redeemed us from the power of evil, reconciled us to God and empowers us with his life "from above." We therefore bring nothing to our salvation. Credited with the righteousness of Christ, we receive his redemption solely by grace through faith.

Third, we believe that new life, given supernaturally through spiritual regeneration, is a necessity as well as a gift, and that the lifelong conversion that results is the only pathway to a radically changed character and way of life. Thus for us, the only sufficient power for a life of Christian faithfulness and moral integrity in this world is that of Christ's resurrection and the power of the Holy Spirit.

Fourth, we believe that Jesus' own teaching and his attitude toward the total truthfulness and supreme authority of the Bible, God's inspired Word, make the Scriptures our final rule for faith and practice.

Fifth, we believe that being disciples of Jesus means serving him as Lord in every sphere of our lives, secular as well as spiritual, public as well as private, in deeds as well as words, and in every moment of our days on earth, always reaching out as he did to those who are lost as well as to the poor, the sick, the hungry, the oppressed, the socially despised, and being faithful stewards of creation and our fellow creatures.

Sixth, we believe that the blessed hope of the personal return of Jesus provides both strength and substance to what we are doing, just as what we are doing becomes a sign of the hope of where we are going; both together leading to a consummation of history and the fulfillment of an undying kingdom that comes only by the power of God.

Seventh, we believe all followers of Christ are called to know and love Christ through worship, love Christ's family through fellowship, grow like Christ through discipleship, serve Christ by ministering to the needs of others in his name, and share Christ with those who do not yet know him, inviting people to the ends of the earth and to the end of time to join us as his disciples and followers of his way.

At the same time, we readily acknowledge that we repeatedly fail to live up to our high calling, and all too often illustrate the truth of our own doctrine of sin. We Evangelicals share the same "crooked timber" of our humanity, and the full catalogue of our sins, failures, and hypocrisies. This is no secret either to God or to those who know and watch us.

Defining Features

Certain implications follow from this way of defining Evangelicalism:

First, to be Evangelical is to hold a belief that is also a devotion. Evangelicals adhere fully to the Christian faith expressed in the historic creeds of the great ecumenical councils of the Church, and in the great affirmations of the Protestant Reformation, and seek to be loyal to this faith passed down from generation to generation. But at its core, being Evangelical is always more than a creedal statement, an institutional affiliation or a matter of membership in a movement. We have no supreme leader and neither creeds nor tradition are ultimately decisive for us. Jesus Christ and his written Word, the Holy Scriptures, are our supreme authority and whole-hearted devotion, trust, and obedience are our proper response.

Second, Evangelical belief and devotion is expressed as much in our worship and in our deeds as in our creeds. As the universal popularity of such hymns and songs as "Amazing Grace" attests, our great hymn writers stand alongside our great theologians, and often our commitment can be seen better in our giving and our caring than in official statements. What we are about is captured not only in books or declarations, but in our care for the poor, the homeless and the orphaned; our outreach to those in prison; our compassion for the hungry and the victims of disaster; and our fight for justice for those oppressed by such evils as slavery and human trafficking.

Third, Evangelicals are followers of Jesus in a way that is not limited to certain churches or contained by a definable movement. We are members of many different churches and denominations, mainline as well as independent, and our Evangelical commitment provides a core of unity that holds together a wide range of diversity. This is highly significant for any movement in the network society of the information age, but Evangelicalism has always been diverse, flexible, adaptable, non-hierarchical and taken many forms. This is true today more than ever, as witnessed by the variety and vibrancy of Evangelicals around the world. For to be Evangelical is first and foremost a way of being devoted to Jesus Christ, seeking to live in different ages and different cultures as he calls his followers to live.

Fourth, as stressed above, Evangelicalism must be defined theologically and not politically; confessionally and not culturally. Above all else, it is a commitment and devotion to the person and work of Jesus Christ, his teaching and way of life, and an enduring dedication to his lordship above all other earthly powers, allegiances and loyalties. As such, it should not be limited to tribal or national boundaries or be confused with or reduced to political categories such as "conservative" and "liberal" or to psychological categories such as "reactionary" or "progressive."

Fifth, the Evangelical message, "good news" by definition, is overwhelmingly positive, and always positive before it is negative. There is an enormous theological and cultural importance to "the power of No," especially in a day when "everything is permitted" and "it is forbidden to forbid." Just as Jesus did, Evangelicals sometimes have to make strong judgments about what is false, unjust and evil. But first and foremost we Evangelicals are for Someone and for something rather than against anyone or anything. The gospel of Jesus is the good news of welcome, forgiveness, grace and liberation from law and legalism. It is a colossal yes to life and human aspirations, and an emphatic no only to what contradicts our true destiny as human beings made in the image of God.

Sixth, Evangelicalism should be distinguished from two opposite tendencies to which Protestantism has been prone: liberal revisionism and conservative fundamentalism. Called by Jesus to be "in the world, but not of it," Christians, especially in modern society, have been pulled toward two extremes. Those more liberal have tended so to accommodate the world that they reflect the thinking and lifestyles of the day, to the point where they are unfaithful to Christ; whereas those more conservative have tended so to defy the world that they resist it in ways that also become unfaithful to Christ.

The liberal revisionist tendency was first seen in the eighteenth century and has become more pronounced today, reaching a climax in versions of the Christian faith that are characterized by such weaknesses as an exaggerated estimate of human capacities, a shallow view of evil, an inadequate view of truth, and a deficient view of God. In the end, they are sometimes no longer recognizably Christian. As this sorry capitulation occurs, such "alternative gospels" represent a series of severe losses that eventually seal their demise:

- First, a loss of authority, as sola Scriptura ("by Scripture alone") is replaced by sola cultura ("by culture alone").

- Second, a loss of community and continuity, as "the faith once delivered" becomes the faith of merely one people and one time, and cuts itself off from believers across the world and down the generations.

- Third, a loss of stability, as in Dean Inge's apt phrase, the person "who marries the spirit of the age soon becomes a widower."

- Fourth, a loss of credibility, as "the new kind of faith" turns out to be what the skeptic believes already, and there is no longer anything solidly, decisively Christian for seekers to examine and believe.

- Fifth, a loss of identity, as the revised version of the faith loses more and more resemblance to the historic Christian faith that is true to Jesus.

In short, for all their purported sincerity and attempts to be relevant, extreme proponents of liberal revisionism run the risk of becoming what Søren Kierkegaard called "kissing Judases"—Christians who betray Jesus with an interpretation.

The fundamentalist tendency is more recent, and even closer to Evangelicalism, so much so that in the eyes of many, the two overlap. We celebrate those in the past for their worthy desire to be true to the fundamentals of faith, but fundamentalism has become an overlay on the Christian faith and developed into an essentially modern reaction to the modern world. As a reaction to the modern world, it tends to romanticize the past, some now-lost moment in time, and to radicalize the present, with styles of reaction that are personally and publicly militant to the point where they are sub-Christian.

Christian fundamentalism has its counterparts in many religions and even in secularism, and often becomes a social movement with a Christian identity but severely diminished Christian content and manner. Fundamentalism, for example, all too easily parts company with the Evangelical principle, as can Evangelicals themselves, when they fail to follow the great commandment that we love our neighbors as ourselves, let alone the radical demand of Jesus that his followers forgive without limit and love even their enemies.

Seventh, Evangelicalism is distinctive for the way it looks equally to both the past and the future. In its very essence, Evangelicalism goes back directly to Jesus and the Scriptures, not just as a matter of historical roots, but as a commitment of the heart and as the tenor of its desire and thought; and not just once, but again and again as the vital principle of its way of life. To be Evangelical is therefore not only to be deeply personal in faith, strongly committed to ethical holiness in life, and marked by robust voluntarism in action but also to live out a faith whose dynamism is shaped unashamedly by truth and history.

Yet far from being unquestioning conservatives and unreserved supporters of tradition and the status quo, being Evangelical means an ongoing commitment to Jesus Christ, and this entails innovation, renewal, reformation and entrepreneurial dynamism, for everything in every age is subject to assessment in the light of Jesus and his Word. The Evangelical principle is therefore a call to self-examination, reflection and a willingness to be corrected and to change whenever necessary. At the same time, far from being advocates of today's nihilistic "change for change's sake," to be Evangelical is to recognize the primacy of the authority of Scripture, which points us to Jesus, and so to see the need to conserve a form behind all re-form.

We therefore regard reason and faith as allies rather than enemies and find no contradiction between head and heart, between being fully faithful on the one hand and fully intellectually critical and contemporary on the other. Thus, Evangelicals part company with reactionaries by being both reforming and innovative, but they also part company with modern progressives by challenging the ideal of the-newer-the-truer and the-latest-is-greatest and by conserving what is true and right and good. For Evangelicals, it is paradoxical though true that the surest way forward is always first to go back, a "turning back" that is the secret of all true revivals and reformations.

In sum, to be Evangelical is earlier and more enduring than to be Protestant. Seeking to be Evangelical was the heart of the Protestant Reformation, and what gives the Reformation its Christian validity for us is its recovery of biblical truth. In some countries, "Evangelical" is still synonymous with "Protestant." Yet it is clear that the term "Evangelical," and the desire to be biblical, both predate and outlast the Protestant project in its historical form, for the word "protest" has increasingly lost its original positive meaning of "witnessing on behalf of" (*pro-testantes*), and the term "Protestant" is more and more limited to a historical period. Other labels come and go, but the Evangelical principle that seeks to be faithful to the good news of Jesus and to the Scriptures will always endure.

2. We Must Reform Our Own Behavior

Our second major concern is the reformation of our behavior. We affirm that to be Evangelical or to carry the name "Evangelicals" is not only to shape our faith and our lives according to the teaching and standards of the Way of Jesus, but to need to do so again and again. But if the Evangelical impulse is a radical, reforming and innovative force, we acknowledge with sorrow a momentous irony today. We who time and again have stood for the renewal of tired forms, for the revival of dead churches, for the warming of cold hearts, for the reformation of corrupt practices and heretical beliefs and for the reform of gross injustices in society, are ourselves in dire need of reformation and renewal today. Reformers, we ourselves need to be reformed. Protestants, we are the ones against whom protest must be made.

We confess that we Evangelicals have betrayed our beliefs by our behavior. All too often we have trumpeted the gospel of Jesus, but we have replaced biblical truths with therapeutic techniques, worship with entertainment, discipleship with growth in human potential, church growth with business entrepreneurialism, concern for the Church and for the local congregation with expressions of the faith that are church-less and little better than a vapid spirituality, meeting real needs with pandering to felt needs, and mission principles with marketing precepts. In the process we have become known for commercial, diluted and feel-good gospels of health, wealth, human potential and religious happy talk, each of which is indistinguishable from the passing fashions of the surrounding world.

All too often we have set out high, clear statements of the authority of the Bible, but flouted them with lives and lifestyles that are shaped more by our own sinful preferences and by modern fashions and convenience.

All too often we have prided ourselves on our orthodoxy, but grown our churches through methods and techniques as worldly as the worldliest of Christian adaptations to passing expressions of the spirit of the age.

All too often we have failed to demonstrate the unity and harmony of the body of Christ, and fallen into factions defined by the accidents of history and sharpened by truth without love, rather than express the truth and grace of the Gospel.

All too often we have traced our roots to powerful movements of spiritual revival and reformation, but we ourselves are often atheists un-awares, secularists in practice who live in a world without windows to the supernatural, and often carry on our Christian lives in a manner that has little operational need for God.

All too often we have attacked the evils and injustices of others, such as the killing of the unborn, as well as the heresies and apostasies of theological liberals whose views have developed into "another gospel," while we have condoned our own sins, turned a blind eye to our own vices, and lived captive to forces such as materialism and consumerism in ways that contradict our faith.

All too often we have concentrated on great truths of the Bible, such as the cross of Jesus, but have failed to apply them to other biblical truths, such as creation. In the process we have impoverished ourselves and supported a culture broadly careless about the stewardship of the earth and negligent of the arts and the creative centers of society.

All too often we have been seduced by the shaping power of the modern world, exchanging a costly grace for convenience, switching from genuine community to an embrace of individualism, softening theological authority down to personal preference, and giving up a clear grasp of truth and an exclusive allegiance to Jesus for a mess of mix-and-match attitudes that are syncretism by another name.

All too often we have disobeyed the great command to love the Lord our God with our hearts, souls, strength, and minds, and have fallen into an unbecoming anti-intellectualism that is a dire cultural handicap as well as a sin. In particular, some among us have betrayed the strong Christian tradition of a high view of science, epitomized in the very matrix of ideas that gave birth to modern science, and made themselves vulnerable to caricatures of the false hostility between science and faith. By doing so, we have unwittingly given comfort to the unbridled scientism and naturalism that are so rampant in our culture today.

All too often we have gloried in the racial and ethnic diversity of the Church around the world, but remained content to be enclaves of separateness here at home.

All too often we have abandoned our Lord's concern for those in the shadows, the twilight, and the deep darkness of the world, and become cheerleaders for those in power and the naïve sycophants of the powerful and the rich.

All too often we have tried to be relevant, but instead of creating "new wineskins for the new wine," we have succumbed to the passing fashions of the moment and made noisy attacks on yesterday's errors, such as modernism, while capitulating tamely to today's, such as postmodernism.

We call humbly but clearly for a restoration of the Evangelical reforming principle, and therefore for deep reformation and renewal in all our Christian ways of life and thought.

We urge our fellow Evangelicals to go beyond lip service to Jesus and the Bible and restore these authorities to their supreme place in our thought and practice.

We call our communities to a discerning critique of the world and of our generation so that we resist not only their obviously alien power but also the subtle and seductive shaping of the more brilliant insights and techniques of modernity, remembering always that we are "against the world, for the world."

We call all who follow Jesus to keep his commandment and love one another, to be true to our unity in him that underlies all lesser differences, and to practice first the reconciliation in the Church that is so needed in the wider world. In a society divided by identity and gender politics, Christians must witness by their lives to the way their identity in Jesus transcends all such differences.

We call for an expansion of our concern beyond single-issue politics, such as abortion and marriage, and a fuller recognition of the comprehensive causes and concerns of the Gospel, and of all the human issues that must be engaged in public life. Although we cannot back away from our biblically rooted commitment to the sanctity of every human life, including those unborn, nor can we deny the holiness of marriage as instituted by God between one man and one woman, we must follow the model of Jesus, the Prince of Peace, engaging the global giants of conflict, racism, corruption, poverty, pandemic diseases, illiteracy, ignorance, and spiritual emptiness, by promoting reconciliation, encouraging ethical servant leadership, assisting the poor, caring for the sick and educating the next generation. We believe it is our calling to be good stewards of all God has entrusted to our care so that it may be passed on to generations yet to be born.

We call for a more complete understanding of discipleship that applies faith with integrity to every calling and sphere of life, the secular as well as the spiritual, and the physical as well as the religious; and that thinks wider than politics in contributing to the arts, the sciences, the media, and the creation of culture in all its variety.

Above all, we remind ourselves that if we would recommend the good news of Jesus to others, we must first be shaped by that good news ourselves, and thus ourselves be Evangelicals and Evangelical.

3. We Must Rethink Our Place in Public Life

We must find a new understanding of our place in public life. We affirm that to be Evangelical and to carry the name of Christ is to seek to be faithful to the freedom, justice, peace, and well-being that are at the heart of the kingdom of God, to bring these gifts into public life as a service to all, and to work with all who share these ideals and care for the common good. Citizens of the City of God, we are resident aliens in the Earthly City. Called by Jesus to be "in" the world but "not of" the world, we are fully engaged in public affairs, but never completely equated with any party, partisan ideology, economic system, class, tribe, or national identity.

Whereas fundamentalism was thoroughly world-denying and politically disengaged from its outset, names such as John Jay, John Witherspoon, John Woolman and Frances Willard in America and William Wilberforce and Lord Shaftesbury in England are a reminder of a different tradition. Evangelicals have made a shining contribution to politics in general, to many of the greatest moral and social reforms in history, such as the abolition of slavery and woman's suffrage, and even to notions crucial in political discussion today, for example, the vital but little known Evangelical contribution to the rise of the voluntary association and, through that, to the understanding of such key notions as civil society and social capital.

Neither Privatized nor Politicized

Today, however, we Evangelicals wish to stand clear from certain positions in public life that are widely confused with Evangelicalism.

First, we Evangelicals repudiate two equal and opposite errors into which many Christians have fallen recently. One error has been to privatize faith, interpreting and applying it to the personal and spiritual realm only. Such dualism falsely divorces the spiritual from the secular, and causes faith to lose its *integrity* and become "privately engaging and publicly irrelevant," and another form of "hot tub spirituality."

The other error, made by both the religious left and the religious right in recent decades, is to politicize faith, using faith to express essentially political points that have lost touch with biblical truth. That way faith loses its *independence*, the Church becomes "the regime at prayer," Christians become "useful idiots" for one political party or another, and the Christian faith becomes an ideology in its purest form. Christian beliefs are used as weapons for political interests.

Christians from both sides of the political spectrum, left as well as right, have made the mistake of politicizing faith; and it would be no improvement to respond to a weakening of the religious right with a rejuvenation of the religious left. Whichever side it comes from, a politicized faith is faithless, foolish, and disastrous for the Church—and disastrous first and foremost for Christian reasons rather than constitutional reasons.

Called to an allegiance higher than party, ideology, and nationality, we Evangelicals see it as our duty to engage with politics, but our equal duty never to be completely equated with any party, partisan ideology, economic system, or nationality. In our scales, spiritual, moral, and social power are as important as political power, what is right outweighs what is popular, just as principle outweighs party, truth matters more than team-playing, and conscience more than power and survival.

The politicization of faith is never a sign of strength but of weakness. The saying is wise: "The first thing to say about politics is that politics is not the first thing."

The Evangelical soul is not for sale. It has already been bought at an infinite price.

A Civil Rather than a Sacred or a Naked Public Square

Second, we Evangelicals repudiate the two extremes that define the present culture wars in the United States. There are deep and important issues at stake in the culture wars, issues on which the future of the United

States and Western civilization will turn. But the trouble comes from the manner in which the issues are being fought.

In particular, what we as Evangelicals lament in the culture warring is not just the general collapse of the common vision of the common good, but the endless conflict over the proper place of faiths in public life, and therefore of the freedom to enter and engage public life from the perspective of faith. A grand confusion now reigns as to any guiding principles by which people of different faiths may enter the public square and engage with each other robustly but civilly. The result is the "holy war" front of America's wider culture wars, and a dangerous incubation of conflicts, hatreds, and lawsuits.

We repudiate on one side the partisans of a *sacred public square*, those who for religious, historical, or cultural reasons would continue to give a preferred place in public life to one religion which in almost all most current cases would be the Christian faith, but could equally be another faith. In a society as religiously diverse as America today, no one faith should be normative for the entire society, yet there should be room for the free expression of faith in the public square.

Let it be known unequivocally that we are committed to religious liberty for people of all faiths, including the right to convert to or from the Christian faith. We are firmly opposed to the imposition of theocracy on our pluralistic society. We are also concerned about the illiberalism of politically correct attacks on evangelism. We have no desire to coerce anyone or to impose on anyone beliefs and behavior that we have not persuaded them to adopt freely, and that we do no not demonstrate in our own lives, above all by love.

We repudiate on the other side the partisans of a *naked public square*, those who would make all religious expression inviolably private and keep the public square inviolably secular. Often advocated by a loose coalition of secularists, liberals, and supporters of the strict separation of Church and state, this position is even less just and workable because it excludes the overwhelming majority of citizens who are still profoundly religious. Nothing is more illiberal than to invite people into the public square but insist that they be stripped of the faith that makes them who they are and shapes the way they see the world.

In contrast to these extremes, our commitment is to a *civil public square—a vision of public life in which citizens of all faiths are free to enter and engage the public square on the basis of their faith, but within a framework of what is agreed to be just and free for other faiths too.* Thus every right we assert for ourselves is at once a right we defend for others. A right for a Christian is a right for a Jew, and a right for a secularist, and a right for a Mormon, and right for a Muslim, and a right for a Scientologist, and right for all the believers in all the faiths across this wide land.

The Way of Jesus, Not Constantine

There are two additional concerns we address to the attention of our fellow-citizens. On the one hand, we are especially troubled by the fact that a generation of culture warring, reinforced by understandable reactions to religious extremism around the world, is creating *a powerful backlash against all religion in public life among many educated people.* If this were to harden and become an American equivalent of the long-held European animosity toward religion in the public life, the result would be disastrous for the American republic and a severe constriction of liberty for people of all faiths.

We therefore warn of the striking intolerance evident among the new atheists and call on all citizens of goodwill and believers of all faiths and none to join with us in working for a civil public square and the restoration of a tough-minded civility that is in the interests of all.

On the other hand, we are also troubled by the fact that the advance of globalization and *the emergence of a global public square find no matching vision of how we are to live freely, justly, and peacefully with our deepest differences on the global stage.* As the recent Muslim protests and riots over perceived insults to their faith demonstrate, the Internet era has created a world in which everyone can listen to what we say even when we are not intentionally speaking to everyone. The challenges of living with our deepest differences are intensified in the age of global technologies such as the World Wide Web.

As this global public square emerges, we see two equal and opposite errors to avoid: *coercive secularism* on one side, once typified by communism and now by the softer but strict French-style secularism; and *religious extremism* on the other side, typified by Islamist violence.

At the same time, we repudiate the two main positions into which many are now falling. On the one hand, we repudiate those who believe their way is the only way and the way for everyone, and are therefore prepared to coerce others. Whatever the faith or ideology in question, communism, Islam, or even democracy, this position leads inevitably to *conflict*.

Undoubtedly, many people would place all Christians in this category, because of the Emperor Constantine and the state-sponsored oppression he inaugurated, leading to the dangerous alliance between Church and state continued in European Church-state relations down to the present.

We are not uncritical of unrestrained voluntarism and rampant individualism, but we utterly deplore the dangerous alliance between Church and state, and the oppression that was its dark fruit. We Evangelicals trace our heritage, not to Constantine, but to the very different stance of Jesus of Nazareth. While some of us are pacifists and others are advocates of just war, we all believe that Jesus' good news of justice for the whole world was promoted, not by a conqueror's power and sword, but by a suffering servant emptied of power and ready to die for the ends he came to achieve. Unlike some other religious believers, we do not see insults and attacks on our faith as "offensive" and "blasphemous" in a manner to be defended by law, but as part of the cost of our discipleship that we are to bear without complaint or victim-playing.

On the other hand, we repudiate all who believe that different values are simply relative to different cultures, and who therefore refuse to allow anyone to judge anyone else or any other culture. More tolerant sounding at first, this position leads directly to the evils of *complacency*; for in a world of such evils as genocide, slavery, female oppression, and assaults on the unborn, there are rights that require defending, evils that must be resisted, and interventions into the affairs of others that are morally justifiable.

We also warn of the danger of a *two-tier global public square*, one in which the top tier is for cosmopolitan secular liberals and the second tier is for local religious believers. Such an arrangement would be patronizing as well as a severe restriction of religious liberty and justice, and unworthy of genuine liberalism.

Once again, our choice is for a civil public square, and a working respect for the rights of all, even those with whom we disagree. Contrary to medieval religious leaders and certain contemporary atheists who believe that "error has no rights," we respect the right to be wrong. But we also insist that the principle of "the right to believe anything" does not lead to the conclusion that "anything anyone believes is right." Rather, it means that respect for differences based on conscience can also mean a necessary debate over differences conducted with respect.

Invitation to All

As stated earlier, we who sign this declaration do not presume to speak for all Evangelicals. *We speak only for ourselves, yet not only to ourselves.* We therefore invite all our fellow Christians, our fellow citizens, and people of different faiths across the nation and around the world to take serious note of these declarations and to respond where appropriate.

We urge our fellow Evangelicals to consider these affirmations and to join us in clarifying the profound confusions surrounding Evangelicalism, that together we may be more faithful to our Lord and to the distinctiveness of his way of life.

We urge our fellow citizens to assess the damaging consequences of the present culture wars, and to work with us in the urgent task of restoring liberty and civility in public life, and so ensure that freedom may last to future generations.

We urge adherents of other faiths around the world to understand that we respect your right to believe what you believe according to the dictates of conscience and invite you to follow the golden rule and extend the same rights and respect to us and to the adherents of all other faiths, so that together we may make religious liberty practical and religious persecution rarer, so that in turn human diversity may complement rather than contradict human well-being.

We urge those who report and analyze public affairs, such as scholars, journalists, and public policy makers, to abandon stereotypes and adopt definitions and categories in describing us and other believers in terms that are both accurate and fair and with a tone that you in turn would like to be applied to yourselves.

We urge those in positions of power and authority to appreciate that we seek the welfare of the communities, cities and countries in which we live, yet our first allegiance is always to a higher loyalty and to standards that call all other standards into question, a commitment that has been a secret of the Christian contributions to civilization as well as its passion for reforms.

We urge those who share our dedication to the poor, the suffering and the oppressed to join with us in working to bring care, peace, justice and freedom to those millions of our fellow-humans who are now ignored, oppressed, enslaved, or treated as human waste and wasted humans by the established orders in the global world.

We urge those who search for meaning and belonging amid the chaos of contemporary philosophies and the brokenness and alienation of modern society to consider that the gospel we have found to be good news is in fact the best news ever, and open to all who would come and discover what we now enjoy and would share.

Finally, we solemnly pledge that in a world of lies, hype and spin, where truth is commonly dismissed and words suffer from severe inflation, we make this declaration in words that have been carefully chosen and weighed; words that, under God, we make our bond. People of the good news, we desire not just to speak the good news but to embody and be good news to our world and to our generation.

Here we stand. Unashamed and assured in our own faith, we reach out to people of all other faiths with love, hope, and humility. With

God's help, we stand ready with you to face the challenges of our time and to work together for a greater human flourishing.

References

Author's Introduction to the New Edition
1. Luke 18:8, *NIV*.

Memorandum 1: Operation Gravedigger
1. See Peter L. Berger, *The Social Reality of Religion* (Harmondsworth, UK: Penguin, 1973), p. 132; published in the United States as *The Sacred Canopy* (Garden City, NY: Doubleday, Anchor Books, 1969); see also David Martin, *The Dilemmas of Contemporary Religion* (Oxford, UK: Blackwell, 1978), p. 54; Roland Robertson, *The Sociological Interpretation of Religion* (Oxford, UK: Blackwell, 1970), p. 43.
2. Noel Annan, *Leslie Stephen* (London: MacGibbon and Kee, 1951), p. 110.
3. Quoted in Ian Bradley, *The Call to Seriousness* (London: Jonathan Cape, 1976), p. 15.
4. Quoted in Paul W. Blackstock, *The Strategy of Subversion* (Chicago: Quadrangle Books, 1964), p. 51.
5. See Noel Barber, *Sinister Twilight* (London: Fontana Collins, 1970).
6. Romans 1:25, *NASB*.
7. "Letters on a Regicide Peace," letter 1, in *The Work of Edmund Burke*, vol. 6 (London: Oxford University Press, 1907), p. 85.
8. H. Richard Niebuhr, *Christ and Culture* (New York: Harper, Colophon Books, 1975), p. xi.
9. Peter L. Berger and Richard Neuhaus, eds., *Against the World for the World* (New York: Seabury Press, 1976).
10. See 1 Samuel 4:1-11; 2 Samuel 6:1-9; Jeremiah 7:1-15; Mark 3:1-6; Romans 1-7; Jeremiah 1:10.

Memorandum 2: The Sandman Effect
1. See Bernard Crick, *George Orwell: A Life* (Harmondsworth, UK: Penguin, 1982), p. 500.
2. Quoted in Herbert R. Lottman, *The Left Bank* (Boston, MA: Houghton Mifflin, 1982), p. 23.
3. See Peter L. Berger and Thomas Luckmann, *The Social Construction of Reality* (Harmondsworth, UK: Penguin, 1967), pp. 174ff.; Berger, *The Social Reality of Religion*, chap. 2.
4. 1 Timothy 3:15, *NEB*.
5. See Sidney A. Burrell, ed., *The Role of Religion in Modern European History* (New York: Macmillan, 1964), p. 95.
6. See Berger and Luckmann, *The Social Construction of Reality*, pp. 1-30.
7. Blaise Pascal, *Pensées* (3. 60), trans. A. J. Krailsheimer (Harmondsworth, UK: Penguin, 1966), p. 46.
8. In the Louvre Museum, Paris.

Memorandum 3: The Cheshire-Cat Factor
1. Quoted in Alistair Cooke, *Six Men* (Harmondsworth, UK: Penguin, 1978), p. 13.
2. *Prospects for the Eighties* (London: Bible Society, 1980), p. 12.
3. *The Times Literary Supplement*, December 18, 1981, p. 1461.
4. Ellul, *New Demons*, p. 2.
5. See Peter L. Berger, *The Social Reality of Religion* (Harmondsworth, UK: Penguin, 1973), pp. 113ff.; David Martin, *General Theory of Secularization* (Oxford, UK: Blackwell, 1978); Martin E. Marty, *The Modern Schism* (London: SCM, 1969); Bryan R. Wilson, *Religion in Secular Society* (London: C.A. Watts, 1966).
6. David Barrett, ed., *World Christian Encyclopedia* (Oxford, UK: Oxford University Press, 1982).
7. Chadwick, *Secularization of European Mind*, p. 9.
8. Quoted in ibid., p. 18.
9. See Berger and Neuhaus, *Against the World*, chap. 1.
10. Ibid., p. 10.

11. See Chadwick, *Secularization of European Mind*, p. 97.
12. See Joseph N. Moody, "The Dechristianization of the French Working Class," in Burrell, *Role of Religion*, pp. 89ff.
13. Quoted in *Context*, November 15, 1981, p. 6 (emphasis added).

Memorandum 4: The Private-Zoo Factor

1. See Peter L. Berger, Brigitte Berger and Hansfried Kellner, *The Homeless Mind* (Harmondsworth, UK: Penguin, 1974), chap. 3.
2. See Peter L. Berger, *Facing Up to Modernity* (New York: Basic Books, 1977), chap. 11; Arthur Brittan, *The Privatised World* (London: Routledge and Kegan Paul, 1978)
3. See Thorstein Veblen, *The Theory of the Leisure Class* (New York: New American library, 1953).
4. Berger, *Facing Modernity*, p. 18.
5. Theodore Roszak, *Where the Wasteland Ends* (New York: Doubleday, 1973), p. 449.
6. Peter Brown, *Augustine of Hippo* (London: Faber and Faber, 1967), p. 248.
7. Karl Mannheim, *Essays on the Sociology of Knowledge* (London: Routledge and Kegan Paul, 1952), p. 269.
8. See Berger et al., *Homeless Mind*, pp. 167ff.
9. See ibid., p. 168; also Christopher Lasch, *The Culture of Narcissism* (New York: W. W. Norton, 1979).
10. *Christianity Today*, 12 Nov. 1982, p. 80.
11. Bryan R. Wilson, *Contemporary Transformations of Religion* (Oxford, UK: Oxford University Press, 1976), p. 87.
12. Os Guinness, "An Evangelical Manifesto: A Declaration of Evangelical Identity and Public Commitment," Washington, DC, May, 2008, p. 14.

Memorandum 5: The Smorgasbord Factor

1. See Berger, *Social Reality of Religion*, pp. 138ff.
2. See ibid., chap. 2.
3. Martin, *Dilemmas of Contemporary Religion*, p. 168.
4. See ibid., pp. 1ff.
5. See Barrett, *World Christian Encyclopedia*.
6. See Berger and Luckmann, *Social Construction of Reality*, pp. 102ff.; Berger et al., *Homeless Mind*, pp. 64-65.
7. Quoted in *The Observer*, 19 Apr. 1981, p. 13.
8. Quoted in Peter Williamson and Kevin Perrotta, eds., *Christianity Confronts Modernity* (Ann Arbor, MI: Servant Books, 1981), p. 12.
9. Ibid.
10. Quoted in *Context*, 15 Dec. 1981, p. 6.
11. See Peter L. Berger, *The Heretical Imperative* (Garden City, NY: Doubleday, 1979), chap. 1.
12. See Peter L. Berger, *The Precarious Vision* (Garden City, NY: Doubleday, 1961), pp. 17ff.
13. Lasch, *Culture of Narcissism*, p. 14.
14. See Wilson, *Religion in Secular Society*, pp. 51-52.
15. Quoted in Gill, *Social Context of Theology*, p. 100.
16. Quoted in *The Times Literary Supplement*, 28 Jan. 1983, p. 83.

Memorandum 6: Creating Counterfeit Religion

1. See Michael J. Malbin, *Religion and Politics* (Washington, DC: American Enterprise Institute, 1978).
2. See Robert N. Bellah, "Civil Religion in America," *Daedalus* 96, no. 1 (Winter 1967); Robert D. Linder and Richard V. Pierard, *Twilight of the Saints* (Downers Grove, IL: InterVarsity Press, 1978).
3. See Berger, *Social Reality of Religion*, chap. 6.
4. Quoted in Marty, *Modern Schism*, p. 139.

5. Benjamin R. Barber, *Consumed: How Markets Corrupt Children, Infantilize Adults, and Swallow Citizens Whole* (New York, W.W. Norton, 2007), p. 7.

6. Quoted in James S. Tinney, "The Prosperity Doctrine," *Spirit*, Apr. 1978.

7. Quoted in Frank S. Mead, *Handbook of Denominations* (Nashville, TN: Abingdon, 1970), p. 217.

8. Quoted in Context, 15 Feb. 1982, p. 6.

9. See Raymond Williams, *Communications* (Harmondsworth, UK: Penguin, 1970).

10. David Rosenthal, "Kid Power?" *Bostonia*, Winter 1979, p. 13.

11. Quoted in Cynthia Schaible, "The Gospel of the Good Life" *Eternity*, Feb. 1981, p.21.

12. Jack Newfield, *A Prophetic Minority* (New York: Signet Books, 1967), p. 157.

13. Horace Bushnell, quoted in Marty, *Modern Schism*, p. 132.

14. Quoted in Schaible, "Gospel of Good Life," p. 22.

15. Quoted in Martin, *Dilemmas of Contemporary Religion*, p. viii.

16. Quoted in P. Fitzgerald, *The Knox Brothers* (London: Macmillan, 1979), p. 259.

Memorandum 7: Damage to Enemy Institutions

1. See Jurgen Habermas, *Legitimation Crisis* (Boston: Beacon Press, 1973), p. 90.

2. Andrew M. Greeley, *The Persistence of Religion* (London: SCM, 1973), p. 14.

3. See Berger, *Social Reality of Religion*, p. 133.

4. Martin, *General Theory of Secularization*, p. 71.

5. Peter L. Berger, "The Second Children's Crusade," *The Christian Century*, 2 Dec. 1959.

6. Lasch, *Culture of Narcissism*, p. 76.

7. Daniel J. Boorstin, *The Image* (New York: Atheneum, 1962), p. 57.

8. Luke 6:26, *NIV*.

9. See Berger, *Social Reality of Religion*, pp. 143-48.

10. See Ivan Ilich, *Disabling Professions* (London: Marion Boyars, 1977).

Memorandum 8: Damage to Enemy Ideas

1. Quoted in *TIME*, June 7, 1976, p. 54.

2. Quoted in Schaible, "Gospel of Good Life," p. 26.

3. Exodus 10:26, *NEB*.

4. Paul Berman, *Terror and Liberalism* (New York: W.W. Norton & Company, 2003), chap. 4.

5. See Boorstin, Image, pp. 130ff.

6. Quoted in *Sojourners*, January 1978, p. 9.

7. G.K. Chesterton, "What I Saw in America," quoted in Raymond T. Bond, ed., *The Man Who Was Chesterton* (New York: Dodd Mead, 1946), p. 235.

8. Quoted in Linder and Pierard, *Twilight of Saints*, p. 164.

Memorandum 9: Fossils and Fanatics

1. See Berger, *Facing Modernity*, pp. 175ff.; Berger, *Social Reality of Religion*, pp. 157ff.

2. See Martin, *Dilemmas of Contemporary Religion*, pp. 75ff.

3. See Berger, *Rumor of Angels*, pp. 17, 18.

4. See ibid., pp. 13, 14.

5. See Martin, *General Theory of Secularization*, pp. 111ff.

6. See Peter L. Berger, *Invitation to Sociology* (Harmondsworth, UK: Penguin, 1966), pp. 130, 131.

7. Quoted in Chadwick, *Secularization of European Mind*, p. 250.

8. Burrell, *Role of Religion*, p. 94.

Memorandum 10: Trendies and Traitors

1. See Berger, *Facing Modernity*, pp. 169ff.

2. Ibid.

3. See Henry Chadwick, "All Things to All Men," *New Testament Studies*, 1954-55, pp. 261-75.

4. See Berger, *Facing Modernity*, p. 165.

5. Ibid., p. 168.

6. See Antoine Lion, in David Martin, John Orme Mills and W. S. F. Pickering, eds., *Sociology and Theology: Alliance and Conflict* (Brighton, UK: Harvester Press, 1980), pp. 163-82.

7. George Tyrell, *Christianity at the Cross-roads* (London: Allen and Unwin, 1963), p. 49.

8. Albert Schweitzer, *The Quest for the Historical Jesus* (London: A. & C. Black, 1954), p. 398.

9. See Berger, *Rumor of Angels*, p. 41.

10. Ibid., p. 23.

11. Walter Kaufmann, *The Faith of a Heretic* (New York: New American Library, 1959), p. 32.

12. Berger, *Rumor of Angels*, pp. 20, 21.

13. Alasdair Macintyre and Paul Ricoeur, *The Religious Significance of Atheism* (New York: Columbia Univ. Press, 1969), p. 46.

14. Walter Kaufmann, *Existentialism, Religion and Death* (New York: New American Library, 1976), p. 3.

15. Macintyre and Ricoeur, *Religious Significance of Atheism*, p. 29.

16. See Ellul, *New Demons*, p. 38.

17. Berger, *Rumor of Angels*, p. 12.

18. Berger, *Facing Modernity*, p. 163.

Afterword: On Remembering the Third Fool and the Devil's Mousetrap

1. Czeslaw Milosz, *Visions from San Francisco Bay* (Manchester, UK: Carcanet New Press, 1982), p. 74.

2. Malcolm Muggeridge, *Christ and the Media* (London: Hodder and Stoughton, 1977), p. 76.

3. Reinhold Schneider, *Imperial Mission*, trans. Walter Oden (New York: Gresham Press, 1948), p. 93.

4. Ezekiel 20:32, *NEB*.

5. *Pensées* (4. 433), trans. Krailsheimer, p. 164.

6. Walt Kelly, Pogo comic strip.

7. Peter Shaffer, *Equus,* Act 2, in *Three Plays* (Harmondsworth, UK: Penguin, 1976), p. 274.

8. D. Martin, *Dilemmas of Contemporary Religion*, p. 88.

9. G. K. Chesterton, *The Everlasting Man* (Garden City, NY: Doubleday, Image Books, 1955), pp. 260, 261.

10. "Holy Sonnet X," in *Donne: Poetical Works* (Oxford, UK: Oxford University Press, 1971), p. 297.

11. *Sermo* 130. 2.